SHOESTRING DREAMS

FAMILY, FRIENDS, AND RIVALS

PART 1

ANDRÉ WADE

Shoestring Dreams
Copyright © 2021 by André Wade

All rights reserved. No part of this publication may be reproduced, distributed, or transmitted in any form or by any means, including photocopying, recording, or other electronic or mechanical methods, without the prior written permission of the author, except in the case of brief quotations embodied in critical reviews and certain other non-commercial uses permitted by copyright law.

Tellwell Talent
www.tellwell.ca

ISBN
978-0-2288-7092-0 (Hardcover)
978-0-2288-7091-3 (Paperback)
978-0-2288-7093-7 (eBook)

This book is dedicated to my loved ones:
Charles H. Wade, aka *"Buddy."*

To my bloodline: The Wades
(Valen, Craig, and Dorien), I love you so much!

To my support system: my dear friends
who have encouraged my thoughts and
ideas and put them into writing.

Thank you all! Nothing but love.

PROLOGUE

We all dream… The makeup of a dream comes from life experiences; some are good, and some are bad. All are a part of you, whether you want to believe it or not. However, "dreams," like visions, don't necessarily need to operate only by getting some shut eye. For dreams last way longer than your bedroom regiment or the daydream you had about your favorite meal, all the while trying to take notes for a class or a meeting. These dreams could be passion-related, goal-oriented, reappearing aspirations, or "signs," even your own premonitions based on your fears.

Being a dreamer is about acknowledging the obstacles set before you and overcoming them with the life tools that God gives us. We are all blessed with our intuition combining with the inspiration etched into our souls since the moment we awoke. We all have our own story to tell about how we get these "dreams" in the first place. To be clear, they don't define us but simply enlighten us if we pay attention to the daily signs giving to us. No matter how ridiculous they may be, these moments in time answer our slightest doubts and keep us pushing. Even with our fear, it keeps us alive no matter how old we are.

With maturity comes wisdom, and with wisdom comes faith, and with faith comes work. This is a great recipe for seeing those dreams come to fruition. So, with that said, go forth and achieve the unbelievable. Conquer that reemerging fear that has had you in a chokehold, for only God knows how long. Understand that failure will happen in life, just as common as breathing, and I guess you are not scared to breathe. Because, for us dreamers, who take that deep breath as we get up in the morning ready to seize the day, or night, by pulling a graveyard shift that so many people couldn't do, unless it was a recipe for your dream. We (dreamers) dust off the failed attempts, take our wisdom from the fall, and push forward to keep our dream alive… And we certain decapitate fear at the head with that.

CHAPTER 1

After hitting the snooze button a couple of times, it was clear that it was time to kick off the day. Wiggling his toes underneath the sheets, and then clenched them tightly. When he released them, he heard every "pop and cracks" his bones gave in the early Winter morning. Switching his feet up and down, he slowly started loosening his ankles which gave way to a slight tightness around his calf region. His sense of tightness extended upward to his quads and buttocks, but the comfort and warmness of his bed combined with the soreness from yesterday's shoot around.

It was the perfect cocktail for not wanting to get out of bed. His bed made it seem like last night's workout was well worth it, as it hugged him through the night. With the number of back screens and cheap shots being hurled last night at the gym, of course, it was all in good spirit. There was nothing like a competitive pick-up game after school. It was a place and time where friends came to assemble. Receiving a well-deserved and "needed" release from an outlet, where everyone there knew the basis of the game.

To him, last night wasn't about the baskets being made but the "love" of being there and around familiar faces.

Similar to how many of us demolish a dessert that our sweet tooth craves. It's not about the calories and sugar rush that is sure to come, but because we "love it." And that's how the kids felt when dribbling up and down the court last night with their fellow teammates. Instead of talking about the way they played in the previous game last week. They decided to talk about the girls they saw passing in school, sports, money, music, clothes, and shoes. These "images" were only flashbacks flickering inside Eric's busy mind as he slept. Their conversations on the basketball court that night, after their 3-hour basketball affair. Everyone was drenched in sweat and seated on the hardwood floor. Some are lying down, facing the ceiling. Suddenly, a teammate asked, "So, who's getting those new J's, Friday?"

No alarm clock was needed for him as he was naturally an early bird. He was still lying in his bed, awake. But still, half-conscience, as his brain had him reminiscing about last night's on-and-off the court dialogue. Flashbacks of him on the hardwood floor. He was drenched in sweat, untying his black Air Jordan Retro 10's, letting his feet finally breathe. One of his friends tossed him a cellphone from a gym bag. And as his memory depicted, he saw the cellphone floating in mid-air towards him to catch. Eric's eyes locked on the twirling cellphone as he came in his direction. Upon opening his hands to grab it, he snaps out of his dream, finding himself in his cozy bed with his eyes half-opened now. He sluggishly stares up at his bare bedroom ceiling for a few seconds before blinking himself out of his cold daze. As he lay there, trying to piece together some of the murky pieces to his dream, it hit him.

"Damn, they come out tomorrow!? I might have to miss class for this," Eric suggested to himself. As a typical teenager, the first thing he did in the morning was roll over to grab his cellphone. He scrolled through his social media timeline as he was attempting to get out of bed. He also began to wipe some of the colds out of his eyes. Seeing nothing that piqued his interest, he set his phone back down on his nightstand and glanced over his left shoulder to read his calendar taped to his wall. It was placed next to the frost-bitten window, which is alerting him of the wintry mix awaiting him outside. "Alright, man, four more months to graduate. You can do this." Eric said to himself as he began to yawn, stretching out his arms, waking himself of his slumber.

Eric Brewer was a 17-year-old graduating senior year at Hollywood High School, located just on the outskirts, in the commercial district of Hollywood Heights, Ohio, also known to the locals as "The Heights." Roughly 45 minutes north, if you took interstate 75 from Cincinnati, Ohio. It was a relatively smaller city than Cincinnati. However, it produced a lot of talent and history to show for it in its hay day, from famous poets, aviation moguls, and even musicians.

Hollywood Heights was once a place where dreams took flight, but today, most people are considered "lucky" to even have an opportunity to move out of the city for a better life. Some often refer to the Midwest as "The neglected fourth coast." A major producer of America's goods and services, spanning decades, started in the '50s. In "the Heights," their industrial section has been reduced to abandoned power plants and factory mills which now serve as homes to the homeless. Most just braving the winter elements. And as a high schooler, seeing all this with his own eyes; Eric wanted a different life once he graduated.

Finding it hard to escape his bed's grip, he reached back to his nightstand and grabbed his phone. Scrolling through his newsfeed on his Instagram timeline, he found some pictures he admired and some memes he found hilarious as a "pick me up" to get the blood flowing. On his cozy full-size bed, Eric had an arrangement of pillows, which allowed him to sleep better and kept his thin-wireframed body insulated from the cold. And sometimes, Eric would wake up and find himself holding one of these pillows at night, easing the restlessness his body brought him. To him, it was a one-of-a-kind bed he will surely miss when he's off to college.

Most college students were provided with a twin-size bed in their designated school dormitory, which, in hindsight, is half the size of his current one. The good news is that he will be able to bring his childhood quilt with him to school. It was a childhood piece he cherished and kept him warm throughout the winter months. It was made by his grandmother on his father's side, Paula, and was gifted to him at the age of 5 years old. And he still uses it to this day, but more for nostalgic reasons. He knew folks were going to make fun of him for bringing it, but he was also humble and cocky enough not to give a damn.

The quilt has a mustard yellow color in design, which tells a story of a black boy on a journey, traveling up a windy dirt road. To Eric, the boy's destination was never made clear to him by his grandmother. Instead, she allowed him to determine where the young boy was going for himself, teaching him to create his own path of imagination. On his journey, the black boy is greeted by a multitude of animals. Happy tigers, smiling bears, and joyful lions, and even hummingbirds were pictured hanging on the branches of the trees. None of God's creatures posed any threat to the boy, nor did the boy pose a threat to them. Also, etched on the quilt were more onlookers, but in the human form. People of all races greeted him on his path; many were depicted, waving at the boy as he continued his journey. As he walked into the golden horizon, and at the tail end of the quilt by Eric's feet, was a sun and a crescent moon. It truly was a piece of work Eric's grandmother hand stitched. He just never could understand the meaning behind it, but it was sentimental enough. So, as years passed and as he got older, he never cared to ask her what it meant.

Eric sat up in his bed, flipped his cellphone upside down on his bed. His ears were alerted to the commotion coming from downstairs. He was hearing the metal pans shuffle over the stove and morning greetings between his parents. It was time to get the day moving.

"Eric B! Are you going to eat this food, or not? A bit of advice- NO isn't the right answer!".

That was Nadine Brewer, the Mother, and Queen of the Brewer household. And usually, the first person to make it downstairs to the kitchen, followed by Eric's father, Ronald Brewer Jr.

"Yea- Uh, Naw. I'm not taking your black behind to school if you miss this bus," stated Ronald Jr. "I have a big meeting at the base today and being early means you're on time. But you know this right, superstar?"

Ronald Jr., 43, has been a civilian worker at the Huber-Kett military base for the past 10 years. He was a well-liked and diligent employee in the office, and in the field, alongside a prestigious resume filled with various accolades. At an awards reception in 2012, he assisted the Department of Defense with their war efforts in Afghanistan, and he was accredited for his logistical expertise and determination to succeed. In a heartfelt speech to his coworkers, he credited his drive to his parents, Ronald Sr. and Paula Brewer, as well as his upbringing. Ronald Jr. is a native to Hollywood Heights; his parents relocated from Chicago, Illinois, to provide a better future for themselves and start a new life in a new city.

In Hollywood Heights, as a kid, Ronald Jr. would recall seeing his father wake up at the crack of dawn to hot breakfast from his wife, Paula. Ronald Sr. would work grueling hours at the steel mill plant, where 12 to 14-hour shifts weren't out of the norm. However, he used to be dirty, exhausted, and hungry after his shift, but would still walk inside his front door all smiles. For he understood love, even if he didn't express it the best. Ronald Jr. remembered his dad as a hard worker man. Therefore, he always says to himself, "He never quit, so, how can I?"

Ronald Jr. was once a defense contractor for the Huber-Kett military base. Ronald Jr. helped construct and supply well-designed vehicles and aircraft to the Department of Defense at a lower cost. And here is where Ronald Jr. found his niche. After a few years and his government contract was set to expire, the Department of Defense offered to elevate him up the chain and offered him a permanent position if he chose to stay, which he accepted.

With the country still at odds in the Middle East, Ronald Jr. got to see a whole different side to the work he did, now being permanent. That side of the government was titled Logistics and Supply-Chain Management.

This new task was indeed a welcoming challenge for Ronald Jr. However, he enjoyed it, which made the work fun—traveling to different parts of the world. He was able to see breathtaking landmarks such as the Taj Mahal, The Eiffel Tower, Big Ben in London, just to name a few. His job even allowed him to rub shoulders with one of his favorite defense strategists, Colin Powell. Huber-Kett was also where he first laid eyes on his wife, Nadine, who was once an intern for the Department of Defense. Her position being a job clerk, she found no "loyalty" there and ended up leaving the department for a chief position at a local bank a year later, which gave her more freedom to lead, and a lot closer to home than Ronald Jr. commute.

Today, Ronald Jr.'s job has skyrocketed. He has taken over the role of defense contract lead at the Department of Defense. Like his previous perks of work, he gets to travel, networking around the globe, looking for well-priced and well-manufactured products suited for the defense's liking. Ronald Jr. thrived at being on the move and always in a fast-paced environment. And, also the same reason Nadine left, she wanted a position that's more "firmly planted," at a location closer to home.

"Mom, can you pack my breakfast up, please!?" Eric yelled down the stairs, "I'm almost ready, just throwing my clothes on!"

It never took any time for Eric to get ready for school. Ruffling through clean clothes in his hamper adjacent to his bed, he found whatever clothes looked "visibly appealing" to him. And trying not to be late, he grabbed the items with the least number of wrinkles and what smelled the best. He gave everything a quick whiff, just to make sure there was still some hint of laundry detergent.

In the past, it wasn't always like this. Before Eric attended Hollywood Highschool, the Montgomery County Public School system had a very "lax code" regarding school attire. However, In the 1990s, through the early 2000s, the dress code swiftly changed from casually wearing whatever fits your mood to receiving harsh remarks because of your clothes.

"What colors are those?"

"What neighborhood are you from, playa!?!"

"Last time I checked... We da the ones to wear dat. Take that shit off...Na-Naw, Matter of fact, let me help ya, G..."

Since then, the Montgomery County Public School board has implemented a strict, county-wide school uniform policy: White Polo shirt, khakis, and black shoes. They were also given the option of wearing their red sweater vest, which all the kids hated. The uniform itself wasn't too bad but still felt like a prison-mandated rule, and the students wanted to rebel against it. However, they understood the reason behind it. Eric never wore his red vest; that was never an "option" for him. The only issue that plagued his morning as he got dressed was debating to himself, "Which shoe am I going to rock with this 'ugly" ass uniform?

Like most kids of his age in high school, he had a profound obsession with basketball shoes. From the original, Chuck Taylors. To the Adidas, Crazy 8's, once worn by Kobe Bryant before he received his own signature shoe release. Eric has dedicated his whole bedroom closet to his shoe addiction; he has at least 75 pairs. However, with the cold weather outside, Eric grabs the closest one to him, his wheat Timberlands.

"Ahh, good choice. The weather looks stupid out there anyway." He said as he hastily tied up his boots, but not too tight. He made sure his boots were loosely tied, with the boot's tongue exposed over his khakis. They weren't tight enough to get joked on by the kids at the bus stop and school, but tight enough to not tweak his ankles outside on some black ice. He proceeded to grab his red-bubble coat from his bedroom closet and darted down the stairs, rushing to eat his breakfast. In the process of doing so, Eric found himself stumbling over his loosely tied bootlace, which unraveled his boot knot. Unknowingly to him, his lace was now completely undone; and in a split second, he suddenly tripped over his right foot and almost crashed, landing at the bottom of the steps. Nadine was startled by the early morning sounds of loud, thick, Timberland's clunking down the steps, blurted out, "Sir, can you take your time going down the stairs," she said to Eric.

As the "clunking" sounds ended, Eric fumbled down the steps, yet he awkwardly stuck the landing and avoided any serious injury before school that day and a critical game in a couple of days.

"Sorry, momma!" Eric, replied, as he took a bow for his dismount landing at the base of the steps and smiled, "Y'all told me to hurry up."

Packing Eric's lunch, Nadine, clarifies, "I told you to eat!... Your father said don't be late. Here's your lunch, baby, now eat your breakfast." As she folded the top of the brown paper bag, she planted a kiss on his cheek, "Be safe."

"Thanks, mom." He replied as he received his lunch bag from his mom. Eric finally acknowledges his father, who has been eating in the kitchen since he came stumbling down the steps. Before he stuffed his lunch in his backpack, He pointed to his dad and said, "Sir, you might be late. I'm headed out the door." Then his father takes a slow sip of his black roasted coffee from his San Francisco 49'ers mug as he soaks in what his son said. As he sat the mug down, he jokingly snapped back at Eric, "Negro, I have a car... Don't get cute. It's cold outside…." He then briefly smiled back as Eric made his way over to him. He extended his fist out to his sons for a quick pound, "Be safe, baby boy."

"Yes, sir," he replied as he dashed out of the front door; he was immediately greeted by the frigid temps his phone and family warned about. The brightly shining sun could have fooled anybody who wasn't outside at this time of day, and it seemed as if the only sounds being made were birds chirping as they flew overpass, and Eric's breath, as he blew into his hands trying to keep them warm. To his observations, nothing seems to have thawed out since he woke up this morning. The murky water that flowed from the curb to the gutters was frozen, and ice cycles dressed the streetlights and street signs.

Checking his phone for the temperature read, it said: *Hollywood Heights, OHIO. 21 degrees- wind gust up to 10 mph."* Sticking his phone back into his bubble coat and pulling his hat closer to his ear, he blew into his hands, thinking about how he couldn't wait to relocate to a place like California when he graduates. "I can't keep doing this shit." He muttered.

As he continued his 4-minute journey to the bus stop, he started to rub his hands more aggressively, applying more friction to his skin to keep warm. Common sense didn't prevail this morning, as it didn't occur to Eric to grab his gloves due to his rushing. However, most teenagers think they can handle the elements anyway, choosing to only sport a trendy windbreaker or a gym hoodie. Eric was one of those kids. Approaching his bus stop, the intersection of Main Street and Union Road, Eric spotted his clique of homies, Jacqueline, Angelo, and Jeremy. They were also waiting for the bus, also trying to stay warm. He greeted Jacqueline first, as a gentleman tends to do, with a warm embrace, and proceeded to give the rest of the gang their signature dap. He pulled out his phone to show his friends the shoe release he saw in bed.

"Aye, man, check out what hit my phone this morning." He showed everyone the phone screen, illuminating a picture of a limited-edition basketball shoe and its release date. It wasn't just any shoe; these were the *Air Jordan 13 Retro, "Bred Edition."* They all gaze in awe, captivated by the shoe display, rotating on the phone screen. There was a "cool factor" to how the layout was presented, giving them a warm, up-close, and personal view. It was a marvel. Using his cold fingertips, Eric zooms in on the Air Jordan shoe, studying every stitch of detail. To his peers, this shoe was a "must-have," and his crew loved everything about the Air Jordan 13's.

The way the black leather wrapped around the toe could make your mouth water. The red suede wrapped the shoe's heel like a Christmas present, complimenting the red "Jumpman" logo. A green, holographic button-like label displayed the number "23", and again, the Jumpman logo finished off the signature shoe. With their mouths wide-open, in awe, the kids were sold on the Jordan shoe without truly knowing the history behind what made these a timeless classic for future generations to come.

Before Eric Brewer was even considered thought to his parents, a man from North Carolina, by the name of Michael Jeffery Jordan, better known as "MJ," dominated the sport of basketball, making him the juggernaut of the National Basketball Association in the 1990s. With all praise to him and his dedication to the game, he took the NBA international, bringing the excitement of the game to people around the globe. "I just wanna be like Mike!" was a famous and catchy 90's saying that most kids would say to themselves after seeing it on TV commercials like Gatorade. Some adults even adhered to the saying, using it for their own obstacles, "Be like Mike." Children adored him, players feared and respected him, and the city of Chicago loved him as if he was born there; and the world adopted him.

In the 1997-98 NBA season, and supposedly MJ's final season, since head coach Phil Jackson announced he was leaving the Chicago Bulls, they marked this season as "The Last Dance." It was their last chance to win an NBA Title and an attempt at being 2-time, 3-peat champions. A feat that seemed impossible to the average man was accomplished by the Chicago Bulls, making them the 97-98 NBA Champions and solidifying their place on NBA's Mount Rushmore. Then to the Boston Celtics and Los Angeles Lakers. However, a fallout began (and honestly, long before) once their 3-peat season ended. The aftermath of the team was hard for any basketball fan to stomach.

The Chicago Bulls soon dispersed their All-star roster, breaking up Michael Jordan, Scottie Pippen, Steve Kerr, Dennis Rodman, and Toni Kukoč. The Bull's front office sent head coach, Phil Jackson, to the Los Angeles Lakers, pairing him with another dynamic duo in the making, Kobe Bryant and Shaquille O'Neal. Michael Jordan refused to join another team and retired for the second time and went home essentially only to come back out of retirement again in 2001 to the Washington Wizards; also, being president of their basketball operations.

During his 1997-1998 NBA season, Michael Jordan debuted his Air Jordan 13's, just not in the "BRED" colorway Eric sees today. The first editions displayed the team's majority colors being white, with a red under-sole and a black leather toe. They premiered in stores nationwide in November 1997, at the mere price of $150, compared to the $250 price tag people are willing to pay in 2017 (20 years later). A popular shoe that even gained prominence in iconic movies such as "He Got Game," starring Hall-of-fame actor, Denzel Washington, Jake Shuttlesworth, and his college-bound son, Jesus Shuttlesworth, played by NBA All-star and future Hall-of-Famer, Ray Allen.

Eric *had a game*, but not 250 dollars' worth of game. He needed a discount, "a hook-up," behind the counter; something. The new retail price for the BRED Air Jordan 13's started at $190. It's still too high for his budget. Regardless of his parents having decent jobs, with his father traveling the world and meeting global leaders and contractors, and his mother, a Chief financial manager at the Hollywood Credit Union.

Hollywood Credit Union is a state-wide bank ranked #2 as the safest state bank, according to Ohio's Bank Finance Magazine. With all that said, the Brewers were still of the middle class. Despite making decent money, they made sure to live within their means. However, being human, they still found themselves trying to keep the family's head above water. Their finances were often tied up in old home repairs, a long and unforgiving grocery list for a growing 17-year-old boy who seems to wipe the refrigerator clean every three days, and medicine for the family as well as any other necessities. For Eric, Air Jordan's didn't fit into the "necessity" criteria to be deemed one; it was a luxury. Nevertheless, the crew loved these shoes, and they all wanted them.

Eyeballing Eric's phone, still salivating over the new shoe release, Angelo ceased rubbing his hands as he was distracted by the shoes, not even feeling the cold air whipping his skin. "Damn! They droppin' tomorrow, my nigga!?" Angelo shouted, and almost immediately as the word "nigga" left his mouth, Eric and Jeremy began to strike Angelo's arm and rib cage with punches, making their way to his back and giving him a few jabs to his ribs. They needed to do this to Angelo, letting him know their stand on this subject. You just never knew who was listening to your conversation, and in a majority-black neighborhood, if the wrong ears caught his pale skin saying that- it's over.

"Come on, my G. What the hell we say about saying that word and out here!?" Eric insinuated as he continued to lay into him. Finally breaking free of the assault, he made a quick dash to where Jacqueline stood, where she was watching all of it unfold and not too pleased with Angelo either. "I ain't ya scapegoat, fool," Jacqueline said as she pushed him away, back closer to the boys. Angelo took a break to catch his breath, caressing himself as he rubbed his battered arm and back from the melee of punches thrown. Angelo lifted his head and laughed, replying, "Man, Ok. Ok. OK, you win... I'm not 'American Black,' per se... But I'm y'all first cousins when you think about it. All Cubanos are your first cousins... It's just whacked that they don't want to claim the darker folks... My, G. Is that better?"

"It's a start," Eric replied.

The crew heard his petty cry out for a plea but weren't too receptive to it; after all, he did look like a teenage white boy on the opposite side of town, from where 'they' usually reside. All they could do was watch him and then roll their eyes in embarrassment. Jacqueline, on the other hand, was trailing Angelo up and down, wanting to give Angelo her own jab. Angelo charismatically brushes off the seriousness of the matter they were trying to reveal to him. Of course, he meant no direct harm in his banter. He wasn't socially aware or "woke," he just wanted to get his jokes off; that was just him. He meant nothing by it, and they understood because they had known him for years. So, they reverted to their shoe discussion.

"But yea, man. Anyway, those kicks look wet, bro. You tryna skip school tomorrow?" Angelo said, trying to change the topic.

"I'm not sure what I'm going to do," Eric replied.

"Anyway, I will see if I can give the cash to grandma to get them or wait in line, but I don't know because it is Winter and all."

Jacqueline, looking off into the distance, redirected her eyes back to the group. "How are your grandparents doing anyway, Eric?"

At the same time as her engagement with the group, their school bus, #739, approached, squeaking to a slow stop. Their bus was like many of the other school buses across the county. The brakes made an awful screech that matched the trail of grey smoke steaming from the exhaust pipe. It was truly an off-putting eye sore for any visitors who chose to visit Montgomery County Public Schools. However, the bus was festive with young teenage energy on the inside. Children are eager to start the day as they are found shouting at one another across the bus aisle. Some were morning people on bus #739. You may find some on their cellphone, face-timing friends on another bus or walking to school, or some still sleeping with their hoods draped over their eyes, simply exhausted from hanging out past curfew the night before.

The gang walked onto bus #739 and were greeted by their schoolmates, some of them knowing their peers on a personal level. Many of the students would run into each other in neighborhoods they visited after school, walking by, or even at the grocery store with their parents. Another common denominator on this bus is that majority of these kids were from the "tougher" neighborhoods of Hollywood Heights, such as Kimberly Quarters, Residency Park, Eastwood, just to name a few. Many of them wouldn't even flex a smile at their bus stop until they were in the presence of their loved ones or individuals they could "let their hair down" with. Today, Hollywood Heights isn't a place to let your guard down in unfamiliar settings, like most places in America. For the kids growing up in Hollywood Heights, they understood their school buses were safe havens.

Some of the school bus drivers also grew a rapport with the children, seeing many of the kids before and after school. Some bus drivers have been with the Montgomery County Public School system for so long, and they could date back to when they bused today's kids' parents. They also witnessed first-hand what the youth really dabbled in and how they spoke amongst each other- for they derived in the same neighborhoods they worked. Bearing an underestimated responsibility to the youth, for the bus drivers, it seemed to be a weekly occurrence that someone would fuss on the bus. One thing was for certain, "don't fight on the bus," and many respected that as they chose to settle it off the bus. Whether at a bus stop or a nearby alleyway, the bus drivers didn't snitch, they were the overseers to make sure everyone made it out alive, and there was no "jumping in."

Nonetheless, there were no issues this morning as they climbed the steps to get on bus #739. Eric sees that most of the seats are taken up, which wasn't too surprising to them. When this reoccurring theme would happen, the gang was forced to take the "less desired" sections of the bus. The seats were decorated and etched with some fancy knife play and encrypted graffiti; mostly harmless tags representing the neighborhoods they claimed, and of course, your usual childish scribble- *"Tisha wants to call all of the boys to the yard!" "#739 home away from home" "yeaaaa hoe!!!"*

Thankfully, everyone found a seat next to each other today. Finally, escaping Old Man Winter's morning bite, Eric removed his hat and rubbed his hands together, creating friction. However, to his surprise, as he touched the brown leather seat, and it was cold. The heat wasn't working on the bus, yet the public school still felt the bus was operational, getting them from point A to point B. Other than that, there was a long list of funding issues plaguing the county, and with no money coming into the county, as once in the past, many of the locals painfully had to accept the conditions as they were.

"Uh, E?... You gonna answer my question or not?" Jacqueline said, staring with confusion at Eric, slightly irritated and awaiting an answer since they first got onto the bus and found their seats. Blowing heat in his hands, Eric answered, "My bad, Jacci... Yea, they are good; I mean, they are old, so you know... old people problems, I guess."

Scrunching up her face at his awkward response to a delayed question, Jacqueline let out a sarcastic laugh as Jeremy chimed in, "You crazy if you're gonna have your grandma stand in the line for those damn shoes, bro, in the freezing cold too? You tripping nigga'. It's like 20 degrees outside!!"

"I gotta side with Jerms on this one," Jacqueline, said drawing her line in the sand.

"What I say about that *Jerms* shit, it's Jeremy!"

"But it's gonna be 40 degrees tomorrow," Angelo replied, also rubbing his hands to keep warm.

Still in disagreement that Eric would even consider the thought, Jeremy got pissed and finished his statement, "Well... it's gonna be cold outside. But you got it, tell her to wear 3 sweaters, *Nigga*".

Jeremy looked in Angelo's direction, begging him to stir the "N-word" pot as he was tempted to at the bus stop earlier. Instead, they both chose to laugh as they sat back in their respective seats, relaxing on their 15-minute commute to Hollywood Highschool. It was early, but the city was up and ready to move. Any traffic? No, but in fairness, the city's population surpassed no more than 150,000. That didn't mean you couldn't see the mother walking her kid to daycare, bundled up equipped with earmuffs. No matter the weather, you would always see the local newspaperman, "Olly," on Pike Rd. and 35th. You would see the cars at the gas stations spewing exhaust fumes, trying to keep their cars warm as they wait for the next available nozzle, as well as the occurring ambulance and cop sirens passing back and forth.

However, it's safe inside the bus, but not warm; the students could talk about all the tv shows they watched the previous night, as round two from the Twitter war most embarked on. Sports highlights were also popular talk, from the games played, ranging from dunks to the ejections on the court. Lastly, the "exaggerated" neighborhood gossip ran by Angelo himself. His stories often consisted of things he claimed to see on his way home from his girlfriend's house or near his own residence in Eastwood. To his peers, the first sign that Angelo's story was bullshit was when he referenced "having a girlfriend." None of which his closest friends ever met. Jacqueline swore up and down that Jesus Christ would reappear in a tuxedo like James Bond before Angelo's dating life would begin.

Eric and Jeremy shared the same sentiment when it came to Angelo's dating life. Like Jacqueline, they both agreed to be multi-millionaires, living in mansions, before someone chose to date Angelo and put with his foolishness. They gave him a rough time. He was a pest, and nobody really cared to hear about his personal life, especially his fictional love affairs. The bus just wanted the "hot tea" for the morning. As exciting as they were, Angelo's stories tended to be all over the place, which made the journey an enjoyable one.

Sometimes it could be situated around a homeless man trying to steal a tv out of a mom-and-pop shop; it could also be a homeless man attempting to rob a store, equipped with only an all-black Nike Air Force One, tucked under his hoodie. Angelo swore up and down it was a gun when he first saw it. This time, he knew that it could also be like a previous story he told when a homeless man saved him from getting clobbered by a Hollywood Heights city bus… One thing was for sure; it always revolved around a homeless man. But the bus and driver soaked it and wouldn't have it any other way.

All jokes aside, Angelo tried very hard to be the life of the party. He tried so much; in fact, it would often rub his friends the wrong way. In the back of their minds, they would often question his motives: "Why make *yourself* a fool for people who really don't care and wouldn't even bat an eye if something happened to you? For the sake of a laugh?" They just felt the bar was low, especially for some of the extremes he would take. As a graduating senior like the rest of them, college wasn't on Angelo's radar in the slightest. However, neither was a life of crime, nor staying in Ohio for that matter.

His burning passion is to make it big and become a stand-up comedian. The joy Angelo derived from seeing people laugh at his jokes, as well as the "Boo's," only added fuel to his fire. However, his comedy routines or lack were really "dark" in humor at such a young age. Nevertheless, Eric and his friends did what they could to support their fellow brother because they didn't want to destroy his dreams before they could ever fully takeoff.

They attended Angelo's Hollywood High School comedy talent show, hosted by himself and *Bucky the Mascot* throughout their school years, to show their support. Bucky, a six-foot-tall, angry-eyed deer, who honestly was more inept than angry. His eyes were misleading and would often frighten the kids who attended these events or any appearance he would make. He was only at Angelo's comedy show as the comedic relief for when things got silent or if there were some technical issues with the soundboard.

Bucky's "go-to" move was a simple hand sway, side to side, finally breaking down into his patent breakdance for the crowd, and to Bucky's delight, the crowd loved him. Angelo saw it as Bucky was stepping on his toes. He was pissed while Eric, Jeremy, Jacqueline, and the front row were crying from laughter. "Go, Bucky…Go, Bucky…Go, Buck!" was all the auditorium chanted as he continued his dance, spinning on the floor.

Even after school, Angelo would walk over to one of the local convenience stores in the Eastwood neighborhood to find the clerk working or any customers there. And just stir up some jokes, pointing at people's hats, commenting on their "accessorized" feather, and asking people, "What da hell kind of shoes are those!??" Even the occasionally and often risky "Yo Momma" jokes. All were his attempts to make people laugh, even if it could cost him his life.

The tagging along crew have advised numerous times "not to joke around those parts" seeing people posted up by the corner stores, with only one mission on their mind, trying to make ends meet to feed their families- no jokes allowed. With that said, most of the hustlers affiliated with the convenience stores in Eastwood were not in the mood to hear anything these kids had to say. And given his lighter-fair skin, they also had to remind their reckless friend, "Don't say the 'N-word." Yet, there they stood, supporting him anyway, standing on the block, and praying not to become a statistic to "collateral damage."

Angelo Alvarez is the only son of immigrant parents from Güines, Cuba; he was 18 years old, and on a mission to prove to his family in America, as well as Cuba, that he was going to be a star. Being 5'8 and fairly thin, he had no passion for playing sports, only commenting on them and giving it his own spin. Angelo also suffered from a severe acne problem, which took a mental blow on how he approached people, especially women. Many direct messages from his social media accounts, sent out to women he taught were attractive, ended up being blocked or left on, "read." So, when all these failed, jokes did the trick, the ice breaker at times, which people were generally receptive to. After a laugh or two, they finally would let their guard down, and Angelo would proceed; however, as a lady, these tactics would never work on Jacqueline.

One thing the fellas understood about Jacqueline is that she hated small talk, ice breaker or not. Not to be confused as someone pessimistic, she was far from that. At the age of 17, she was a girl full of passion and charisma, and she always wanted to make the best out of her life, or any situation presented to her.

Jacqueline Henderson, or "Jacci," as her friends do call her, stood 5'5 with mocha brown skin and hazel-brown eyes that almost everyone admired but her. She hated the attention her eyes brought when she would look at someone and the unwarranted stares that soon come after. She was a slim girl, petite at best, with long black hair and red highlights. The boys in high school all wanted to date her but found her extremely hard to approach, even with how often she smiled at school. Wiser than most, she knew the majority of the high school boys didn't want much besides sex. That wasn't her focus, or her three "brothers'," who didn't want anything from her. Their bond helped her find peace, instead of being off to the side "in the cut" and away from the crowd. Social gatherings weren't necessarily her cup of tea, but she was the life of the party without even trying around her friends.

She was the only girl in a clique full of young boys; however, the boys looked to her as the "voice of reasoning." With her calm and soothing characteristics, she was able to take critical thinking to a new level, and they admired her for that gift. Some of the boys at Hollywood High School saw those same characteristics and thought, "girlfriend potential." Always wanting to lend a friendly ear or provide her expertise in any situation her peers found themselves in. They trusted her protective guidance, and the fellas always watched over her in return. Also, to some, she was the sister they never had but could always count on.

In her own private household, it was a different story. Jacqueline was the youngest of 4, and like her mob at school, she was the only girl. She had 3 older brothers, Pierce Henderson, 19, who graduated high school last year and now attends Central State University, just outside of Xenia, OH, majoring in Bioengineering. Her eldest two brothers, Joshua Henderson, 32, and Carter Henderson, 26, took on a different route to obtain their "American Dream."

Cater decided to enjoy life, making tax-free money up and down the freeways of the Mid-West, traveling state to state. Her oldest brother, Joshua, is 3 years in… serving time for a lucrative yet, illegal business venture that ultimately ended up being charged for fraud. Speaking with Jacqueline on the prison phone, he told her it was "only a failed attempt at trusting friends," instead of putting the accountability where it lies. It always confused Jacqueline; why her oldest brother could rack up fraud charges spanning from 3 separate counties in southern Ohio as bright as he was.

To her benefit, it seemed as if he was operating a legitimate roofing business, and being gullible, she deemed him too intelligent to dabble into anything else other than what he said. However, inquisitive to most in Hollywood

Heights, he laid low throughout his affairs, only keeping his "Day 1" by his side. But to his demise, it got him locked up and serving a hefty 15-year sentence with a parole hearing at year 5 on good behavior. Jacqueline would often write to her brother in prison, updating him on the newest music and trends. He would update her on the day-to-day prison life, the food, the "laws" around the yard, and the God-awful cold showers with grown-ass men. There wasn't a hint of "correction" in this *correctional* facility.

Jacqueline would always recite and pray at night before bed, hoping that her street-running brother, Cater, would realize the risk before finding himself where the oldest is. She adored all her brothers, but not without fear, even for Pierce. At the age of 4, Jacqueline's father died in a head-on collision with a semi-truck on the freeway. As devastated as the family was, they had to move on, and her brothers became her role models as a kid, tutoring her on the "rights and wrongs," the difference between a boy and a man, and through their mistakes. The hard lessons of life.

Jacqueline wanted to go to college like her brother, Pierce, at Central State University, far from Ohio. Her mother, Sasha Henderson and the real MVP of the household is a full-time registered nurse, wanted more than Ohio for her daughter. To rake in some extra pennies, her mother finds ways to work extra hours and graveyard shifts to support her dreams. As her kids get older, she could stay back at the hospital and work more, as they are rarely home now. But it was a sacrifice Jaqueline was all too familiar with and tired of. However, nobody would know due to the radiant smile on her face every time—a harsh dilemma.

Jeremy Sharpe, 18, has been Eric's best friend for well over 10 years. He also grew close to Jacqueline and became her closest male friend over time. They would always exchange thoughts with one another, bouncing odd theories and ideologies back and forth. Lastly, Angelo and Jeremy's daily joke partner because Angelo desperately needed the practice if he wanted to make it. He is what people consider today, "A man's man." He had style, flare, and a way he carried himself in public, chin up, that let everyone around him know that he's approachable, a rarity in Hollywood Heights.

As a kid in middle school, Jeremy once sacrificed his new school clothes to protect Jacqueline from getting teased by a group of petty children for her outdated shoes. Crying and overwhelmed with embarrassment, Jacqueline was frozen in the middle school hallway as the kids carried on. Seeing this in passing, it wasn't in Jeremy's character to witness anyone feeling belittled, especially his friends. With that said, before going to his P.E. class, Jeremy did what he felt needed to be done; he socked one kid in the side of the head, blindsiding him; he then grabbed another student and slammed him up against the lockers before the last 3 remaining kids jumped at him. He just wanted them to stop their silly antics, but it resulted in him being blooded, beaten, and pissed off.

After being suspended by the principal, Jeremy's mother, Irene Sharpe, spanked him relentlessly for his childish antics, for ruining his new clothes, and for her leaving work early. She worked hard for that attire, being a manager of a customer call center. Jeremy's father, William Sharpe, was a construction worker and a man who also had a different outlook on the events that got him suspended. Instead of scolding the young boy, he took him out for ice cream and a movie of his choice, for what he considered was him being a gentleman. Jeremy chose the movie "I am Number Four." Jeremy's father always had a rule in the house, "Stand up for what's right," and in hindsight, Jacqueline never forgot that, and they became close.

Jeremy was the true X-factor in the group, and everyone loved being around him, including the ladies. It was something Angelo admired but also secretly envied in a positive competitive fashion. Standing at 6'3 and 185 pounds, Jeremy took a different approach than his best friend, Eric, to high school activities. While Eric approached the sports realm of basketball, Jeremy sought after the theatrics and photography.

Ms. George, Jeremy's high school freshman English teacher, is the reason for the "spark" that ignited him for the stage and bright lights as well as an in-class reading of *William Shakespeare's Romeo & Juliet*, which had his curiosity. But as a treat to the class for finishing the book, seeing the dram-action movie starring Leonardo DiCaprio and Clara Danes had his undivided attention. To Jeremy, it was poetry in motion. It wasn't just the love scenes or the battles between a Capulet or Montague that intrigued him. But the scenes, as well. And the lighting displayed by the camera as they acted out a scene. Even the still shots. It was also Mercutio, played by Harold Perrineau.

At first, it was weird to see a black man, in a major role, regarding anything Shakespeare granted, Jeremy didn't understand why he needed to wear a dress for the costume party, but overall, he was the man in his eyes and was sold. The way Shakespeare's composed his words, free-flowing and with imagery, made him think, "I can do this…I want to do this." His newfound commitment resulted in Jeremy doing a complete 180. Now with the recommendation of his guidance counselor, directing his focus strictly to the theatrical arts and signing up for photography elective classes, putting basketball on the back burner.

Jeremy was still exceptionally good at sports, being a natural athlete. But he consciously knew that wasn't the direction he wanted his life to go. He had plenty of AAU and 1st place baseball and basketball trophies from his youth, but now in the basement collecting dust in a trophy case erected by his father. He had other various dreams of designing clothes or being a thespian and part-time model. The choices were up to him, and he loved that control of his future. With a GPA of 3.7, the ball was in his court.

CHAPTER 2

By the time Eric arrived at school for classes, just on the other side of town, his grandfather, Ronald Sr., was just opening his eyes and wiping the cold out. He was greeted with a small, soft peck on the lips by his wife, Paula. Ronald Sr. smiled but quickly pointed to his mouth, indicating his "morning breath" if he opened his mouth. But of course, his wife didn't mind.

"Good morning to you too, baby," Paula said as she chuckled. "How did you sleep?"

"Not too bad at all," he replied, as he lifted himself from the bed covers to have a good morning stretch, reaching his hands to the sky. He also gave his stiff neck a good cracking on both sides, then slowly rotating it around in a circle just to get things moving; the cold wasn't the kindest on the old bones.

"How about you, baby girl? Do you sleep well?

Walking back towards the doorway, Paula spotted a mirror on the dresser, fixated on her hair; Paula answered, "Good, baby. You seem to be… up, looking good. I'm gonna get moving here soon and prepare breakfast for us while you wash up."

Ronald Sr. nodded in agreement, "Yea, I'm not feeling too bad… I mean, I'm here. For whatever that means, I'll take it." He proceeded to let out a sighing exhale, finally removing the warm blankets covering his legs. Paula, still standing by the doorway, began to look at her husband of more than 45 years; and smiled in his direction. Ronald Sr., who is still trying to come to his senses, was oblivious, missing the passionate gaze she gave him before she left for the kitchen, giving him time to get himself together.

Being married for this long, with time and understanding, one will learn when to give someone their space, and nothing is wrong with that; it's all in the process of getting to know one another. Paula knew he liked his morning kisses, regardless of how hot his breath was that morning. She also knew he liked his peace when he was getting ready for the day. Even though she had left the room 3 minutes ago, Ronald Sr. smiled as he could still smell his wife's honey-sickle perfume by his bedside, lingering to the doorway. Taking one more deep breath, he planted both of his bare feet on the soft brown yet, outdated carpet.

"Let's start this day right, Lord," Ronald Sr.'s daily message to the heavens above as he awakes- a "Thank you," in the sort. However, it's become something he hasn't been too sharp with over the recent years.

Regardless, as the morning builds, Ronald Sr. freshens up as he gets out of the hot shower and is welcomed by a steaming bathroom, only to stare at a foggy glass trying to notice his reflection. With no immediate luck, he turns on the bathroom ceiling vent to assist with his poor eyesight. There, on the white bathroom counter, Ronald Sr. grabbed his Donepezil from his pill organizer. He gently rubbed his fingers over the indented grooves that represented the days of the week. Then highlighted in a bright green were the letters "THUR," which was the correct day. If he were to slip up, fail, and take the wrong day, it wasn't going to be "Do or Die," at least not suddenly. So, Paula would always come back and double back after leaving the bathroom, ensuring the right day and dosage was taken.

Turning on the water from the bathroom sink, he wanted cold water to combat the steaminess of the bathroom. As he filled up his glass left on the counter to take his medicine, he popped the proper dosage in his mouth. In three strong gulps of water, he sat the glass back down to clear the remaining condensation from the bathroom mirror. It was still blurry to Ronald Sr., but at least he could make out the figure he saw in the mirror.

Moments like this, thinking of how the ending scene of your life will be, can be hard for anyone, and this is the stage of life Ronald Sr. finds himself in. And these moments seem to occur more often than not. Looking at the mirror, he tried to remember what it was like to be a kid again, but his memory continued to draw a blank. He was a decent-sized man, standing just above 6 feet and weighing 210 pounds. He had the typical "old man belly," one acquired with age, but nothing gave way to him being out of shape. "Life" was just taking its toll and still holds an undefeated record. Physically, he could hold his own, but mentally, life was running its course.

With the bathroom vent doing its job, the bathroom mirror became clear in a matter of minutes. And there he was. The reflection of old man Ronald Sr., who couldn't help but stare at his receding hairline in the mirror, and the touch of bare skin on the middle of his scalp indicated his growing bald spot; he quivered at the feel of it, rolling his eyes. However, he loved his salt and peppered beard. Life was doing what it's supposed to do. But being diagnosed with

Alzheimer's disease just wasn't on his list of things he wanted nor expected to tackle in his personal life.

Still hot in the bathroom, Ronald Sr. reached for the bathroom doorknob, leaving the bathroom door cracked, letting out any excess steam as he poured another glass of cold water. As he finished up his grooming, he brushed his teeth and flossed, leaving the mouth wash for after breakfast since he heard his wife in the distance screaming for his attention.

"Ronald! Your phone is making noise on the nightstand. I can hear it," Paula yelled from inside the kitchen as she finished up the breakfast spread. On hearing nothing from him, she left the kitchen briefly, setting the home fries on the back burner to stay warm. Entering their bedroom, she grabbed his vibrating phone and noticed on the front it read, "***Text Message: Eric-Grandson***." Being nosey with Ronald Sr. still in the bathroom, she opened the text message to see what the fuss was about…As innocent as the two were, she was still curious.

"Hey G-Pop!!! Wut u think of these?" (emoji face)

Included in his text message was a picture of the Air Jordan 13 "BRED Edition," a basketball shoe, her grandson has categorized as "major" on his *must-have* list.

After 20 minutes or so, Ronald Sr. came out of the bathroom, whistling to himself as he looked down to fasten the last button on his favorite shirt. It was a black and grey bowling shirt, with the initials "R.B" on his pocket square, and on the back of his shirt read, "Soul Runners." The writing on the back was hard to make out given the wear and tear, and years in his possession. Ronald Sr. was a competitive bowler in his league bowling days; long gone days due to a hip replacement 5 years prior. It's not necessarily the hip surgery that hindered his bowling. Ronald Sr. averaged a

225 in his past bowling leagues. It just seemed to have lost the competitive edge when he went under the knife, often saying to his old leagues' friends, "Nah. I'm good this year… Maybe next year".

As he walked into the bedroom, still slightly damp, he found Paula holding his cellphone and admiring the Air Jordan sneaker while waiting for him, but it looked as if she was nosey again to him.

"Uh woman, I heard you say my phone was going off; I didn't need you to go the extra mile…"

"Oh! Here you go, babe… And hush, it was just your grandson," she replied as she handed the phone over to Ronald Sr. as she leaves the room to finish her cooking.

"Yea, I could smell it when walking out of the bathroom; smells great so far."

"Don't push it. But yes, breakfast will be ready shortly. I'm about to whip those eggs up while the potatoes finish cooking… What else did you say you wanted?"

As the question caught him off-guard, he quickly frowned and began to scratch his head, then palming it with his hand and finally giving himself a quick pop to the head to get the brain juices going. However, that was a red flag to Paula, who was becoming too familiar with his hiccups. As she takes a deep breath, she continues, "I mean, I know what you requested, my love… I know that, but what I need from you is to repeat it for me, ok? Don't fret…"

As Ronald shook his head vigorously, trying to recollect his memory, he fixed his mouth to answer before he was abruptly cut-off by Paula, reinstating the purpose for this test.

"Don't go sucking your teeth at me, Ron," she said, sternly addressing her husband, "Remember, this is key for you and us."

Paula, now standing back at the bedroom doorway, let a few seconds gloss over, allowing him time to gather his thoughts, or as he assumed, "enough time for the medicine to kick in." And just like that, it clicked...

"Two eggs, cheese, toast slightly brown and buttered, like you," he said as he winked, "Oh yeah, and some fruit. But please, baby, hold the eggshells."

Her eyes began to widen, as Paula was surprised by her husband's witty response, and so early in the morning too. She shifted her posture from standing to leaning against the doorway with her arms folded. A few seconds passed while they stared at each other, and both began to chuckle... until Paula abruptly stopped.

"You ain't funny, honey. Now...check your little phone. I'm talking to you, and the home fries are still on. I'll let you know when breakfast is ready."

"Ah! Yes! That is what I smell!" Ronald responded.

She proceeded to look him up and down, still amazed he took a cheap shot at her cooking. Taking it with a grain of salt, she sucked her teeth, slowly rolled her eyes, and departed to the kitchen. The smell of roasted dark coffee and home fries was in the air, urging Ronald Sr. to get dressed swiftly.

Paula and Ronald Brewer have been happily married for 48 years. They were high school sweethearts since the 1960s, and when Ronald Sr. chose to serve in the Vietnam War. Throughout the years, they have been each other's foundation, not letting one another succumb to life's trials and tribulations, in which there are many over the past 48 years. So, it goes without saying that not even Ronald Sr.'s recent diagnosis of Alzheimer's did break their bond. Tested? Yes. Broken? Never.

Instead, Paula made certain his medication was taken daily; he is quizzed constantly, keeping his brain active, and exercising daily with brisk walks in the morning after breakfast. She even has prepared meals for him every day since it became a challenge for him to eat consistently in the last 3 years.

To help save the house some money, Paula picks out some of his favorite items he enjoyed eating over the years; and puts a healthy spin on them.

This week:

BREAKFAST: Home Fried Potatoes cooked in Olive Oil, scrambled egg whites, with cheddar cheese, ½ slice of wheat toast, and assorted fruit breakfast.

LUNCH: Cold Turkey sandwiches, Iceberg lettuce, light mayonnaise, with Dijon mustard, paired with almonds and dry cranberries.

DINNER: Pot Chuck Roast with assorted vegetables and cornbread, a top-tier dish for Ronald Sr., and for reasons he can't quite recall. However, Paula knows. It was a dish his mother made him on special occasions when he was a child and even in high school when they first dated.

Love and support are what every relationship should promote in this selfish world. With 48 years under their belt, they were the living example.

"Oh wow! These are cool! -cool, cool, cool!" Ronald Sr. said, looking at the text from his grandson. His eyes lit with excitement as he was eager to respond. Not being as savvy with his cellphone, unlike his grandson, he carefully typed out his message, sounding off every word as he typed:

"*Did…you…buy…those? -* Send".

Ronald Sr. knew his grandson was a shoe fanatic. After all, the child had his own closet dedicated solely to his shoe collection. Eric couldn't take all the blame, for Ronald Sr. knew he may have created this shoe-grabbing monster, spoiling his grandson since he was born. It's practically every dream of a grandparent when their grandchild comes of age, and they can form more memorable bonds. For instance, on June 13th, 2012, 5 years ago, on Eric's 13th birthday, Ronald Sr. bought Eric his first pair of Air Jordan's, the black Air Jordan 13's, to honor Eric's age. Ronald Sr. purchased two pairs at that time, costing him well over $300 in total. One for Eric, and one for himself.

Ronald Sr. found his shoe giveaway to be playful in good nature at first. He saw it as childhood memories for his grandson to cherish a lifetime for when he is gone. On the flipside, with Eric just turning 13 at the time and becoming a teenager, he saw it as a pact and a friendship between two men. And as kids tend to do with what they love, they latch on, and it seemed from that point forward that these two were going to be together forever.

Flash forward to the present, January 18, 2018, and the purpose of this bond couldn't be more dire. Ronald Sr.'s cellphone vibrated in his hand as he walked to the kitchen for his breakfast. It was another incoming text from Eric. His reply was, "*No.*" His cellphone shakes again; Eric wasn't finished with his statement, "*But boyyyy I do WANT them, they come out tomorrow 2!*".

Eric made sure to get his point across regarding his interest in the shoes; he completed his text message with a sunglass emoji face. Ronald Sr., on the receiving end, was still fascinated with how advanced technology had gotten, since his days of using payphones, when he was 17 in the 1960s. However, he knew what he had to do.

"Hey Paula, want to head to the mall with me tomorrow?" Ronald Sr. asked, "Look at these."

He held the phone up to her face, as she took a brief look at the phone, then back to him; then the phone one last time, "So… you're buying these?" Paula asked, confused, and wanting clarity.

"Yes," Ronald Sr. answered, "I plan to buy a pair for Eric and me. You know the routine… He's graduating this year, and I've bought him a pair every year since he was 13." He began to smile at Paula and continued his plea, trying to win his wife's approval. "Come on, Paula. You know this is our thing". After cooking, Paula decided to sit back just staring back at him, waiting for her tea to cool down. Ronald Sr. stared back, awaiting a response. At this point, she began to skim the magazine articles that usually occupied her breakfast time besides shoe talk.

"So…yes!?" Ronald Sr. asked, but more hesitant not to poke at the situation to frustrate her, but he wanted answers and support in his decision.

"Your food is getting cold," Paula, shot back, not in the mood to entertain his foolishness. However, being the smart-ass he was, he quickly sat down. And not missing a beat, he said a 5-second prayer to bless the food and took a fork full of eggs to the mouth. "It's so good, baby," Ronald Sr., said, still trying to swallow his food, "So… the shoes?"

"You are 'REALLY' serious about this!?" Paula stopped her reading to reply, hoping to provide some wisdom to this situation and avoid any ill-advised purchases he may make.

"Firstly, it isn't even his birthday; you still have like 6 more months. Secondly, you are not 18, sir. And you know these shoes are more expensive every year. I do like them, though, and I'm not sayin' that..." Paula paused as she took another glace at the phone screen sitting on the table. "How much again?"

"...I didn't say," as he took a sip of his orange juice. Looking down at his phone, he squinted his eyes with a little more force, since he didn't have his glasses nearby,

"$190.00..."

A blank and silent stare swept over Paula's face, finally taking her first sip of tea. She tested the temperature using her lips to cool it down and the tip of her tongue to measure the intensity of the heat as she swallowed. "Sir... and you're thinking of buying two pairs!? And with who's money!?" At this point, Ronald Sr. felt she was poking fun at the thought of him proposing such a ridiculous idea. Paula was firm on her stance, being the voice of reason. "Seriously, What about your meds, Ron? We still need those... And that is a necessity. Not these shoes."

Ronald Sr. knew in hindsight that she was right. He's currently paying $180 a month on Alzheimer's medication; two pairs of shoes would cost him at least $380.00, plus tax. As a retired Army veteran who served his country and toured proudly. However, the military didn't look out for him as he thought once returning home for some odd reason.

As a matter of fact, on a wider scale, most black communities, both urban and rural, that served in the Vietnam War were still cast aside returning to the United States. And at what a time, too. Many soldiers came back home to their families and loved ones with more than just post-traumatic stress disorder. At the height of the Civil Rights movement, boycotts became a way to "make noise" on American issues, both by bus and dine-ins. The establishment of the Black Panther Party, and the rise and fall of Martin Luther King Jr., Malcolm X, and John F. Kennedy, who were all assassinated, only added fuel to the burning transgressions plaguing America. This is what many of the Veterans had to come home to once the war ended, and all the above if you were a minority.

To be clear, Veterans of all races returned home riddled with drug addictions. Some got hooked on heroin as a means to cope with their time fighting overseas, which often plagued the question many blacks at home pondered, once their families return, "When will we finally get the help, we need for the sacrifices we made for this country?" Thankfully, Ronald Sr. was not an addict. Yet, in the same breath, he wasn't a respected veteran either. Majority of black communities in American knew this, so many tried to look out for their veterans and men and women that are still serving today.

Giving his scrambled eggs another, go. He mashed them up with his home fries before stuffing them in his mouth. Ronald Sr. pondered on his wife's very valid question for a quick moment while he chewed his food, then replied, pointing at Paula, "Woman, I got this! Now... kiss me!" A quick peck on her forehead assured Paula that he was only poking fun back at her. It was the result of the slight shoe interrogation he felt he was under. "I love you, too," Paula replied, unfolding her arms, as she grabbed her piece of toast for a final bite and another sip of tea before their morning walk.

CHAPTER 3

As the student's chit-chat and slide notes amongst each other in Physics class. Eric was uninterested in the lesson today and was doodling across his notepad, daydreaming about the Jordan shoe announcement that alerted his phone earlier that morning. He figured that if he scribbled in his notepad, the teacher would assume he was taking notes. Before drawing Nike logos on his paper, he sent his grandfather a text message and was waiting for his reply.

Eric was simply trying to gauge whether his grandparents would be up for the challenge, braving the cold, and attempt to get his "exclusive" shoes. The other option, Eric, was dreading to have would be for his grandmother outside, alone; just to bear the burden of waiting in a shoe line. With all the different types of characters out there and the panhandlers that can make anyone feel uneasy. It was still, a risk he thought about trying. He did take account the suggestions provided by Jeremy. But for the sake of the shoes, this was at the expense of a long-standing tradition.

Chivalry aside, being a young teenager and desperate for the hottest shoe, Eric still wanted to stand out amongst the crowd. He even had the thought of floating over him and skipping class that morning. It was, in fact selfish, but a necessary evil to him. Yet, he quickly rejected that idea because everyone was on his coach's radar with this week's game approaching- "If you skip anything this week- your class, a shower, ya teeth, your dinner, your homework- you skip the game…"

Eric was in such a deep trance as he weighed his options; he forgot to put his vibrating phone away, he left it on the desk as it alerted him, instantly reminding him of where he was, and the other students also did.

"Shit! Shoot! …I meant 'shoot,' Mr. Holloway…"

Simultaneously, he quickly tried to find any button on his phone to stop it from disrupting the classroom, and he finally tossed it in his backpack on the classroom floor.

"Shoot, man," and to the class's amusement, they heard a faint reply to Eric's shooting call in the background.

"Bang! Bang!" a random girl's voice in the back-corner desk of the classroom was caught pointing a finger gun at him and laughing. In fact, they all did, besides Eric. For now, he was humiliated because he was caught slacking in class.

Eric's explicit outburst and recovery were all a little too late due to the sound of his classmate's giggling and the grave death stare from his physics teacher, Mr. Holloway. Mr. Holloway was an odd-looking man, as most of his students claimed. He had ghostly pale skin that looked like it hadn't seen the sun in ages. He had icy-blue veins that would protrude in the winter months, accompanied by beady blue eyes and a black beard. To add insult to appearance, he was known for sporting a black bowl haircut, which is extremely off-putting and comical, on a 34-year-old man.

Generally, the class didn't give a damn about his physics class, as the majority ignorantly said it had no place in the

Hollywood High School curriculum. However, to the benefit of the doubt, Mr. Holloway didn't make the subject of physics seem too exciting. He teaches at a snail's pace. The disconnect in the classroom was clear; however, they are not to be blamed, but Mr. Holloway, who was too intimidated by a group of teenagers from the inner-city Rhode Island where he came from. So, Hollywood High School students simply didn't want to learn it, and their antics in the classroom back it up. Some even considered it a "complex class credit," and Eric was one of those students hence, why he was caught at the expense of laughter from the class.

Now, looking up at the whiteboard to only God knows what's on it and what the numbers and letters mean, Eric was caught with his tail between his legs. Mr. Holloway tries to silence the uproar in the class to the best of his ability, waving his two hands in the air, "Shhhh, class!" and puts them back down. As the uproar simmers to a murmur, Mr. Holloway was hoping that Eric could follow up on the lecture before being interrupted.

"Mr. Brewer! perhaps you could provide the solution to this quantitative relationship given in this equation?"

The classroom redirects their eyes over to Eric, clearly embarrassed as he fidgeted with his fingernails. He adjusted his eyes to the whiteboard in front of the classroom, confused at what he was seeing and unable to compute the equation into standard English; he instead provided a witty rebuttal; hoping that could save his reputation one more time for the school year.

Eric's responded, "No, but did *'you'* know you can charge a cellphone with just an apple? Not the China phone y'all use…I'm talking about the fruit". A few giggles emerged, as well as someone randomly yelling "Droid!" in the background. "Due to the acidic juices of the apple, combined with the reaction to the power charging cord... Ta-da! Did you know that Mr. Holloway, Sir?"

With the look of both curiosity and excitement by their fellow classmate's answer, they unconsciously dropped their heads in unison. They tapped into their cellphones; simply fact-checking Eric's off the wall counter for Mr. Holloway. One student couldn't help but co-sign Eric's statement, "Damn... He's right. Good shit, E! Aye, that's my dog there!". Eric pointed at the student who had the decency to acknowledge a "genius" when he saw one. He knew he was smart, despite what Mr. Holloway would throw his way, and even though he secretly knew that he didn't apply himself as he should. It may not have been the answer he was looking for, but it was something "exciting." Whispers followed, traveling desk to desk, which irritated a still dumbfounded Mr. Holloway because of the lesson he was teaching.

"Ok...Class! Phones up, the bell hasn't..."; despite of his efforts, Mr. Holloway was interrupted by the classroom bell ending the period. That bell also meant it was Eric's last class of the day before basketball practice. At the end of the day, like most high school teens, the group usually reconvenes downstairs near the high school gym, adjacent to the main office. However, to Eric's surprise, Mr. Holloway wanted to share a few words with him before walking out the door.

With his chapped lips in need of some moisture, Mr. Holloway's smile grew bigger as he approached Eric, who was honestly fascinated with his off-the-wall response. "Mr. Brewer! ... Hey, smart guy, I like what you said there... that was natural science. But statistics, percentages," he said as he pointed to the whiteboard, "Yet, you don't like quantitative research and equations?" Eric was caught off guard by Mr. Holloway's statement and asked for clarity as he readjusted his backpack. "What's that, sir?"

"Do you not want to pass this class, let alone go to a good college?" Eric looked at him, dumb, "of course…my parents would kill me if…" Mr. Holloway cut him off right there, "Bingo, that's all I needed to hear, man… Come with me right quick; it won't take long, I promise."

Standing side-by-side, it was clear that Mr. Holloway was a rather short man. Instead of standing, straining his neck to speak to Eric, he escorts him to his work computer located on his teacher's desk. Before Mr. Holloway sat down, he pulled a chair out from one of the empty student desks nearby so that Eric could sit next to him and discuss how he wanted to close out the second half of his senior year. Whether Eric wanted to, believe it or not, Mr. Holloway; and like many others, cared about his future.

As they both settled down, Eric became overwhelmed with anxiety in the pit of his stomach, wondering what his teacher had up his sleeve. He quickly began to regret the sassy comment he made aloud in class, which he assumed was why Mr. Holloway stopped him at the door in the first place. Eric's objective was only to ruffle Mr. Holloway's feathers for picking on him so much, which was a success, but now, at what cost?

Mr. Holloway pulled his seat up to the computer desk and quickly typed his password. He then hit "Enter" and rotated the monitor as he went into the Student log database. He continued to type in Eric Brewer's name and showed him his grades for the semester and cumulative GPA for the four years at Hollywood High School.

"It's 2.59," Mr. Holloway said, looking over to Eric, who isn't happy about what he saw on the monitor. "That's your current grade in my class, but the good news is that I also noticed that you have a 2.9 GPA overall in school."

"I know it can be better," Eric chimed in. Mr. Holloway began to scratch his dry scalp, flickering dandruff from his hair, unknowingly landing on his teal dress shirt. He was trying to find the right words to ask Eric about his work ethic or lack thereof without his student being offended, but he couldn't find one and just came clean with the truth of the matter.

"Mr. Brewer, why is this class holding you back from getting a 3.0? ...Or any class, really."

Eric was somewhat relieved it wasn't a personal attack at his earlier explicit language in the class, but just his grades and a whole different beast as a student who wanted a scholarship... Eric simply answered the best way he could to Mr. Holloway's question.

"Well, Sir," Eric, now beginning to scratch his own head, seeing dandruff fall from Mr. Holloway's head and land on his shirt, made him itchy as well, but he came clean with his truth... "Math interests me, and science doesn't. That's it, basically. No secret there for me."

Mr. Holloway's eyes began to squint with perplexity, trying to understand Eric's immature rationale but with no success. Instead, all he could say to his inattentive student was, "You know science is math Eric...And math is science. Yes, they may be different categorically, but they also depend on each other when something doesn't make sense, like your grades." Eric began to roll his eyes, ready to leave, but Mr. Holloway continued, "Think of it as a relationship... I'll say that instead. Cool?"

"Ok…" Eric said, still seated with his backpack in hand, was ready to leave the classroom and the conversation. He wasn't being too receptive to the advice at the time; all he could think about was his friends and the time being wasted right now. However, Eric did nod his head in agreement, just for the sake of keeping the conversation moving, in which his teacher pushed on, "But, on the subject of not making any sense. You have an 'A' in Pre-Calculus, and you're struggling to maintain a C in here!? All I'm saying is that sir, get it together before graduation. Mr. Brewer, please."

"I mean… you could make it a little more exciting in here. Get on your Bill Nye or Magic School Bus bag!! We just don't care!!"

A simple reply was all that was needed from this discussion, but after feeling like he was scolded, a "Yes sir" wasn't going to cut it. Eric responded as he gave Mr. Holloway a *peace sign*; he stood up and walked out of his classroom, finally ready to locate his friends who were probably posted up at the lockers cutting up and playing games.

As he was walking down the steps briskly, Eric first spotted Jeremy in the distance. The dead giveaway was not just his obvious height and frame that caught his eyes, but his sparkling cubic zirconia stud earrings were sticking out like a sore thumb, drooping from his ears. As Eric reached the school lobby, he found the rest of the gang; Angelo held Jacqueline's water bottle playing a "keep away" game with an overexcited Jeremy, eager to catch Angelo's throw. This whole scene wasn't too far off from Eric's assumption about what they may or, may not have been up to after class. He knew his friends well.

As the games continued with each throw, Eric saw the frustration build on Jacqueline's face with every attempt she made at catching her water bottle as every toss went over her head. As one person caught it, they would toss it back to the other, leaving Jacqueline in the middle trying to catch it midflight, while the other teased her. Shaking his head in disgust, Eric still couldn't help but laugh slightly, looking at Jacqueline leap an inch off the ground.

"This shit ain't funny, E! Help!" Jacqueline yelled frantically.

She was right, and for the sake of keeping their 'only' female friend around, he decided to break up the childish play by walking over and intercepting the bottle midair from Angelo's throw to Jeremy… And just that easy, their teasing stopped.

"Ah, Damn, man. We were about to break our personal record," Jeremy shouted overhead to Angelo. Simultaneously, they both yelled aloud, "Forty!" as the pair broke out into their celebratory dance, which consisted of high stepping and swaying their arms in a circular motion as if they were man-made helicopters. While the two were goofballs carried, always feeding off one another. The attention in the lobby was now directed at the four of them and the racket they were causing. It never sat well with Jacqueline being teased by boys, especially in a public setting with friends. She cared deeply for them, but she wouldn't hesitate to slap them. But in this instance, they were just being immature boys who enjoyed screaming obnoxious numbers to the masses at her expense.

"Forty! Forty! Forty!"

Eric handed over the water bottle to Jacqueline while Angelo and Jeremy continued their pointless celebration. "Thanks, E… Took you long enough. How was ya day?" She asked as she took a quick swig from her water bottle before putting it back in her bag.

"I can't complain too much," Eric said, still looking at Angelo and Jeremy dance. Deep down, Eric felt they were making the crew look like a joke around the high school. "But I personally think Mr. Holloway hates me," Eric said.

"That pasty-ass looking, science teacher?"

"Physics… But yea."

"Physics is science... I see why you flunkin' now, dummy."

"See you off-topic, but yes, the real-life White Walker from Game of Thrones. On top of that, he always picks on my ass in class. It's just like how Gelo and Jeremy were just messin' with you, and I had to save ya...In there, I gotta save myself, G." Eric began to snicker at Jaqueline, who didn't expect her water bottle hero to turn on her so fast with his jokes.

"Too soon, playa... Too soon," Jacqueline fired back.

"My bad," Eric recanted, "But, yea. For some reason, Mr. Holloway picks on me and expects me to give him the wrong answer...every time."

"Well, do you?" Jacqueline asked.

"Naw, Hell naw! Check this out; today, I had to give him some dumb fact he could appreciate, or at least I thought... That's why I was so late getting down here; he held me up!"

Jacqueline proceeded to chuckle and shake her head, "Well, what was the fact, Mr. Bill Nye?"

"OMG, you can read my mind!?!"

"Huh?"

"Nothing... I explained to him, well to the class, and his ungrateful ass, that you can charge a phone using an apple; you know, like the fruit?" To the story, Eric's icebreaker came off to Jacqueline as more of approval for his actions than convincing someone he was right in his childish behavior.

"Go ahead... No, you didn't!!" Jacqueline said, continuing to shake her head. She was fixing her mouth to provide her two cents to Eric's classroom debacle before she was interrupted by the school intercom overhead. It was an upbeat followed by a raspy voice and cleared throat before delivering the school's "Last Call" announcements.

"Good Afternoon Bucks and *Buckettes*! It's ya boy, Jacob Teely, with your Lassst Caaallll Announcements!! Now, not many of you listen in comparison to the morning announcements... And I get it that it's time to go home... But not before I address you people!!"

Eric and Jacqueline's ears are lifted towards the intercom above, trying to catch every word from the announcer. His uncanny enthusiasm kept many, who were still in the hallways, attentive to his delivery and message. Given his tone, he always seemed to be upbeat in spirit when sounding off throughout the school.

"...The boy's... my bad... The men's varsity basketball team is currently undefeated; A feat that hasn't been achieved here since we first got electricity in this building, Ha!" A loud smack was heard over the intercom. "Ouch! Mom! Come on. I was just joking!" Jacob, unaware he still had his finger on the intercom button, it was safe to say the hallways throughout the school got a nice laugh.

"Oh no!" Jacob uttered, realizing he was still on the air. He cleared his throat once again and proceeded with the rest of the announcements, but not without trying to save face and correct his misfired joke... "That good ol' principal... Ha, I love her. We call that 'mother treatment,' wouldn't y'all say. But anyway, the Men's basketball record hasn't been broken since it was set in 1986! Go, Bucks!!"

A sound of cheers and applause swept over the hallways as Jacob used a sound clip, he found online that would fit the cause. Students alike all felt good to be a Hollywood Buck student. "Last week's victory was brought to you by our two starting seniors. Our big boy, Leo Capernati; sheesh, what an awesome last name... And our shooting guard, Eric Brewer!!

Someone, please get *ESPN* on the line, *Twitter*-something! That man Eric dropped a smooth 35 points! "Dropped," if y'all didn't know, means a score for the un-woke folks. Uh, I think used woke wrong... Who cares? He was droppin' 'em!! So, whatever y'all do out there, make sure you say hi to the team when you see them in class or passing... They have a big game coming up! Don't be selfish; give them your homework answers!!" One last slap was heard over the loudspeaker, with a faint, stern voice in the background saying, "J, get in my office now!"

"Ok, mom... 10 seconds," A tremble in his voice assured the crowd that his mood shifted. The remaining students in the school loved every second of this escapade. Jacob let out a heavy sigh and decided to speed up his Last Call announcements, trying not to poke the bear waiting for him in her office. "Sorry, y'all... They are playing the Roosevelt Bears, and I'm just saying they need to focus on these rivals, ok? Playas and Playettes, this has been your Lassst Caaallll Announcements!! Now, let me get off before I get written up. It can get pretty, "Petty Betty," in here! Love and Peace!" Jacob concluded as he got off the loudspeaker.

As the intercom clicks off in the main office, Jacob takes one last exhale before heading to the principal's office. By that time, laughter had spread around the school because the students knew that the announcer would get chewed out by his mother, who was also the principal. There wasn't a shortage of characters attending Hollywood High School. On the other hand, Eric had his eyebrows raised with his head still titled towards the ceiling intercom, wondering if there were any remaining messages Jacob could have forgotten. After a few seconds passed by, nothing. Eric summed up the announcement to Jacqueline the best way he could, "That boy is hella odd. I swear to God."

Jacqueline let her laughter be her agreement to his sentiments. "Facts! And no lie, I just found out today that Jacob's mom is also the principal. What a time!!"

Nodding his head in agreement, all Eric could do was reiterate his expression to the zany announcement they all heard, "Yup, very odd indeed, Jacci."

Jacqueline found it hysterical, and now in tears from laughter, she continuously played the "slap" heard across the school in her heard; for free, wiping away her tears. After a minute, she regains her composure, taking deep breaths and exhaling out slowly. She brought her undivided attention back to Eric, who was standing there with a blank face. He didn't find an ounce of amusement in Jacob Telly's Last Call Announcement, or at least to Jacqueline's level. The only thing he could think about now was the rival game coming up on Friday.

"But…See, that's why he hasn't been fired or suspended yet… The principal is his mom!!" Jacqueline broke out into laughter again.

During the announcements, Angelo and Jeremy had a mission of their own; they happily approached some girls gathering their belongings from their lockers to take home. The two decided to "chop it up" with the girls and walk them down the hallway to their buses. Jeremy found a way to get the phone number of the girl he was talking to in the hallway. On the other hand, Angelo got a genuine "Thank you" but politely declined to give him her number; however, he still had another day to fight the good fight. After parting ways with the girls, they rejoined Eric and Jacqueline with their heads held high to see the plan for after school.

"Eric, you gonna meet us at Barion's Pizza after practice?" Jeremy asked, looking down at his phone, locking in the last letters of the girl's name before hitting "SAVE," he then pulled out his black skull cap, a sign he was ready to brave the weather once again.

Shuffling in his backpack, Eric replied, "No, I can't. I need to swing by my grandparent's house after practice, then homework."

"That's true," Angelo interjected.

"I disagree; he's gonna try and convince them to get those shoes," Jacqueline replied.

"Yup, because he ain't shit," Jeremy said, looking at his best friend, displeased with their earlier convo, "You are a wild boy, E."

"Ahh, don't do that, man. Y'all gonna make me feel bad. I hate y'all"

"Ok, bet!! Our job is done, y'all." Jacqueline said, sarcastically convinced their strategy worked.

"Yea, this weekend can be cool, though," Eric replied, "Y'all some assholes, though." Joking aside, the gang understood he had other priorities, and they had no choice but to respect his grind. On the other hand, Angelo could only do what he knew best in these situations, joke.

"Uh huh, you do need to work on that broke ass shot, boy," posing his hand in the air, imitating a jump shot. Eric's face began to scrunch up, "Boy, your form looks like Shawn Marion's... Ol' broke ass shot." Surely Angelo was mistaken. Jeremy provided some jokes of his own as he stepped towards Jacqueline, "I wonder what's more broke? E's shot, or the back of Angelo's momma? Cause, I swear I *broke* that thang outa commission." Angelo, thinking he had a knee-slapper, began to nudge Jacqueline's arm with his elbow. Yet, Jacqueline started to roll her eyes, repulsed at the thought. All it took was a provoking smile from Jeremy to Angelo, and it was enough for them to start the third round of their daily hallway rumbles.

"Boys will be boys," Jacqueline thought to herself.

Opposite of a comedic roast, everyone just erupted in laughter, besides Jacqueline, who had her nose up like she smelled something rotten. Nevertheless, it was a solid ending to a Friday-eve school day. Departing handshakes were exchanged between the fellas, and a hug, to the first lady of the group as Eric left for basketball practice. Besides his cozy bedroom, which was perfect for braving the cold temperatures, the basketball court was his haven, almost like heaven to him if he were to every visit. It was his calmness, his serenity when tensions were high outside of basketball. And he always felt it was God telling him, "There is so much more to life than the Heights." Eric felt that personally and on a spiritual level. This grateful game of basketball helped expose him to the entire state of Ohio, as well as the occasional AAU tournaments held in Orlando, Florida, when money wasn't an issue.

Even with basketball at the forefront now, Eric's wisdom led him to believe there's more to life than basketball itself; basketball just provides that possible outlet, Lord willing. As the school lobby clears and the hallways begin to empty, teenagers close their lockers after retrieving personal belongings and race down the hallway after hearing the final bus departure bell. Some kids would typically walk home with their friends, talking the whole way home. But due to the temperature being a mere 44 degrees and windy, many resorted to taking the bus home or tried to catch a ride with friends from nearby neighborhoods who did have a car and a license; Even if they didn't have a license, someone had a car.

CHAPTER 4

Basketball practice on the hardwood was always a success, even when Eric felt he under-performed. To him, and the way his mind worked, there was always something to learn in practice. He was a diligent student when it came to basketball, and it rewarded him for his efforts.

The past 6 years really took off for him in the sports division, and with the assistance of his parents, Eric got to travel through most of the Midwest, playing basketball for his high school and summer AAU travel team. In Ohio last year, he was named the All-State Defensive Player of the Year, to which he credited that award to his horrible offensive game in the beginning stages when he first started playing the game.

Fast forward to this moment, which is Eric's senior year, a year where he has thoroughly improved offensively and defensively. From grades 11th through 12th, his game has matured into a solid "two-way" player so much that colleges have started to take a late gander at the 6'3 star. The word around town was that "Hollywood Heights has a prospect that's gonna make it out!"

Granted, he hasn't quite reached his personal goal of maintaining a 3.0 GPA. However, he's still on par to make the grade by the end of school if he stays focused. From division 3, all the way to the mecca of collegiate basketball, D-1, people behind the scenes have expressed their interest in Eric Brewer to others. On the flip side, nobody has formally spoken to Eric, his parents, or even his head coach, Mr. Shawn Walker; not even a letter.

"Great practice, gentlemen. Clap it up, and bring it in," Coach Walker stated, clapping alongside the players as he moved in closer, inviting them in to form a huddle. Chewing his gum profusely like a cow, Coach Walker stopped clapping as the players picked up the momentum where he left off, leaving them to clap on their own tune as they walked to mid-court. It was enough time for Coach Walker to reach behind him and pull out the white towel he had tucked in his sweatsuit pants. He started to blot his forehead dry from any sweat resulting from screaming at them; they all practice with a coach's love, something only players can understand.

With a raise of Coach Walker's hand, he signaled "cut," as he waved it across his throat. The team was locked in tonight, and there was no need for a whistle. "Fellas! Y'all still feeling good?"

"Yes, Coach," the team replied in unison.

"Good…good," Coach Walker said as he scanned the players around them, gauging their body language; they looked solid. "We have a huge game this week against the Bears." A mumble of "*Boo's*" and slick-sassy talk began to fill the huddle among the players. Coach Walker didn't mind the enthusiasm; he encouraged it. "But that doesn't mean we won't make this win look easy. Right men!?" The team agreed. "Yes, coach!"

"Alright then," Coach Walker was receptive to the responses; he tucked his towel back into his pants and began to rub his hands casually; perhaps, plotting his next move in practice. "Except for our senior starters E and big Leo, I'll make a final decision tomorrow morning or afternoon on the remaining starters for tomorrow's game. In the meantime, Fellas, I need 'everyone,' yes, even you, John, to work on your free throws... Also, review any game tapes on Bears, and remember what we talked about on Tuesday during the game-film review. They trap, they trap...they trap!"

"Yes, Coach!"

"Now, it's still early in the season, but I want you all to pick up on any weaknesses they may have, as well as yourself, because they are also studying you all." Coach Walker's index finger shot straight in the air; his brain had sparked an idea. He used the same index finger and directed it to his assistant coach, who was standing just across from him in the huddle.

"How many free throws did we miss last week, Coach Lawry?"

Assistant Coach, Marco Lawry, wasn't your ideal image of a basketball coach or even someone who had played the sport. His was a short and stocky, blonde-headed white man, standing all of 5'7- with boots on. However, he took to the kids well, and the love was reciprocated. He had several special connections with the players, strictly basketball, but it drove Coach Walker up a wall. The envy would often cause conflict between the two coaches, primarily behind closed doors.

Coach Walker felt it was the assistant's job to do just that, assist. Assistant Coach Lawry hated to bicker. And when it came to confrontations, was the opposite of how the head coach handled his. He was more of a statistical and analytical man and a blessing to the Hollywood Bucks' Men's Basketball Team.

Ruffling through his notes on his white plastic clipboard, which doubled as an eraser board for plays he would draw up during a timeout, he found the answer. "We missed, sorry... correction. We 'made' 7 out of 19 free throw attempts," he said, licking his fingertips. He flipped the page over and continued reading the next category of stats. "Last week, the Bears made 9 out of 11 free throws in their win against the Monarchs. In comparison, that is our- 37% made, against their- 81% made, which is..."

Coach Walker raised his hand toward assistant Coach Lawry, cutting him off in his tracks. He's had enough. Pacing back and forth, he was trying hard to find the right thing to say that would expound to the team in detail on how he felt about their play last week, and he found one.

"ATROCIOUS! Downright, atrocious!" Coach Walker yelled.

"What if the game comes down to the wire, huh? What if we need some key buckets? If we get fouled, which we will, and we must shoot a free throw... Who can we count on?" His boisterous voice and dominating stature left many of his young players speechless. A few were even looking down at the ground, hoping not to be called upon. As a man first, he despised no eye contact and hated a weak handshake. Granted, these were still kids, high schoolers. Coach Walker wanted to prepare them for the ugly, selfish, and toxic part of life, and as men in this world, you need to be aware of your surroundings and adjust accordingly, but always stand tall.

Standing a towering 6'8, Coach Shawn Walker was a Texas Southern University ex-collegiate basketball star. He was locally known around Heights before his rise to fame; he attended the same high school he is currently coaching.

After his collegiate playing ended, and came up short of an NCAA championship title, only making it to the Sweet 16. With no offers from the National Basketball Association and refusing to join the NBA's G-League, Coach Walker decided to play basketball overseas for 5 years; 3 years in Spain, with the remaining 2 years in Austria.

In the last year of his overseas contract with Austria, before contract negotiations, Coach Walker sustained a fractured kneecap from a shattering fall driving to the basket for a dunk. The defender caught him mid-air, clipping his legs from underneath him, resulting in a devastating collision with the court. It was an injury he would never bounce back from… People in the stands at the time called it a "cheap shot." Coach Walker just chalked it up to being "life," an unfortunate outcome. However, in his prime at the time, and being only 26 years old, his pride took a heavy blow, and depression crept in.

Today, which is ten years later, the depression never really went away, but it's manageable. Shawn Walker finds himself as the head coach of his high school alumni, now preparing them for an epic rival match-up against the Bears.

Coach Walker's imposing height, toned muscular physique, and deep voice tended to have most of his players on edge. The team didn't want to disappoint him, knowing if they did, they would surely hear his roar. On the basketball court, he was a hard man to please, at least on the outside. Yet, given his resume, and clout around the Heights, the players respected him.

They didn't like him but knew he did not joke, especially in rivalry games. Could he be a hard ass? Yes, most head coaches are by nature. But Coach Walker had his own ways of easing the tension around the team, something he learned from his years overseas. So, every now and then, but rarely, he would attempt at a dry joke from time to time. Nothing "funny" really stuck to his players, though. However, some were smart enough to give their head coach a couple of sympathy laughs to avoid running suicides.

Coach Walker's eyes locked in with his star guard player, and proud to see he didn't have his head hanging low, "Eric, Eric, Eric, my man! Come on down. Brother, you are on; the Price is Right! ...Not that y'all youngins' really know what that show is," Coach Walker said, signaling him to stand next to the coach.

One player blurted out, "I know Price is Right, though, coach!"

"That wasn't really the point... Shut up, Khalil," Coach Walker fired back, silencing any other eager players that wanted to chime in with their two cents.

"Eric. My man. This is your time, and your team is on the line," Coach Walker smiled, "Y'all like how that rhymed?" as he proceeded to wink at his players who were visibly unimpressed. Eric rolled his eyes, for he knew the consequence if he missed a free throw shot. Yet, in question form, he still replied to Coach Walker, "With what, Coach?"

Grabbing a basketball from one of the players, Coach Walker said to Eric, "Don't look too frustrated, E... You know it's suicides. I mean... It's y'all favorite thing to do," as he slowly grinned, ready to see what unfolds. "I want you to make two free throws in a row. If you do, you all can go home for the night; my treat." The team's mood swung up and down from excitement to pure anxiety in just an instant. The team began to mumble words on top of one another, creating a chaos of noise for Eric in the background. They were all expecting the worse from this situation because Eric had a critical task at hand.

"Two free throws. Come on, E, baby." Coach Walker said as he walked over to the sideline where assistant Coach Lawry was positioned. He asks for the stats from last week one more time. "Coach Lawry, my brother. What were Mr. Brewer's stats from last game, please, and thank you?"

With his nose buried into his clipboard, the assistant coach was looking at rival defensive schemes to counter, oblivious that Coach Walker had walked next to him. It was the deep-low bark in his voice, especially so close to his ear, that alerted assistant Coach Lawry's attention, almost fumbling the clipboard when called. He regained his composure, clearing his throat, and began to read the stats:

> ***Eric Brewer***
> ***Field Goal- 5/12***
> ***3PM- 1/3***
> ***FTM- 3/6***
> ***2 turnovers***

"Again, let me just stop you there, Coach. Thanks," Coach Walker's grin began to fade. "So, you mean to tell me, we went 7- for freaking- 19. And out of those 7 made... Eric, gave me half of those? Yet, we still missed a combined, 19 Goddamn free throws!?" The team grew silent. So, Coach Walker repeated himself, "19 Goddamn free throws!?... Or am I speaking to myself here?" Without hesitation, the team answered swiftly and with conviction.

"Yes, sir. Coach!"

Satisfied by the team's united response, Coach Walker nodded his head in agreement and continued with Eric. "So, Eric, you have been tasked, young king. Is it in you to make these two shots? Given your stats from last game... this should be a lay-up."

Coach Walker threw a crisp pass to Eric, a perfect bounce pass with some slight English on the ball because it came from the sideline to where Eric was positioned at the free-throw line… And just that easy, the pressure was on. Sweaty palms and all, but as a true Alpha male, he welcomed the pressure and wore his poker face well as he approached the free-throw line and positioned his feet for the perfect shot.

With basketball in hand, trying to calm his nerves, he went back to a time when he remembered a saying his grandfather recited to him as a kid, "Release and shoot for the stars, Eric. It's gonna land where it needs to; just follow through with the destination." In other words, "relax," and don't let the moment get to you. He never knew what that saying meant as a kid, and he thought he probably never would. It just sounded cool at the time. Now in high school, going through the flames himself and battling elite teams in high school. He better understands the word "patience," especially when it's an uncontested shot- like a free throw. It's all mental in the grand scheme of things.

His teammates clapped their hands, encouraging him to make these two shots so they could leave early. He took one dribble on the hardwood and took a deep breath. Eric bent his knees, popping back up, with a good release, and followed through as the basketball left his hands. Unfortunately, it was short, bricking off the front of the rim. Grunts and moans filled the court, echoing to the bleachers, dreading their upcoming run.

"Damnit E!" One player yelled aloud, his hands over his head as he walked to the baseline, "You had 'one' job my, G."

"Man, you suck, bro…" another teammate, piling it on and scorning him.

Eric didn't care, though. He knew he was better than 90% of the team anyway, and that was him being humble. Eyeing down his teammates who disapproved of his missed shot had some blunt remarks for his team as he also walked to the baseline clenching his fists.

"Yea… Fuck y'all too," Eric shot back, "You gonna be ok. Some of y'all need this run."

Whistle in hand and his grin reappearing on his face, Coach Walker silenced all the side chatter and jawing at the sideline. The shot was over and done with. He blew his fox-40 whistle once more and recited three words, "Line up boys!!"

CHAPTER 5

As Ronald Sr.'s watch alarm goes off, the clock on the dresser displayed 4:45 pm, reminding him to take his Donepezil medication. However, in a heavy sleep, he had flashbacks of a darker period in his life, the Vietnam war. In a war where the casualties surpassed 58,000 American troops, not including the P.O.W.'s. Many had a hard time shaking off the experience they endured, and Ronald Sr. was one of them. Graphic memories of shrieking screams, near-fatal explosions, and of course, gunfire. Even cries out to God, from soldiers who thought all was lost; Atheist included. These were all remnants of a past he surely thought was decades behind him. Yet, it was like a dark cloud continued to rain over him from above, drenching him in his sorrow for his lost ones in combat.

At least that's how Paula envisioned it when she walked in the room and saw him. The only reason she was in there was that she heard his alarm ringing from the family room nonstop for the past two hours. It made Paula curious, and she came to check on her husband. That was the moment she walked in and discovered him zoned out in his chaise, in the right corner of the bedroom. Struggling to awake her husband from his daydream slumber, she began to yell at him… nothing worked, and he couldn't snap out of it.

"Ronald! Ronald! Baby!" Paula, repeating herself as she simultaneously snapped her fingers. "Are you okay, baby?" She looked down and caught Ronald Sr.'s right-hand twitching, which wasn't so when she first walked in the room. She grabbed him by the arms and gave him one good shake while he lay on the chaise before calling the cops. And slowly, his hand had ceased the twitching, and he slowly began to open his eyes.

The first thing he saw was Paula's light-brown eyes. They were marvelous to see first while waking up from a nightmare. Her brown eyes popped from the remaining sunlight reflected off the bay window before dusk decided to set in. Yet, encased in her beautiful eyes, was a look of fright.

"Thank God!" Paula said, "Did you have another bad daydream again?"

Shaking his head to clear the cloud over him, Ronald Sr. takes a deep breath and calmly responds, "Something like that, Paula. I suppose." They both look down at his right hand to find it still clinched firmly to the chaise.

Ronald Sr. also found his t-shirt, which was once clean and dry drenched in sweat. Maybe due to his "dark clouds" of the past. They seem to become more realistic than the couple once thought. Each flashback seemed to be more intense. With credit to the Vietnam War, their reactivated feelings were now embedded in his soul, till this day. To make matters worse, Alzheimer's coming into play makes him completely oblivious at times as to why he even has some of these recollections. It has now become a true mental and emotional struggle for Ronald Sr., and he just wants it to end.

"This felt a little more intense. Like last week, I think. How long was I out?" He enquired.

Paula was still concerned but gave him the honest answer, "I was only at the door for a few seconds before I walked over to cut your watch off. But you weren't saying anything when I called your name…" Paula uses her hand to scoot Ronald Sr. over as she sits at the foot of the chaise, "So, that let me know something was up with you, babe… You scared me."

Ronald Sr. just laid there in his sweat. He was trying to gather the floating fragments of his thoughts. Paula continued, "I was even snapping my fingers, at cha,' a few times, but no luck. Shall I click my heels like *Dorothy* next time, love?" she said smiling, not trying to hinder his already damaged ego. She wanted to make him laugh, which is one of life's best antidotes.

He ultimately let his guard down as he cracked a smile and rolled his eyes, "Maybe *Dorothy* can take me back home and away from you!"

Not impressed with her husband's sly remark, Paula playfully slapped him on his arm and fired back, "You are home, Negro…" He suddenly tried to reach down to the foot of the chaise, attempting to grab Paula and pull her in for a hug.

"NO!" Paula screamed, "You are soaked!" She jumps up and yells, trying to dodge his outreached hands. With no success in his attempted grab, they both spend a few seconds laughing over the whole, back and forth.

Smiling at each other, she walked closer to Ronald Sr. and gently held hands for a moment before reaching in and giving him a passionate kiss on his salty forehead. "You might wanna wash up again, my love," she said as she grabbed the kitchen towel, she threw on the bed. She still needed to get back into the kitchen to finish cleaning for the morning.

Through their brief conversation, poking fun at one another, Ronald Sr. wasn't speaking of going home in the literal sense when referencing *"Dorothy"* to take him home; he was speaking about his childhood home on Chicago's Southside. A time he believed was a pivotal moment in his upbringing, pre-war Vietnam. As a black man in the 1960s, the options to be successful came with limitations; and most of it involved something illegal. Ronald Sr., only a teenager at the time, always heard about the white folks on the north side of Chicago that where they had 'limitless' options.

Not to mention, with America's introduction to heroin in the 1960s, Ronald Sr. quickly saw the change for the worse in his community. Around the same time- he was looking for a way out. A gift and a curse; as bad as it's kept, the Vietnam War saved many people from the perils of their own home front, but only to fight in another. You could pick one, the war in the streets of Chicago or the war on the other side of the world. Ronald Sr. felt it was best to serve the country, leave the USA, and protect what's *home*. Plus, he was always in for an adventure to see new sights because he was still young.

At that time, Ronald Sr. was a 17-year-old high school dropout, which wasn't so uncommon. He wanted a better way to provide for his family, and he felt he wasn't getting that at school, nor did they pay him. Paula was his only childhood friend at the time, so she tried to encourage Ronald to stay in school, trying to persuade him not to enlist in the war. Paula always felt that war was for everyone but black people. To her, that wasn't a war worth sacrificing, especially for people she had never seen a day in her life. However, being hardheaded in his teens, Ronald Sr. didn't take heed to the advice.

An Englewood neighborhood native, where he grew up, *"running the numbers,"* was a popular commodity in the 1960s and usually thrived in poorer neighborhoods. At the same time, it was a nice hustle for a 17-year-old kid. He felt the risk of living in a white America and knew many things were in his favor, especially gambling with people's money. It was a high-risk, low-reward situation, and even worse if you didn't know how to network or smooth over a money discrepancy; character was everything when you have nothing.

A couple of his friends became heavily engaged with the Civil Rights movement, but he wasn't so much. Nonetheless, his views did lean towards that of the Black Panther Party; and especially because he saw them actively in his neighborhood.

You name it, he saw it everything ranging from community protection, schooling for kids, free meals, clothes, and hygiene products. It was love for self. However, in 1966, he heard an 18-years-old kid say, "There needs to be peace in Vietnam, and the North should win that unjust war." And Ronald Sr. couldn't have been at odds more with him than that day. "What the hell is that boy, Fred, talking about?" He said to himself because he wanted to leave Chicago and explore at any cost. "Fred Hampton don't know the ins and outs of my life!" Something Ronald Sr. would say when Fred was brought up in convo amongst friends.

In the summer of '66, Ronald Sr. decided to abandon his old life of running numbers and enlisted in the Army; his friends back home discouraged him from doing it, but he didn't care. He wanted out. Ronald Sr. wanted to travel the world and see more than any of his friends in Chicago could ever imagine. He wanted stories to tell once he came back home. Women of different hues and nationalities, languages, styles of food, and the climate and humidity were the complete opposite to Chicago's weather.

Indeed, it was a true culture shock, but it was one Ronald Sr. embraced wholeheartedly. There was no time he talked about visiting a place like this again. Even through a war. A losing one at that, there was still a refreshing feeling about being away from Chicago. However, the "dark days" consisted of intense battles on the Thanh Hoa Bridge and Ia Drang Valley, leaving a sour taste in his mouth. He lost countless fellow soldiers-friends, he knew since he was stationed in Vietnam, only to never see them again, an imprint on his mind forever.

In moments like this, Ronald Sr. went from leaving Chicago, feeling powerful, and on a quest for identity and independence, to now feeling powerless, losing battle after battle, and losing fellow soldiers as a bloody cost to war. "Fred Hampton might have been onto something," Ronald Sr. would think to himself, laying down for the night, in a thick jungle, still able to make out the stars at night, wondering if Paula saw the same ones.

After serving three consecutive years on tour, Ronald Sr. returned to Chicago just after Thanksgiving in 1969 without a *physical* scratch on his body. And two weeks later, Fred Hampton was assassinated. As the community wanted answers, Ronald Sr. just wanted to apologize to the man. The loss of Fred Hampton cut him deep, just as if he lost another soldier, but from a different fight.

Around the spring of 1970, he was reunited with Paula, unknowingly spotting her at a deli market on the southside of town, and they rekindled. A year later, they decided to marry and chose to relocate to Hollywood Heights, Ohio. Ronald Sr. found a job working at a steel factory plant. They only had one child, a son, and they named him Ronald Brewer II, aka Ronald Jr.

So many thoughts had crossed Ronald Sr.'s active mind. Looking at his wristwatch, which his wife silenced, he knew Paula was right. He hasn't been much of his old self in a long time. Finally, finding the strength to get off his chaise, he removed his soggy grey t-shirt, exposing some old war-time tattoos with one word, "Mom," on his left breast. Beneath it was a US flag and a brigade shield. He put on a fresh white t-shirt, ignoring the advice of his wife to retake his bath.

"Paula is out of her mind. I'm not about to shower because of a dream," Ronald Sr. said to himself.

Once Ronald Sr. changed his attire, he headed straight for the bathroom to take his pills. Glancing at his watch one last time, he then turned his face up to the ceiling, rubbing his bristled, peppered chin. He was trying to utilize his brain to remember a significant event that needed to occur.

"Paula!" Ronald Sr. shouted, "Eric is coming over, right?"

Paula, who was now busy, about to vacuum the hallway shouted back, "Yea, should be swinging by after practice! You know he has a big game this week!"

Nodding his head, acknowledging her response, Ronald Sr. walked out of the bathroom and entered the hallway and said with confidence, "Oh, I'm sure he will play fine." He said with conviction, "The team will do well... Who are they even playing anyway?"

Paula was in the hallway, shaking away the loose dirt from the walkway rug; she answered, "...Those Bears. You remember them, right?" she asks, as she flings the rug off to the side, preparing the vacuum. "Move!"

Ronald Sr., not taking kindly to the bark in his wife's voice yet, complied and carefully sidestepped around the dirt pile in the hallway that Paula made to vacuum, "Well, damn! My fault, baby... I'll let ya finish!" He said and continued to walk on the edge of the wall in the hallway, making sure not to disrupt her flow. "But yea, I remember those crazy Bears," Ronald Sr., responding, late.

Paula grabbed the vacuum cord, making sure not to get it caught underneath the vacuum against the suction. Hearing her husband's answer to her question and the fact that he remembered made her heart skip a beat. As the vacuum revs up, making a whistling noise, it makes it virtually impossible to have a normal conversation, so Ronald Sr. decided to make his way into the kitchen.

He grabbed the *Hollywood Heights Observer* on the kitchen table, a local newspaper that kept everyone in Hollywood Heights up to date with what was happening around the city. Different stories, ranging from traffic construction reports, crime, politics, science, and sports. Ronald Sr. sat down and opened it up to the local sports section; he began to review each of the school's statistics from the previous week's matchups. When he made it to the Roosevelt Highschool section of the report, he thought to himself, "The Bears are a damn, defensive machine!"

- 13 total forced turnovers, with 8 forced in the second half
- Their All-star, Shila Rooks, is a top pick for offensive player of the year- Averaging 27 points, 4 steals, and 4 blocks a game.

But the icing on the cake is that they have held every team they've played all season, from scoring more than 8 points in the last quarter.

"What'd you think of that line-up?" Ronald Sr. uttered, closing the newspaper as he stood back up. He remained in the kitchen with the newspaper tucked underneath his armpit and leaned against the white door frame, with his eyebrows raised, admiring his wife as she cleaned.

Lately, she has been a real warrior in the household by taking a hefty load of responsibilities, and he appreciates her more than he can even realize, even with his occasional mood swings and day-to-day slip-ups of the tongue. For Paula, it started to be a thing of the norm; to where she had to readjust her mind as well as the house structure.

Paula was still working the vacuum back and forth, making sure she didn't miss a spec because she couldn't stand doubling back around for something that should have been swept up the first round. As she looked up, she was startled to see Ronald Sr. standing there and staring at her. With her eyebrows now raised, she replied to him, "What!?"

Uncrossing his arms, he responded, "Nothing."

Now frustrated her work is being interrupted, she took a deep breath in; she hated a "nothing" response when asked, "What's up?" especially if you're going to stand there while I'm working. So, she decided to take a brief pause from cleaning, cutting off the vacuum, "What, baby?" Her full attention was now directed to her husband.

An enticing smile covered Ronald Sr.'s face, and he repeated the question, "What'd you think of those stats?" Unfolding the newspaper, he re-read some of the key statistics Roosevelt had over the season, as Paula playfully bumps into Ronald Sr., who was blocking the kitchen entrance. She was still irritated she had to stop her work to tend to something that wasn't serious at the time. Nevertheless, she was a team player and gave him her undivided attention. "And, The kicker, baby… You ready?" Ronald Sr. said, setting the mood and recapping the statistics off.

"Yes, what is it, Ron," Paula asked.

"It reads that the Bears held every team from scoring more than 8 points in their last quarter all season." A look of blatant sarcasm and shock engulfed his face after he finished. And there, stood Paula, unimpressed with her husband's dramatics said, "Why couldn't you just say, 4th quarter?" She then turned her backside to him, making her way to the kitchen sink. Lustfully, Ronald Sr. was tempted to smack her with the newspaper but wasn't in reach. Walking away, she decided to repeat herself, hoping he might get half as annoyed as she had been all afternoon with him and his questions. "You just had to be extra… Next time, just say 4th quarter, old man."

"I got cha 'old man," Ronald Sr. lustfully said but whispered it under his breath.

With Paula now at the kitchen sink, and Ronald Sr. still at the kitchen doorway, they both took a brief pause for each other. While one was taking in the sights, the other was actually doing work and cleaning up the house. Paula's sly remarks were to wear down her husband. Ronald Sr. started to resent the word "extra," coming out of her mouth and being directed at him. Yet, he bit his tongue and instead smiled.

"Yea. It's cheaper to keep her," he mumbled, but not low enough.

Hearing and seeing everything, like most mothers have been equipped with since the beginning of time, she swiftly responded, "Boy! I heard that!"

"Heard…what?" Ronald Sr. asked.

"If you don't get yo ass outa here with that mess!" She said as she pulled her hands out from the sink water and started to sprinkle whatever water left that was on her hands.

Ronald Sr., still agile for his age, dodged the droplets of water leaving her hand. Smiling through all the commotion, he retreated to the opposite side of the kitchen wall and said jokingly, "Don't worry... I won't let 'our' son know I said that. You know I love you, woman."

Peeking his head out into the doorway, he looked at his wife, snickering and smiling as she waved her man over, in which he obliged. They shared a slow, intimate, and loving kiss but shortly lived by the doorbell ringing. "Ah! That must be the grandson," Ronald Sr. suggests as he untangles his wife's wet hands and hightails it to the door.

In the process, he almost stumbled over the vacuum cord still plugged into the wall socket. Opening the door, he was greeted by his grandson, Eric, who was bundled up in his black bubble coat, and what appeared to be two knitted caps on his head. He was still sweaty from practice and couldn't afford to get sick before the big game.

"Grandson!" Ronald Sr. said.

"G-Pop!" Eric replied.

Ronald Sr. looked outside his doorstep; he saw no passing cars to the left then to the right. "How did you get here?" He asked Eric.

"The homies, they just left. Can I come in? It's... uh, cold out here," Eric muttered.

"Oh, ok, ok," With a head nod to Eric, giving him the green light, Ronald Sr. then pointed to the welcome mat that his grandson always seems to overlook. "Wipe ya feet, boy. Ya grandma has been cleaning, and I don't want to hear her shouting. Hey! Want some pizza!?" Ronald Sr. said as Eric hopped in.

CHAPTER 6

As the evening sun retired for the day and the city retired for the evening, many spent their weekdays at home, saving their funds for whatever the weekend could provide for entertainment. Weeknights were about family dinners and discussing the day's affairs. Happy to be childless for the night, Ronald Jr. and Nadine decided to take full advantage of their intimate setting.

Soft R&B played as Ronald Jr. lights a scented, vanilla bean candle. Suddenly, he breaks out in a smooth two-step dance, just to release some of the excitement he has balled up for the evening, snapping his fingers to the background music. Nights like this were special to Ronald Jr. and Nadine because Eric wasn't at home and also because they adored each other's company.

On Thursday nights, before games, and after his practices, Eric has made it a routine to visit his grandparents on the other side of town. It was also enough distance away for mom and dad to have fun- undisturbed. A second candle was lit and placed onto the coffee table adjacent to the roses he bought for Nadine before returning home from work. The ambiance was perfect. He had just enough lighting to where they could gaze into one another's eyes, complimented by the flickering of the candlelight. As Ronald Jr. hears the bedroom door crack open, he knows it's time for dinner. And on cue, the R&B music station shuffled to a more enticing song; Johnny Gill's, "My, My, My." Nadine emerged from the bedroom.

"Hey, babe, do you… need any help?" Nadine asked nonchalantly as she was toying with her hair when she walked out, only to be surprised by the immaculate layout her husband provided. The calming scent of the vanilla bean candles filled the room as the wick burning. She looked down to notice a trail of red rose petals leading from the bedroom door through the hallway and ending at the dining room table where her seat awaited her.

"Oh, wow! It looks so nice in here, Ronnie! I knew you said you had 'something' planned…but wow…"

All she was told was, "Dress nice, be ready to eat." So, she took it upon herself to make sure she met the demands and dressed in a classy yet, informal black dress. She straightened her salt and kinky pepper hair, often in its natural state, and brushed it back with not a curl in sight. She wore her favorite earrings and a pair of red rubies, gifted to her by her grandmother on her 10th birthday. Tonight, she felt it was a special occasion, with her husband's given rules on what to wear, so she didn't mind pulling them out of her jewelry case. It was all about how *she* felt. Nadine topped off her ensemble with a complimentary black chocker and her wedding ring. It was perfect.

"Hot Damn! Whatcha name is, girl?" Ronald Jr. said jokingly; however, staring in amazement- with a hint of salacity. "No ma'am. I don't need any help, pretty lady. Just sit your fine butt down over there and let ya man get dinner ready… Walking out like that, you've done enough".

"Oh, yea?!" She replied with a wink.

"Hell yea…" He continued to eye his wife, captivated by her dinner attire as he headed for the kitchen to plate the dinner. In the meantime, as the music continued to play, she took another glance at everything her husband did before grabbing the remote to find another track to play on the R&B shuffle that Ronald Jr. found on the internet. Finally, she found it; Eric Benét featuring Tamia, "Spend My Life with You." It was their wedding song and Nadine's personal favorite, and she began to hum along with the opening notes. Nadine couldn't help but take another gander at the arrangement of roses placed throughout the house as she approached the dining table where dinner would be served. The way the candles flickered gave no need for lightbulbs. The mood was set, and Nadine was sold.

"I was so nervous that day!" Nadine shouted towards the kitchen, only to whisper to herself, "I'm glad I said, 'I do,' though." Then, putting a little more volume back in her voice, she continued to talk over the music to Ronald Jr. "Well… besides this whole 'rose pedal trail' thing you got going on, you do look nice too, Ronnie. All of this is so nice… We really needed this."

Re-entering the room, holding two empty wine glasses and a bottle of Cabernet Sauvignon, Ronald Jr. agreed, only catching the tail end of her statement. "Indeed, my lady." He placed the glasses on the table and glanced at her with his bright brown eyes. The candlelight gave a glow around him while standing, which his wife loved. Then, passionately, he reached in for a kiss.

"Happy Anniversary too, baby," Ronald Jr. said.

"Oh, I didn't forget, sir… But I see you clearly didn't either, with this special dinner and your request for me to dress up."

"I'm glad you picked up on the clues," Ronald Jr. said as he smiled and returned into the kitchen to grab the dinner plates. On the menu tonight; Two crab cakes, spinach, with minced garlic on a bed of jasmine rice. Dessert; chocolate-covered strawberries. Walking out with hot dishes in hand, she was amazed at the spread, the skill it took, and the presentation. It was amazing.

As a unit, they blessed the food before them. Ronald Jr. then placed his napkin on his lap and said, "Well, let's dig in and enjoy this food! I stepped it up a notch with the crab cakes... Given it's our anniversary and all. Enjoy, Nay."

Little did Nadine know; he was secretly feeling ashamed. On the exterior, he looked good, and things seemed to be in place as he would want her to see. But internally, he was crushed. Instead of an in-home dinner, realistically, he wanted to take his wife out to eat. However, due to some financial restraints, they opted for this. Ronald Jr. was fixing his mouth to apologize for their anniversary dinner's "Plan B" option. But Nadine didn't want to hear his bickering, cutting him off before he could even finish his statement.

Nadine refused to have her romantic night bombarded with things neither one of them could fix today or tomorrow. Instead, she simply wanted to bask at the moment. Placing her silverware back on the table, Nadine took a moment to explain to Ronald Jr. how grateful she was to even have someone attempt a gesture like this. This night was worth more than a fancy steakhouse dinner in Hollywood Heights or traveling to Cincinnati.

"I know money is tight, my love, and Eric going to college next year could be added expenses. But it's good debt in a sense. Even still, we have his first two years already saved up until, hopefully, he can come across a scholarship or a grant." Nadine, starting to see the emotion in Ronald

Jr.'s face shift, reaches across the table, grabbing his hand and wanted to dig into what "really" has his emotions running amok. Then, Heartfully, she expressed, "I know your father's sick, but baby, these are the sacrifices we must make as a team. Not just you."

As soon as the word "You" left her lips, Nadine began to see tears forming in her husband's eyes and tried to empathize with the concern for his father and her father-in-law. His sweaty palms confirmed what she expected, he's not at peace with how things have been lately, and it's secretly eating at him. Bottomline, all Ronald Jr. wants is for his son to go to college, to stay out of trouble, and for his own father to remember the man he raised, which is currently deteriorating.

As the candle wax dripped from the flickering flame, the flame itself gave off an affectionate type of energy. Now, Nadine was only in a rush to comfort Ronald Jr… "All that matters is that we are together, and we continue to work as a team," she urges, as she grabs her silverware, trying to finish off her plate, "We will face anything or anyone that comes our way, Ronnie."

He attempted to rekindle the smile he had at the start of dinner as she continued, while Ronald Jr. took another sip from his wine glass.

"Remember, Eric won't have to live like this… God! He hates it here!" she said and laughed.

The two began to snicker together as she went on. Ronald Jr. didn't want to be a mood killer; he just didn't feel like laughing anymore.

"Shoot, his kids won't live like him either! And so on, and so on. Now, will we ever reach '*The Man*' status? Probably not… But it's our anniversary, and that's a whole different topic, honey. So, I just want you to relax. Sip some wine, please… Get drunk. I'll take care of ya."

"Now you know I gotta be at work tomorrow," he smiled at the thought she took in to look out after him. Sometimes that is all someone needs. Nadine returned the smile.

On the downside, Ronald Jr.'s smile appeared for 5 seconds before his stale look of agitation returned. Nadine only took a few more bites of her crab cake before resting her fork back down. She again grabbed Ronald Jr.'s hand and held it a little tighter as he took a sip of wine with the other.

"I don't even think Eric knows the depth of his condition," Ronald Jr. said, breaking his silence, "It hasn't even got horrific yet… Looking at WebMD and talking to the fellas… I don't know; I'm just mentally drained." He got frustrated and released his grip from Nadine, just at the thought of the downhill spiral his father would face.

"Well, let's not run to WebMD for all of the answers," Nadine quickly said, warning him, "Nor your crazy ass friends… Remember that one time when Keith thought the style in his eye was some form of 'eye tumor.'"

Ronald Jr. instantly busted out with laughter, reminiscing of that time, "Yea, that never gets old; he was crying and writing out his will." Nadine grabbed her glass to take a sip, as Ronald Jr. carried on laughing, "He had us in a group chat asking for advice like we are the docs." He chuckled some more, which was a better tune than the song from the shuffle playlist. "But in all seriousness, Nay, I don't want Eric to know right now, especially with trying to finish up his school year. I just want him to be a kid because nothing will be the same for him once he finds out."

"What makes you think he doesn't know already? He has a cellphone, and he sees his grandfather every week. Do you really think your son, as sneaky as that boy is, doesn't know about his own grandpa? Understanding loss was something Nadine had ample wisdom in because she lost her grandparents back-to-back years, 16 years ago, and neither by natural causes. Her grandmother had succumbed to stage 4 Pancreatic cancer, and her grandfather was killed when his truck slid over some black ice into a half-frozen river. Nadine understood the notion of adapting to one's surroundings, being more flexible, and empathizing with someone going through something greater than oneself. She wouldn't dare to judge her husband's current emotional state; it was a personal battle with his father.

"I just know that nothing will ever be the same when he finds this out," Ronald Jr. said, "No matter how you dress it."

"And the only thing that is consistent in this crazy game we call life is change," Nadine shot back. She looked into Ronald Jr.'s eyes with assurance and added, "He has to know, and you must tell him as his father… Or would you rather let him find out through WebMD?"

"God, No!"

"Precisely," Nadine replied as she sat back and took another sip.

Hearing his wife's valid reasoning over their anniversary dinner, Ronald Jr. sat back in his chair, looking at the spread he took hours making. He didn't touch one grain of rice, which is now lukewarm. All he had was wine. A few seconds of silence filled the room as they sat at the table. The track changed on the shuffle mix, and now playing Avant featuring KeKe Wyatt, "You & I." It was enough time for Ronald Jr. to take a deep breath in, then exhale. "You know… I'm not as hungry as I thought I was going to be, Nay." In a span of 40 minutes, once a look of admiration to Nadine, on their anniversary night, transformed to a look of sorrow and despair as he grabbed his wine glass and finished it off.

Back at Eric's grandparent's house, it was a different atmosphere as they were having a night consisting of jokes and laughs and two supreme Barion pizzas they had delivered an hour before. Local TV commercials play as Eric sits with his grandfather in the den. One commercial that always made them laugh was an ad for a local insurance company, *Fossil Insurance*. They always had popular and humorous commercial segments. According to the commercials, Fossil Insurance CEO, Donovan Rex always found himself in a pickle. He was a heavy-set black man who sported a prominent gold tooth and always sparkled when smiling.

One commercial, in particular, had Donovan Rex stuck on the side of the road with a steaming radiator. It was a hot day, and there he was, with nobody in sight for miles and miles. Thankfully, he had the "Rex app," which is supposed to supply you with a tow service and low repair cost, in reality, depending on your membership. All the while, a dancing dinosaur by the name of *Tyranno-Save-us Rex* would catch everyone's eye in the background doing the "the Hustle," a popular song and dance in the 1970s.

At the end of every commercial, Donovan Rex would recite his popular motto, *"We drive other companies to extinction cause we're bad to the bone!"* It was always the cheesy commercials that intrigued Eric and Ronald Sr. the most. They hated the serious ones, for nights at home should be about laughter and love.

Thursday nights before game days were nights shared with Eric and his grandfather. NBA and NCAA games consumed most of their TV fixation while they indulge in pizza, as Ronald Sr. tries to give pointers to Eric. Ronald Sr. is a persistent quizzer and would present "What if?"

scenarios just to see where his basketball IQ lies. With a critical game against the Bears tomorrow and Eric being the team captain, Ronald Sr. is praying that his grandson can win in front of the masses and against some harsh local rivals. "Will he be an asset or a liability?" A thought that constantly ran through Ronald Sr.'s mind. Yet, a question that is so simple, gave the old man slight stress to Friday's game. Honestly, a situation that's out of his hand… He just wants his grandson to succeed way further than he ever did.

"Hey grandpop, could you ever do this?" Sitting on the carpet, Eric slid his phone across the coffee table to Ronald Sr., who picked up the phone and held it sideways for the perfect cinematic view. It was a Throwback Thursday clip on a cellphone app Eric downloaded called *Jam-a-Gram*. Eric wants to show him a video clip of the vintage, grainy footage of dunks from the NBA's past greats; Shawn Kemp, Hakeem "the Dream" Olajuwon, and Michael Jordan, one being his dunk on Alonzo Mourning, against the Charlotte Hornets.

Analyzing the clip, Ronald Sr. looked back at Eric and replied, "Could I do this!? Son… I could do this in my sleep!" Eric sucked his teeth, "You a liar, granddad." He proceeded to shift his lips up to the side, knowing his grandfather didn't play at that level. "Matter of fact, I had dunked on quite a few fellas in my day. An afro, and high socks, just shining."

"Oh, God! Not the short-shorts!" Eric yelled, laughing on the floor, "I'm dead."

"My shorts were not that short, boy."

"Yes! Yes! They were baby," Paula interjected with perfect timing as she entered the den, refreshed from her shower. She smelled of fresh, minty soap as she was draped in her salmon-colored nightgown. Her hair was wrapped up in a black silk cloth. She wanted to end her day on a high note and see what her "boys" had been up to.

Paula greeted Eric, first, with a soft kiss on his forehead, "Hey, my main man. How's my grandson?" Grabbing his cellphone back from his grandfather, who reverted to the television, Eric was trying to show his grandmother some of the video clips they were looking at. "My week has been good, grandma. Busy, but not too bad," he started skimming his phone, looking for the perfect clip to show his grandmother, and he continued speaking, "Practice was too rough today. Coach can be a complete asshole sometimes."

"Eric!" Paula shouted, "Watch your mouth," as she tried to slap Eric's hand, he began to fumble his cellphone but eventually held on. Ronald Sr. wasn't amused either by his explicit outburst, giving him a cold stare; that was one way to draw his attention away from the television.

"Don't beat me up, G-pop! I'm sorry…" Ronald Sr. acknowledged it, so Eric continued, "But overall, it was good, grandma. It's just a huge rival game tomorrow, and all the kids and teachers have been talking about it."

"I've heard you; your grandfather and I were just talking about it earlier today. Are you ready?"

"Yea, I think so…" Eric replied.

"These kids always 'think today,'" Ronald Sr., chimed in, "What do you actually know?"

"Come on, G-Pop, for real?"

Laughing off his grandfather's comment, Eric finally located the perfect Jam-a-Gram clip and asked his grandmother, "Do you want to see some of the clips I've been showing G-Pop and the ones he's lying about!?"

Waving her hands slightly, Paula signaled, "No."

"I'm fine, baby. Thank you. But why do they have the team practicing so hard before a big game? It makes no sense to me… Don't you need to rest your body?" Paula commented.

"They're in high school. For crying out loud!" shouted Ronald Sr.

Sitting comfortably in his *La-Z-Boy* recliner, Ronald Sr. shifts his body weight to face his wife, making sure he was heard loud and clear… "Back in my day." Paula put her hand up, cutting off the point her husband was trying to make, to provide her own. "But, Ron," she said sternly, "This is 2018. Nobody is 'talking' nor thinking about how anyone from the 50s played basketball… Or whatever year you played with them little booty-shorts".

Paula looked down at Eric, sitting next to her, and gave him a wink. He tried to hold his laughter in but failed. It was rare he found a joke from his grandmother funny, and this one was amusing. "Well, I'm glad you found that funny," Ronald Sr. said, in response to the upchuck of laughter by Eric and Paula.

"I just know it was way tougher for us back then, so stop it! Not much wiggle room for back talking to coaches or lazy play." He continued taking subtle jabs at his grandson. So, Eric naturally defended himself by not even looking him in the eye.

"Grandpop, I have way too much heart for you to beat me one on one. 1950 or now, you stopped it."

The snickering continued as Ronald Sr. looked down at Eric, sitting on their old red carpet and playing with his phone next to Paula. He tried to read his face or look for any clue that his grandson was just teasing him but saw none. Eric, oblivious to the 20-second death stare that scolded him, carried on with his phone. Trying to save face and some of his dignity, Ronald Sr. uttered the first thing that came to mind.

"Hm!! Please… Y'all just flop and shoot 3's now anyway… Leave me alone, boy."

"Love you too, G-pop!" Eric replied.

Unbeknownst to Ronald Sr., Eric was still fully engaged with their back and forth, which kept Paula downstairs in the den. She was curious to see where it was going to lead. Suddenly, all three busted out in laughter over how serious yet, comical Ronald Sr. was behaving. Because, deep down inside, he knew his grandson was a far greater basketball player than he ever was.

As basketball continued to show on the television, five minutes later, Paula was over it as her eyes became heavy. "Well, I'm off to bed, fellas," she said, retiring for the evening, "I just wanted to check and see if you two needed anything?" After dinner, their nights usually consisted of freshly baked chocolate chip cookies for dessert and some milk, all courtesy of Paula. And all night or until one passes out, the pair would watch basketball games and highlights. They would review plays, analyze basketball moves and a player's footwork, defensive schemes, and final two-minute drills. Over time, these became pieces of their in-home studies, and Eric didn't mind it one bit. He was always trying to find a counter over his opponent.

Tonight, was a rare occasion for dessert; they both shook their head, letting Paula know they were 'full' from dinner and possessed no sweet tooth. Basketball highlights and late-night conversations were the only dessert items they craved for the night, leaving Paula free to sleep. "Okay, well, I'm off to bed. The kitchen is closed. Love You, Goodnight."

"Goodnight, grandma. Love you, too!"

"Goodnight, baby girl." Ronald Sr. said.

When he's able, Ronald Sr. tries to find things for his grandson to improve on. He never wants to see his grandson get exposed on the court, especially in a big game like the upcoming one. Granted, Eric knew what his grandfather was doing, and he thought it was cool that he still looked out for him, even as they both became older. However, Ronald Sr. still knew every player had a weakness. Like most right-handed dominant basketball players, Eric also had trouble finishing left-handed moves with his weak hand. At times, he struggled to drive the ball using his left hand, getting it picked apart by any defense in his early years. However, if you give him the option to go left or right, he will keep going right 9 times out of 10.

Ronald Sr. knew that was his grandson's Achilles heel. The good news is that Eric is just a teenager, and he just needed to execute repetition in practice and in the game. However, he can sometimes be stubborn and feels he knows everything, making him difficult to be coached. The immature mind-state of thinking that only your raw talent and ability will excel you in life is a unicorn. Most of that stops at AAU now.

What about those individuals waking up at 4:00 am to work on cone dribbling exercises? What about the girl who is trying to sink 50 free throws in a row before the school bell rings? That's passion and dedication to the craft that Eric needs daily; that's repetition. He swore up and down to his family that he knew what he was doing with this basketball future—often disregarding his parents' help, who were high school competitors in their own time. Nevertheless, stubborn teenager and all, Ronald Sr. loved that boy. The older they both got, the more they enjoyed these moments in the den.

After about 4 hours of straight basketball talk, 1 two-liter of Pepsi, and a bag of Cool Ranch Doritos that he snatched from the pantry. After grueling basketball practice, Eric was stretched out on the carpet, holding a pillow to his chest.

Ronald Sr. was still awake, looking at him and always fascinated with how fast and how hard he could sleep, with the television still blaring highlights of the night's games. Ronald Sr. was exhausted himself. After all, it's now 11:30 at night, but instead of being in his bedroom, tucked away sleep next to Paula, he found himself bombarded with thoughts. Some fuzzy ones about his past. Some about the future; his health, his mind, and his family.

Even with retirement, it was rare for Ronald Sr. to have an in-depth moment to himself, a moment to reflect. There he sat, trying to come to terms with his own health battles. Looking at his grandson, who is now drooling in a deep sleep, he wonders, "How did his life get to be so blessed?" Despite any ailments, he wanted to soak up as much as he could in his den. Taking a double take at Eric's feet, he noticed he still wore his Timberlands in the house, something he *never* allows in his house. Especially since Paula vacuumed earlier that afternoon. Ronald Sr. smirked and chalked it up to Eric being young and him being forgetful.

The earth tone of Eric's wheat boots matched the red-carpet layout in the basement, even complimenting the wood panel wall furnishing the basement den, which got the initial attention of Ronald Sr.… "Shit, those shoes come out tomorrow?" he whispered to himself, trying not to wake his sleeping grandson. Not that his whisper caused much disturbance, as the TV was still on. He knew he had to try and find a way to get those shoes that Eric texted him for earlier that morning. It wasn't his birthday, but it was still a tradition, after all. An unspoken bond between a grandfather and his grandson. These were no doubt a necessity to them, regardless of price. But how? "How can I get these?" Ronald Sr. asked himself, "There must be a way," He concluded.

CHAPTER 7

It was 6:00 am the next morning, the match day. Eric awoke still curled up in the den, lying on the carpet. The smell of country thick bacon frying, and a warm batch of Cream of Wheat mixed in the pot tingled his nose and alerted his sense. Since Eric is eating breakfast there, Paula deviated from her healthy breakfast routine and swapped it out for something that will stick to your ribs. Slowly opening his eyes, he found his grandfather sleeping and snoring, with his mouth open. It wasn't a horrible snore, but enough for Eric to toss his pillow at him.

"Grandpop! You're too loud!"

The pillow landed right in the middle of Ronald Sr.'s face, waking him up pissed, confused, and flustered.

"Boy! You need to stop before I spank ya!" He yelled at Eric.

Eric smiled and started to sit upright, pleading with his grandfather not to hit him. With no remorse, Ronald Sr. chucked the pillow back at Eric. "You, boy! I'm talking about you! Go help your mother with breakfast! ... I gotta get ready for work. Where's the paper, momma?"

And just like that, a moment of joking between family turned sour, as a look of confusion swept over Eric's face. He looked over his right shoulder, then his left, and asked a very reasonable, rhetorical question. "Who the hell is he talking to?"

Ronald Sr. knew something was off… He didn't even really recognize where he was for a second. But the sheer terror of calling his grandson "Momma" had him stuck in his seat for dear life, blinking into the abyss. Then, Eric began to wave his arms back and forth in the front of Ronald Sr.'s face trying to bring him back to the year 2018.

Secretly, and to Nadine's point about their son, Eric knew of his grandfather's condition. But as a teenager, he had a hard way of processing the whole ordeal. So, he took the safe route around his parents and played the "naive" role, internalizing the situation at hand. He would try to play off his grandfather's Alzheimer's diagnosis as a "hiccup" in mental lapse. Of course, they both knew it was more than that. Yet, both continued to beat around the bush, which is common amongst families, when serious topics arise.

"Yo! Grandpop, you okay over there, man? Eric proceeded to ask basic questions, hoping he could bring his grandfather back to reality.

"Where do you work? You know you retired, right?... What year is it, Granddaddy?"

Ronald Sr.'s face became confused and no longer irritated with no immediate answer; he was lost. He couldn't even comprehend what he said to his grandson, let alone even recognize him.

"Grandma, grandpop is talking crazy! … He called me, Momma?!"

Standing to his feet, Eric cried upstairs for help as he walked over to his grandfather to get a closer look. He possessed a cold stare as if his deep brown eyes said, "Who are you!?" It was a sober look that also crushed Eric's soul, and so early in the morning. It was a horrible way to start the day, yet Eric will do his best to play it off, still trying to portray the absent-minded teenager.

"Ronald! I'm coming, babe," Paula said, cutting the fire off on the stove as she rushed down the steps to the den to usher her husband upstairs. When Paula called his name, her voice was that of a light switch, cutting his brain back on, bringing him back to the present until he could reach upstairs and take his medicine. Ronald Sr.'s face became more relaxed as the seconds went on. He jokingly laughed as he tried to play it off, "Boy, you know I was just playing. I know you're my 'granddaughter." Eric's look of confusion now turned to one of anger and sadness; he didn't know if he was joking or not. He even had to look at his grandmother for confirmation of what his ears heard.

"Granddaughter... Oh, hell naw, G-Pop!" Eric shouted.

"Language! Sir!" Paula quickly corrected his hot-tempered grandson. She was not in the mood for any of her grandson's games, and it was only 6:10 a.m. However, Ronald Sr. quickly corrected himself, only trying to shed light on the situation... "Grandson! Duh, I know that Eric. I know you're my grandson. My annoying grandson."

"Are you sure, granddaddy? You looked a little out of it, really confused and lost everywhere... You also called me a girl..."

"You could have helped your grandfather up, child," Paula said, continuing to lay into Eric. She was distraught to see her husband looking like a deer caught in the headlights. She grabbed him by the hands and assisted him up from his La-Z-Boy recliner.

"We had a conversation, grandma... And we just woke up."

Ronald Sr., finally standing on his own two feet, tries to laugh off his most recent episode, keeping all the attention on Eric. "You need to go shower, eat and get ready for your big game! From the smell of it, it seems your grandma has something good cooking."

That was something all three could agree with. The smell of the cooking bacon already gave Eric an extra pep in his step to get showered and dressed, eat, and off to school. Knowing he has a big game tonight, he hoped to get some shots up during lunch if the school would allow. Being one of the top athletes at your high school can come with perks- i.e., gym usage during school hours. And lunchtime for Eric was feasible. With that in mind, he darted upstairs to take a shower and freshen up for school, leaving his grandparents downstairs.

With Paula and Ronald Sr. in the den alone, Ronald Sr. sat back down in his *La-Z-Boy*, replaying the last few minutes of the previous conversation between him and Eric. It left him scarred. He awoke, not to the smell of food but a cloud of fog in his head. As the minutes passed, his recollection of things did too, and he knew he had an important mission for the day; and that sat well with his soul.

First things first, he needed to take his medicine. Arm to arm, the pair walk upstairs from the den. The aroma of the morning breakfast began to spread throughout the first floor of the house. The smell provided a sense of life and a new day to fix whatever was going wrong yesterday, today. Time is always of the essence, and the Brewer family understood this concept very well.

Ronald Sr. was hungry and made his way to the kitchen, where he spotted 6 delicious-looking, crispy pieces of bacon on a white plate. Naturally, he was tempted and decided to help himself to some pieces as nobody was there. Paula had taken a brief detour to their master bathroom to grab his medicine. Ronald Sr. overheard the shower running in the guest bathroom, figuring Eric would finish up in there soon. As the bacon rested by the stove, just underneath the overhead cabinet, Ronald Sr. saw it, tucked away, hiding from greedy people like him.

Licking his chops, Ronald Sr. could only say three words, "Come to Papa." Inching closer to the white plate, he overheard a noise coming from his bedroom. "You can only get 3 pieces, Ron! And the other 3 are for Eric! ... And I'm not joking!"

As much as he loved his wife, he felt she could be a buzzkill at times too. Yet, on the contrary, she could say the same. Making her way back into the kitchen, she gives Ronald Sr. his prescribed dosage of medicine. Also in her hand was her wallet.

"Hey baby, are you going somewhere?" Ronald Sr. asked as he grabbed his first piece of bacon for the morning and how he missed its greasiness. As he took a bite, his eyes began to roll to the back of his head. Paula handed him a white napkin, which contained his pills, to take alongside his breakfast. She then turned around to grab her resting purse on the dinner table.

Putting her wallet inside, she proceeded to leave the kitchen, walking down their burnt orange painted hallway, another piece of the house that needed remodeling. Ronald Sr. always wanted to tackle that hallway. It was something Paula made she put on his "Honey-do-list." But, unfortunately, he may never be able to do it with his current condition, leaving the work for his son or Eric.

The color scheme around the house had become an eyesore over the past years; and very retro. Not to mention the brown carpet on the first floor leading down the hallway was a mess. Everywhere you would look on the carpet was riddled with stains that not even a vacuum or cleaning solution could resolve.

Moving quickly, clearly on a mission of her own, Paula gets ready to walk out the door. She had on her sports coat, black faux fur hat, and grey sweatsuit with a hint of perfume. She hated attention; however, she still appreciated feeling and smelling good whenever she stepped out as a lady. With her back still turned from Ronald Sr., she reiterates her statement, "Don't forget to finish those pills." Walking her to the door, Ronald Sr. was curious as he took another bite of his bacon and said, "Ok. But where are you going?" He has known his wife for over 50 years, and for some reason, he felt something was going on behind his back that he had no clue about. So, he began to eye her up and down, curious to know her true whereabouts.

"Oh…. I'm going to step out for a few hours and meet the girls for a morning mall stroll. I haven't exercised in a while."

"Who… are you trying to look good for?"

"You…"

"Ok, just checking." Ronald Sr. gave her a smirk before kissing her on the lips and then her forehead, as he finished, "Be safe… on your walk".

"Don't do that, Ron," she laughed, "Take your meds, crazy."

"Oh, so now I'm crazy," he chuckled.

Ronald Sr. wasn't trying to cause another early morning rift; he's done enough. But being older now and not as mobile as they once were, he just wanted to make sure his woman was safe. On the other hand, Paula hated to be interrogated going back to her days as a teenager in Chicago. Now, as a wife and an older woman, she knew these questions were more for safety purposes, so she knew it came from a place of love and not control. They just wanted peace in their castle. Regardless, it wasn't that serious to either one of them to argue over; it just wasn't worth it. That's the outcome of being married for 5 decades.

The only person in the household who really didn't comprehend the conversation in its entirety was Eric, who was secretly trying to be nosey. He had been out of the shower for over a few minutes "drying off" through their whole verbal exchange, and without a shadow of a doubt, he now knows that his grandfather takes medication.

A heating sensation began to consume his whole body, anxious at the thought of his grandfather being sick and with confirmation. Then, to his curiosity, Eric turned to face the medicine cabinet directly in front of him in the guest bathroom. It was something he didn't really think about before and opened it, finding nothing other than toothpaste, floss, cotton balls, and a spare bar of yellow soap. No medicine, but he still knew… as their conversation continued.

"I'm going to give Jr. a call this morning," Ronald Sr. said to Paula, "I wonder if we can get a ride with them to the game tonight?"

There hasn't been a game Eric's father has missed. Ronald Sr. simply wanted to participate in the festivities with his son and create better memories. He's hoping that a phone call will do that. Ronald Sr.'s objective was to "play it cool" and casually check on his son without looking or sounding too dogmatic. They have had those issues in the past. However, they are now in a "better space" with time, growth, space, and maturity. In addition, Eric being born was a major component to both parties maturing as men; and showing compassion for one another. It wasn't always like that in Ronald Jr.'s childhood. So, he pledged himself and Nadine never to have that level of disconnect with his son, even though his job keeps him on the move frequently.

"That sounds good, Ron," Paula said, grabbing her grey leather driving gloves off the mahogany console by the front door. "Tell my son I said 'Hi.' I'm going to get out of here. Love you!" she said as she rushed out of the door.

"Well, she seems to be in a hurry," Ronald mumbled.

Back in his own world, he walked back to the kitchen and started nodding his head again as he finished his first piece of bacon, savoring the flavor and the grease. He loved when Eric would spend the night. For his own gluttony purposes, he can binge on food a little more. Needing something to drink, he headed to the refrigerator to pour himself a glass of orange juice to take with his medicine. In the background, he heard a rumbling being made in the guest room, assuming Eric was getting dressed for school. And he was right, for he was in a rush not to be late for school. Still replaying his grandfather's morning incident in his head, he didn't really have the time to internalize it or the conversation he overheard between his grandparents. Eric quickly zips up his backpack and gym bag and heads for the kitchen to grab his breakfast.

"Yo! Sup, G-Pop, I heard grandma say three pieces were for me while I was in the shower."

"And you heard wrong, even though she went for a morning walk which is odd for her," Ronald Sr. said, correcting his famished grandson. He sat in his favorite spot at the table, next to the refrigerator. While he sipped on his fresh glass of orange juice in front of Eric, he continued,

"But you can have an extra piece if you want... Just cause' I love ya, and don't forget your Cream of Wheat. It's cold out there."

Eric, tired of being played for a fool, wanted to bluntly reply, "No... I know '*exactly*,' what I heard... And you're a liar". But with no time to act on those actions, he decided to focus on his breakfast. The paper towel now see-through as the runoff grease welcomed Eric as he drooled at the plate of bacon by the stove. He was trying to choose the *best* pieces for himself. He ended up grabbing three, mostly with fat on the ends. Paula gave Ronald Sr. a clear message to leave the fatty pieces alone. "Save that for, Eric." She said before leaving. But like most humans, the fatty parts are what he loved the most.

Checking for the time on the clock on the kitchen wall, it read- 6:41 a.m., "Oh snap, Grandpop! I don't have time to sit here and eat... I'm going to be late! Else, I won't play!"

He laughed, "Boy, they need you... you gonna play," Ronald Sr. said, sipping his orange juice. Quickly thinking on his feet, Eric rushes to the cabinet- leaving his food on the table, unattended. He pulled out an old *Tupperware* bowl, clearly aged by the telling microwave lines etched on the sides. He also grabbed some aluminum foil from the side drawer, hoping it would trap the heat. Unfortunately, there were no lids that matched the shape of the Tupperware bowl; everything seemed to be mismatched.

"Boom! Breakfast for champs," Eric said as he found a bowl, giving it a blow and removing any particles that remained. "Uh, do you want the bowl back? The plastic is like-orangish... it looks like microwaved spaghetti." Taken aback by his grandson's "spoiled" remarks.

Ronald Sr. responded. "Sure, you can throw it away if you want, but it may cost ya; Say, 5 bucks as compensation."

He got up and walked towards the plate of bacon to grab his second piece. "Or an extra piece of bacon could work."

"Naw… that's dead," Eric shot down the offer.

"Well, hmm… It could be something else, but I won't say it."

Eric was rushing to finish up his food, and he paused for a second, thinking of what his grandfather was hinting at. "Like my new shoes, maybe?" Eric's eyes began to light up with excitement, trying to gather more clues as to what his grandfather was alluding to. But all Ronald Sr. could say was, "Go have a good game tonight, E."

"Yes, sir!" Eric smiled, quickly putting his food away.

Eric rushed out of the building, trying not to be late, and was high tailed up the street, juggling his school bags and food. The morning sun was playing tricks on him again. It was another cold one; partly cloudy with a slight breeze and just under 40 degrees. However, the warm bowl of wheat cream, toppled with bacon, was inviting to his bare hands. It must do the trick. Halfway on his journey to school, which was a 15-minute walk, he finally removed the aluminum foil from his *Tupperware*, which he abruptly stopped. He began to squint at his breakfast; something was missing. Somehow, his grandfather pulled a fast one on him while he was rushing to prepare his breakfast.

"Oh, Wow! How in the hell? That's how you feel, G-Pop? This man 'got' me." Using the spoon, he took with him, he swirled it around in the bowl, hoping an extra piece would emerge. "Oh Yea? This *Tupperware* is trash now. Fuck that!"

CHAPTER 8

After a grueling anniversary night, with no romance for the couple and no sleep for Ronald Jr., he was running on fumes and still had to make it to work on time. With his occupation, work tended to slow down around Christmas and New Year's Eve. Now, with both holidays past them and a new year has emerged, work is back to full operation without skipping a beat. Yet, work wasn't on his mind. Instead, it was the replaying of last night's conversation with Nadine that left him feeling demoralized.

A multitude of questions ran across Ronald Jr.'s mind "What if he doesn't get better? What if he gets worse? What, or when will the unimaginable happen? Or the unthinkable?"

The family van was also running on fumes. He needed to make a pitstop nearby the house at the local gas station, roughly 10 minutes from his workplace and about 15 minutes from his parent's house. Next to the gas station across the street was a neighborhood shopping center, *Hollywood Heights Plaza*, written in bright, neon-yellow cursive letters. Being 3 weeks after Christmas, the lights and decorations were still visible, and illuminated throughout the parking lot. The plaza's Christmas tree was still positioned near the main entrance of the plaza doors.

Hollywood Heights Plaza had been around well before Ronald Jr. was even conceived. A signature staple to the westside of Hollywood Heights; known for always serving and providing to the community. An abundance of black-owned stores operated in the plaza, such as Gigi's Nails, Brooke's BBQ and Rotisserie, a Hollywood Star Convenience Store, Zeek's Cellphone Store, and Feet Justice, which is a popular shoe store. These are just *some* of the Mom-and-Pop shops many have come to love and trust. They were permanently embedded in the community.

As he pulled up the gas station, he put his car in park, meanwhile daydreaming as he sat in the family van. With the window slightly cracked, a gust of cool air blew into Ronald Jr.'s van, shaking it slightly and snapping him out of his deep thinking. Blinking vigorously, trying to bring himself back to his present location, a couple of minutes had passed when he finally takes the keys out of the ignition. Thirsty, and needing a jump start of his own he gets out to retrieve some coffee and fuel before finishing his journey to work.

"Morning. 10 bucks. Yeah, let me get it on Pump #6. Alright… Appreciate it."

Walking out, he bypassed some panhandlers standing near the doorway. He didn't quite see them before walking in, as they surely asked for change. It's so much a preoccupied mind can attain when it's- occupied. Walking to the pump, sitting his coffee on the roof of the van he blew into his hands before grabbing the cold nozzle and lifting the lever to activate the pump. Fueling up the van, Ronald Jr. looked to the grey sky, into the clouds, staring off in the distance; he was getting lost again in his thoughts. Ronald Jr. tried to avoid daydreaming while pumping gas; he hated the cold and wanted this to be a quick trip. But, in a funk, he still couldn't care less about the frigid temperatures, but more so his old man.

As the nozzle clicked off, it snapped his second daydream in the last 10 minutes. It also ensured he got his $10 worth of gas. As his eyes refocused across the street, it was then he noticed a long line forming at Hollywood Heights Plaza. As he checked his watch, it was already 7:05 am, and they were at the Feet Justice store from the angle he was standing.

"What the hell? What's going on over there?" Ronald Jr. said rhetorically, speaking to himself and shaking off the gas nozzle, making sure not to waste any remaining fluid. He closed and locked his gas cap and quickly hopped back in his van to see what the fuss was about across the street. He figured he could be nosey on his way to work and eye hustle the crowd as he drives by. However, God "always" laughs at our plans.

Starting his engine, he put the van in drive and drove across the street. Taking a sip of his coffee, he slowly took his time as he approached the line. Ronald Jr. was contented with what he saw in the line. The usual suspects, some kids skipping class jawing at each other just trying to keep warm; until he recognized a familiar face. There she was, his mother, Paula, in line, sipping her own warm beverage of hot tea. She was wrapped tight in her black scarf, protecting her neck, lips, and nose from the cold and the blustery wind. With that said, she was in good spirits and company. Ronald Jr. immediately stomped on his brakes, almost spilling his own cup of hot coffee on himself.

"Well, damn!?" he said, confused, "Why is she- What is going on!?"

The line consisted mostly of shoe enthusiasts, shoe bloggers, and college students from nearby universities on the outskirts who rather buy shoes than books. The crowd was the total opposite of anyone Paula would typically be around. Yet, there she was, carrying on a hefty conversation while Ronald Jr. observed from a few parking spots away. He assumed she was only engaging with the crowd with hopes that it would take her mind off the cold. He was still lost as to why she was there, by herself.

Taking his foot off the brake, he sat his coffee down in the cup holder, and crept a little closer to the line outside of the plaza. He couldn't believe his mother was here; outside. He again, began to slow down his old-blue minivan, and the brakes picked a perfect time to provide a roaring screech. It immediately drew the attention away from the '*Powwow*' the line was having, to the van.

Finally coming to a complete stop, and to the attention of onlookers, Ronald Jr. yelled, "Yes, folks! I know… I need them fixed! Don't focus on me!"

Trying to keep his embarrassment under control, Ronald Jr. greeted his mother, who was also embarrassed with a forced smile, not wanting this to be any more awkward than it was already.

"Hey, mom," Ronald Jr. said, sounding dry but, smiling.

And being an expert in motherhood, she played the situation off like a true veteran without a hiccup in transition. "Oh! Junior! Hey, baby. You headed to work?" Paula looked at her watch and proceeded to say, "You're gonna be late, aren't cha? It's almost 7:30…" She said, then smiled back at him gracefully, but her eye's read, "I'm busted." She wasn't doing anything naughty. Truthfully, she didn't even need to explain her whereabouts to her son. However, Ronald Jr. still wanted answers about why she was here in the early morning and in the freezing cold.

With his left hand on the steering wheel and his eyes locked with his mother, Ronald Jr. could only fix his lips to say, "Is there something I don't know about?" No immediate words were exchanged as Paula was just taking her time, trying to find the right words to say to her sensitive son and around a bunch of talkative strangers. Never losing her smile, Paula tried to save face in front of the crowd said, "Do you have some time to meet me for lunch? There are some things I want to update you on… I figured your father hasn't done so."

She tried to hint to her son what the issues were, using as few words as possible. After all, she was still in the shoe line with mostly teenagers and young adults who love gossiping—any excuse to take their minds off the cold too. Decoding the message, Ronald Jr. got it and tried his best to harness that burning fire in his stomach that something wasn't right. A wave of new troubling thoughts raced through his mind as he gripped the steering wheel, turning his knuckles white. His mind was his worst enemy.

"What's going on with Dad, mom?" Ronald Jr. pleaded.

Intrigued by the back and forth between a son and his mother, the shoe line now started to whisper among each other, awaiting Paula's response… She said, "Nothing," but breaking code, she could only stare at her son in low spirits.

"Ok, Mom. I'll see you at lunch." He replied.

A disappointing groan swept over the entire shoe line. Upset that they couldn't get the "juicy" gossip coming from the Brewer household. Ronald Jr. bit his bottom lip to fight the uncomfortable feeling he had with his mother. The intense but short exchange left him with more questions than he once had at the gas station, and all because he was curious about the affairs across the street. Ronald Jr. rolled up his passenger side window and proceeded to work, leaving his mother in line.

Seeing him drive off, Paula took a quick sip of her hot tea, just to give her something to do. She knew that her secret mission had been exposed; she was hoping to grab a pair or two of the new Air Jordan shoes Eric wanted to surprise the family. Now that her cover has been blown, she surely feels this will get out to Ronald Sr. She quickly, double thinks about her decision. However, still in line, she fixed her eyes straight ahead to the Feet Justice entrance, written in bold red and black letters. As for the onlooking peanut gallery, she told them abruptly, "And all y'all can mind ya damn business. I'd love to know about some of y'all family's issues… need to be in school, anyway." All they could do was look down or away from her snap. Whip out their cellphones or, rekindle the conversations they had before the van cut it short. But one thing was certain: Ronald Jr. would not miss the scheduled lunch with his mother.

Back inside Hollywood High School, cafeteria trays slap the cold metal railing as they slide down the lunch line to retrieve their food for the afternoon. Lunchtime was always a chaotic scene in the high school cafeteria. Boys and girls alike always race down the stairs and hallways once the bell for lunch has sounded to feast or gossip. Today's menu consisted of Steak Stromboli with marinara sauce, Green beans, Assorted fruit cups, and Whole milk or Fruit punch.

Many high schoolers skipped the traditional lunch altogether, opting for the alternative: an ice-cold soda and some freshly baked chocolate chip cookies from the dessert section of the cafeteria. Sure, the parents wouldn't approve of this under any "normal" circumstances. But this was high school, and lunch wasn't under adult supervision, for the most part, so anything goes for food consumption.

Overall, gossip reigned supreme in the cafeteria at Hollywood High School. Word slithering like a snake, going around the lunch tables, bouncing from one person's mouth to another's ear, either true or false. The people always wanted more. "Who got caught cheating on Mr. Harrison's exam?" "I heard Rick's dad, strung out…again," "So, check this story out about, Nika… you won't believe this shit, nigga…"

What made Eric and his friends unique and a standout amongst their peers was that they pushed each other to be better, not falling into normal constructs that kept other people at bay. They all wanted to achieve big things in their young hearts. None of them were angels by a long shot, and they knew it, but they still wanted more. They deserved more. They had similar mind frames, feeling like this; they believed that friends really could become *family*. It was rare they missed lunch together; this time was used to catch up with each other and not feel rushed. The time here was more than the 10-minute intervals between classes; texting in class can only go so far.

Midway in the lunch line, Jeremy feels his pocket vibrate, and as he reached in and retrieved it, he saw a text message from Eric:

"Hooping during lunch playa. get me a cookie yo! Pause…lol"

Jeremy chuckled as he continued to slide down the lunch line, "I guess E isn't coming today," informing Jacqueline and Angelo, who were also in line behind him.

"I mean, it is a big game tonight, and you know how hard he is on himself," Jacqueline replied, "It's supposed to be a lot of scouts tonight too, I heard. So, yea, his ass needs to practice and get it gear."

Angelo was bored of the conversation and unimpressed with the lunch menu; he opted out, seeing the student's food being plopped carelessly onto the lunch tray, leaving marina sauce covering half of it. "I don't want this shit... they're mixing the red sauce with the green beans! I'm getting cookies, dude" he said, rubbing his belly. It was something about the buttery, sugary, and saltiness he couldn't resist.

"My G, you look like a cookie," Jeremy snapped back, "A soft. Sweet. 'Moist,' cookie."

"Can y'all niggas please chill with that damn, '*M*,' word? Subjecting my ears to that ratchet mess," Jacqueline pleaded.

"Ha, Ha... Ha," Angelo, sarcastically firing back, "Please, Jeremy, don't quit your day job, or your 'fantasy modeling' gig for that matter, Foolio." Angelo's joke drew some snickering from the nearby students' ears hustling in the back and front of the lunch line. And to the group's surprise, because it wasn't a gut-wrenching pull like Angelo may have wanted. But the laughs, nonetheless, ensured him his work there was done, hoping he could stir up some giggles in the dessert line.

"Fuck ya'll laughing for!?" Rolling his eyes, Jeremy wasn't impressed with Angelo's half-witted joke, "Says the man who wants to be a comedian," he said, trying to save face, "But hey! go get some extra cookies for E, since he missin' lunch."

"Say less, my brother. Say less." Angelo replied, and as he was walking backwards and out of the cafeteria line, he saw Jeremy giving him "The Bird." So, he fired one back at him, in common courtesy. As he continued to backpedal out the cafeteria, he bumped into a few fellow students. "Oh! My bad my G," Angelo apologized, playfully dusting off the student's white polo shirt, the uniform shirt for all students.

"Bro get the hell out of my way," slapping Angelo's hands away from his chest.

"Yea, watch out, Lil nigga!" the students grunted and mumbled for Angelo to clear their path.

Short on patience, as most teenagers are- for whatever reason- one of the students decided to grab Angelo's arms, physically moving him to one side so that they could proceed to the main lunch line. These interactions weren't something out of the norm for Angelo. He was always causing a commotion or in somebody's way. And the kid's Angelo ran into didn't want to beat his ass, as they even smirked at him, just giving him a hard time. Like most kids at Hollywood High School, Angelo meant well, and everyone took to him in good taste. He just wasn't as funny as he thought he was.

Jacqueline and Jeremy were not feeling sorry for their friend. Looking on as they continued to slide down the cafeteria line, they started a new conversation of their own. "So, how's the college search going, Jeremy? Time is ticking; Tick tock, tick tock." Jacqueline asked.

Jeremy shrugs his shoulders just as he sees his food plopped forcefully on his plate, just as Angelo imagined.

Another thing that turned his stomach upside-down was discussing his future. It never sat well with him talking about grades and college life; he was a humble kid. On the inside, he knew he was intelligent with a bright future ahead. Besides that, Jacqueline kept him encouraged to leave like he wanted to. "With your GPA, I know you can go anywhere," Jacqueline said, smiling at Jeremy. Her gorgeous smile exposed her pearly, white teeth; it could make anyone melt.

Jeremy was also slightly caught in a gaze as she looked his way. He, however, quickly shook off his "curiosity" and said, "Yea, Jac, you're right... Xavier, Western Kentucky University. Shit, even Howard. I worked hard for this GPA, and I do want to get out of Ohio."

Jacqueline replied, "Well, please pick more places than Kentucky and Ohio, nutso! You always loved taking pics, shit, since middle school... And now with your acting bug, how is Ohio or Kentucky gonna help that?" She let out a slight chuckle, poking fun at him but hoping some of her advice sticks to his brain.

Jacqueline's small pep-talk did get his brain flowing with the possibilities for his future- a hopeful one. And for a moment, he started to ponder on it with a little more insight, but it was at the most unwelcomed time. Now, at the front of the lunch line, and Jeremy didn't realize the cashier was asking for his lunch payment.

"Hey, big man, that's $2.25," the cashier said, repeating herself; she got mad that he was holding up her line and disrupting the flow. "Are you awake!?" She yelled at him.

Jeremy came to life in a daze and paid for his lunch, "My bad, Ms. Sheila," he responded.

"Mhm... You better be glad you so handsome, young man," Ms. Sheila said playfully, winking at Jeremy. Now, making his cash transaction between the two relatively uncomfortable, trying not to make matters worse with the cashier, so he awkwardly winked back before walking out of the lunch line.

And Jacqueline, witnessing it all, said, "You are such a funny man, and without even trying. If you do choose to act, please, go the comedy route."

Jacqueline and Jeremy found a couple of empty seats at a lunch table by the dessert station. They saw Angelo there, cracking jokes while retrieving his "lunch." Next to the lunch table were a pair of double doors, which led to a separate high school hall, mostly woodshop and mechanic classes. Sitting down, Jacqueline and Jeremy resumed their conversation from the cafeteria line. Jeremy was praying and hoping that the second round of this talk could provide further clarity.

"Damn," Jeremy said, scratching his head, "Maybe you're on to something because 'this' is bogus." He began to poke at his steak Stromboli, unimpressed with the decision he made. Jacqueline looked at him and nodded, "I just wanna be great... I don't want to come back here." She quickly blessed her food, then took a small bite of her Stromboli.

"So, what sense will that make by you staying here?" Jacqueline continued, "You want to do 'X, Y, and Z,' but... your ass wanna stay in Ohio, or Kentucky... for what? What has this place done for you to stay?" Her eyes gradually began to widen with every word she recited, trying to get Jeremy back to a reasonable understanding. She continued and assured him, "The world is yours to get. So, get it!"

Jeremy smirked, acknowledging the wisdom given to him by Jacqueline. "Ain't no damn acting headquarters for you in Kentucky, fool."

"Yea, fool!" Angelo interrupted.

The pair at the table turn their head off instinct, seeing Angelo running over to the lunch table with cookies in hand. He took a headfirst slide onto the bench lunch table, smashing into Jacqueline. She has already been irritated by his shenanigans all week.

"Dude, relax! Damn!" Jacqueline shrieked.

"Oops... that's my bad," Angelo replied cheekily.

"You are doing entirely too much... hitting me in the face... move!"

"Aww, come one now…. What cha' gonna do, Missy?" Angelo passively responded, smiling in her face.

Pissed off, Jacqueline pounds the table, ready to let him have it. "I'll tell you what-" however, stopped short, mid-speech. A green bean in aerial flight flung from across the table and ended up smacking Angelo directly on his forehead, with perfect execution. He reacted, snapping his head back, in dramatic fashion, once he felt the juice of the green bean starting to trickle down his face.

Now, it was Angelo's turn to be pissed off. "What the hell, Bro!?" Wiping juice away from his head, looking in the direction of where the vegetable flew from in the first place. Jacqueline and Jeremy found the aerial assault rather amusing, yelping with laughter. For once, someone pulled an "Angelo" on Angelo. He fixed his eyes and locked into the three boys on the opposite end of the table, laughing and pointing at Angelo. Which was an admission of guilt as far as Angelo was concerned.

One boy named Terry Sully, who was sitting in the middle of the trio, fixed his eyes right back at Angelo. He had a husky build and stood around 5'10. He was a charmer with the ladies at Hollywood High School, and they adored him, especially Jacqueline. Granted, this wasn't a love interest of hers, but he was easy on the eyes.

"You doin' okay over there, Miss lady?" Terry asked, nodding his head as he waved his hand in her direction.

Jeremy, sitting next to Jacqueline, could only roll his eyes, hearing Terry's "smooth operator," he was trying to lay onto his friend. During the school day, whenever they ran into each other around school, Terry always made it his goal to greet her with the utmost respect, which Jacqueline and her older brothers could appreciate from a gentleman. It was also far from the normal routine of male interactions with her "Day-1" friends. They were too rough around the edges.

Trying to downplay the flirtatious interaction in the lunchroom, Jacqueline looked back at Terry, acknowledging his greeting "Yea… I'm good; I'm cool. Oh, Angelo? He's lightweight… But thanks, Terry."

"Ok, love… I'm just checkin' on ya… you know?" Terry replied with a smile.

Being snide, Jacqueline hated her personal business on front street. Playing things cool was her way of downplaying her true feelings, not just for Terry alone, but in general. Similar to Jeremy's inappropriate encounter with the cafeteria cashier earlier. No fault to his own, but the situation just made things more awkward than they needed to be, and that's how Jacqueline felt. She did have a small crush on him, though. So, whenever he did come to her rescue, she would try to find the right words, other than a boring, "Thank you."

"But… I'm sure you would've had my back if I needed you, boo." Jacqueline, inclined, with a smirk.

"Oh my God…." Jeremy whispered to himself and repulsed, diving back into his food.

"Damn, right!" replied Terry, and with no hesitation, he turned to Angelo, who also had no issue staring back at his suspected culprit, "The green bean flicker."

Jacqueline, just let out a quiet *sigh*; her infatuation on Terry Sully grew that day.

Angelo and Jeremy were sitting alongside Jacqueline, eating and overhearing every word said between the two lovebugs. Angelo was still pissed he got hit by a food object. But being instigators and for the sake of stirring the pot, Angelo and Jeremy began to point at each other. Telepathically and with some hand cues, the pair would confirm that what their eyes were witnessing was not an illusion.

Jacqueline was in awe while the boys couldn't wait to let their jokes fly once lunch ended. Like many high schoolers, they were childish by nature and couldn't resist the temptation of poking fun. Or redirecting their secret jealousy.

"I hate y'all," Jacqueline mumbled under her breath. Seeing them mimic her mannerism as she was talking to Terry. She then took her eyes off her crush and dove back into her lunch.

CHAPTER 9

Dripping in sweat, Eric licks his lips as he regains composure at the free-throw line. This was his "lunch" today; practice and an appetite to win against the rival Bears. Wiping his forehead with his left wristband, he took one more dribble, followed by a deep breath to clear his thoughts. Eric bent his knees and released his shot, hitting the front of the rim. However, the rotation the basketball provided gave way to a friendly bounce along the iron before falling in.

"Lucky as shit," Eric mumbled, frustrated it wasn't the typical *swish* of the nets he was used to. A sound, truly, therapeutic to a basketball player; no one gets tired of 'that' noise.

"37 out of 50," Assistant Coach Lawry said, onlooking as he finished Eric's workout notes for the day, analyzing Eric's weaknesses and strengths. "Coach Walker will be very pleased to hear you're improving on the free-throw line. And hey! Your mid-range game is improving too." He concluded.

"...36 out of 50, coach," Eric quickly corrected him, "That last, 'bogus,' shot doesn't count."

Assistant Coach Lawry snickered, "Ah, don't be too hard on yourself. That's the coach's job."

As they walked to the empty bench, ending a quick but necessary lunch shootaround, Assistant Coach Lawry was glossing over his clipboard. He proceeded to read more of Eric's stats. "Just 3 weeks ago, you were 22 for 50 in practice free throws and averaging only 47% from the field. Your passion and dedication to the game have improved in ways I can't really put into words, but remarkable... You're now averaging over 53% from the field."

Eric, cheerfully, smiled.

"Not too bad, huh? Keep it up, captain. The team needs you." Assistant Coach Lawry lauded him.

Eric was pleased to hear the praise his assistant coach gave him, soaking up the good news, he replied, "Thanks, Coach."

"I'm ecstatic for you. From a statistical standpoint, of course. But keep it up, man!"

Eric popped open his water bottle, taking a long-needed drink of water while sitting on the bench. Liked like his grandfather in the morning, he attempted to internalize everything his assistant coach addressed, figuring out what the next play to make is?

"So, I still have a lot of work to do, huh?" Eric replied, happy but not satisfied.

"Yes, of course, Eric. Nobody is born 'MJ,' besides, MJ- and *he* even got cut from his high school basketball team; You're young, grasshopper. There will always, and I mean *always*, be room for growth. So, never get too comfortable because, well, that's when you lose, statistically speaking".

Eric's smirk said enough; he loved Assistant Coach Lawry's energy and direction. To Eric's standards, he was far greater leader than Coach Walker. Also, he trusted the assistant coach more because he wasn't full of himself.

"You really are a 'stat,' man, huh, coach? That's your favorite line, '*statistically speaking*,'" Eric started to laugh, taking a sip of his water bottle.

Assistant Coach Lawry was also laughing, "I mean, yea; It's a lifestyle for me. Whether you're hooping or trying to start a business, there will always be room for growth, improvement, and reviewing 'these 'numbers,'" as he pointed to his clipboard. "Even grade-wise, scholastically speaking, you are doing a darn good job."

Eric looked at him and shook his head, "There you go with that phrase again."

"I said, 'scholastically,' sir."

"I got you. But no, I'm not even where I wanna be in that either. Yesterday, Mr. Holloway said that I needed to 'apply myself' more if I wanted to graduate with an overall 3.0."

"Wait, that ghost-looking dude?"

"Yea, he was on my ass about my lack of focus, but he's so boring. Shit, oh well, I gotta do this."

Knowing how hard he can be on himself, Assistant Coach Lawry put his arm around Eric's shoulders, embracing him briefly, and said, "Ah, you're gonna be aight, dude."

"Thanks, Coach," Eric replied.

In Eric's mind, the rivalry game tonight was going to be nothing short of epic. Hell, the whole school had that same anticipation that it was going to be a challenge. Rival schools, possible playoff contention, even college scouts, who have caught word of Eric's talents, might be present. However, to Eric and most of his teammates, the real pressure revolved around their family and friends attending. With ample support, it can also come with ample nerves to perform well at home. So, errors need to be at a minimum tonight. Everyone in the stands will be looking and critiquing their smallest mistakes.

Wrapping up his quick shoot around, Assistant Coach Lawry asked Eric a critical question about his future since they were on the topic of academia. "Have you given any thought to the college you would like to commit to or even attend?"

"Ohio State, Penn State, Arizona… Uh let me think. Oh, Georgetown too!"

Eric, being sarcastic, "Naw, coach. Not really, why?"

"I think Coach Walker still wants to talk to you about that issue next week if you have time. I think he wants to write you a letter of recommendation."

Taking another swig of his water bottle, Eric was confused and replied, "I mean, I haven't received any offers, if that's what you were hinting at…"

"I see, I see," Assistant Coach Lawry said, pushing up his reading glasses. He wanted to make sure he covered his ground before letting Eric off to shower before his next class.

As they part ways, another comment that Assistant Coach Lawry couldn't hold in, catching Eric in his tracks while walking to the locker room, "And Eric, trust me, it's a recommendation that is well deserved."

As an assistant coach, he wishes he could do more, but this was their moment to bond. He smiled at Eric, who only paused for a moment to take in what was said; he was proud of all his high school accomplishments over the last 4 years. He proceeded to turn around and head back to the office, shutting the door.

Eric still needed to freshen up. The lunchtime bell just ended, and he now knows he'll surely be late for his next period, even if it was woodshop. A prominent rule at Hollywood High School, "No show. No Play."

On the other side of town, at the Hook's Diner, there was another lunch appointment that couldn't be missed, and Ronald Jr.'s face said it all. For about 15 minutes, his fingers were fidgeting on the diner-table, completely losing track of time. Looking at the window, his lost gaze from his booth seat bothered his mother, Paula, who sat opposite him. He then reverted his eyes sharply back to his mother; the man was worried. Ronald Jr. knew that as he got older, so did his parents also. And sometimes with age... comes problems and more responsibility.

"Is it getting any worse?" Ronald Jr. said, finally breaking the silence; instead of the overbearing sound of dishes clashing in the background. He reached for his glass of water, still full as he wasn't here for the food. However, his nerves would increase with each passing thought, grabbing for anything within reach to help ease his hands from being all over the place. So, a sip of water couldn't hurt. Paula could tell that her son was stressed. But the issue that concerned her most was knowing that there's nothing *anyone* could do to reverse this soul-sucking disease... or at least, for the time being.

Ronald Sr.'s fate was inevitable. No amount of money, savings, medicine, sacrifice, or prayers could reverse his condition. A hard reality to adjust for the Brewer family. Paula knew she needed to protect her family at all costs, even from the inconceivable. Clearing her throat calmly, she said, "Well, it's not improving. But it's not becoming unbearable." It was hard to grab words from the sky and piece them together while your firstborn looked like his world was about to end. She tried to do the best she could, but his face said otherwise. So, she quickly corrected herself.

"I mean... It's never 'unbearable,'- Such a wrong word... I'm so sorry, son. What I mean to say is, 'it's not killing me.'"

Missing his facial cue completely. Ronald Jr.'s eyes widened with shock as they then began to squint with anger… and confusion. Selfishly, he felt his mother didn't have the same cause of concern as he did. And due to his ignorance with his busy schedule at home and work, he hasn't seen the recent steps Paula has taken to care of her husband. He was still stuck on the last three words she recited at the diner.

"I don't think that phrase is going to cut it either, momma," he said as he took another sip from his glass.

"I'm so sorry, baby."

"Stop saying 'sorry,' mom… Just do better, please."

"I know. You're right. These moments in our life now are very sensitive. I can only really imagine how Eric…"

Ronald Jr. had to cut her off, especially when it came to the well-being of his only son, his only child. He ensured he would do whatever to protect his child's emotions, given how he lacked empathy growing up as a kid. With an Army veteran father at home from war, that impacted him more mentally, than physically. And a hardworking mother with two jobs and taking care of the house. Ronald Jr. had little time to be shielded from life's curveballs. But to his credit as a child, he always wished they could have been a little more sensitive to his needs in the late '70s.

"I'll worry about how he feels, momma," Ronald Jr. said, driving the point sternly, "Nadine and I will handle that." He grabbed Paula's hands and looked at her intensely. His look of worry shifted to a look of love and even empathy. He saw how his stress affected how she responded to his questions as if she was walking on eggshells.

"I love you, mom," Ronald Jr. said, kissing both backsides of her hands.

"I love you more, son," was all she could utter as a tear rolled down her cheek. This was their new reality, and it was a tough one to cope with.

About 5 years ago, Paula had a firsthand account of when things took a turn for the worse with Ronald Sr. Caring for a loved one battling a life-alternating illness, such as Alzheimer's, can take a toll on more than just the patient. And often, there's usually more than one victim in these circumstances.

Ronald Sr. has been diagnosed with Alzheimer's for the past 3 years. A simple procedural check-up with his primary physician was the only thing he was going for at the time. He took pride in going to the doctor, opposite of the negative stigma of black males and their doctor visits, or lack thereof. He never missed an appointment. However, it was at home and with the keen attention from his wife that persuaded him to speak to his doctor. Paula couldn't ignore the red flags anymore when it came to her husband and his health.

Ronald Sr. was the family genius. Especially when it revolved around math problems and number crunching, he could budget his finances better than most people, always set money aside for bills and home repairs.

One precious moment that Ronald Jr. always held close to his heart were the days his father would come to his room, rescuing him from solving tough homework problems alone. Ronald Sr. would see his son huffing and puffing, frustrated after work. And in walks his father, with no real need for a calculator, unless they were complex equations. Patiently, the two would work out the problem together, showing step-by-step how to derive the answer. Not to mention at

Cracker Barrel, he would always leave one peg standing in the triangle peg game. That was his forte.

Besides those "rare" loving moments shared between a father and son. Trips to Hollywood Heights Plaza as a kid, he always saw items he wanted, asking his father, "Oo! Can I have this, Daddy, Please!"

"Sure!" would often be Ronald Sr.'s response, following up with, "It says it's 35% off $30.00. How much is that, son?" If Ronald Jr. solved it correctly how Ronald Sr. saw it, he would buy it, no questions asked. However, Ronald Jr. would get frustrated, and more times than not, then take himself out of the game to get it. Let's just say Ronald Jr. didn't get to pick his clothes as much as he wanted to as a kid.

Over the years, Paula saw an uncomfortable, slow, and steady decline in her husband's mental health. His difficulties with the basic necessities such as self-care and hygiene turned to forgetfulness; he did not remember his name or what street he lived on- plagued with mental confusion and mood swings aimed at Paula. To say the least, it was taxing for her own mental health.

That was 3 years ago; that ended up being the last straw. Still uncertain of his condition at that time and why he was acting in this manner, she took him to see his doctor. There was when they received the unsettling news. Sadly, with her pride on the line and the pride of her husband, she held back from telling her son the condition of his father. And today, this was something Ronald Jr. had a hard time shaking off. "How can you go that long and not tell your son? And why didn't I know?" Yet, the unconditional love he had for his parents never waived. It only strengthened as he tried to envision himself in his mother's shoes.

At the diner still, and a half empty glass of water, Ronald Jr. looked down at his watch- it was a quarter past 1:00 pm- and realized he needed to wrap up this lunch and head back to work. "Check, please!" Ronald Jr. asked, raising his hand, alerting the server. He looked back across the table to his mother, trying to smooth over a rather rough discussion. He looked at her and instantly, memories from his youth, till now replay in a flicker. And in those moments, she always saved the day. That was his veteran, too. Ronald Jr. smirked as he reached in his back pocket, pulling out his wallet only to snicker again.

"Damn"

"What's so funny?"

"I'm turning into dad... I have a coupon for this joint- 20% off."

"Ooh... use it then! We do discounts 'round here!"

After paying the tab, using the coupon, they leave Hook's Diner. Outside in the parking lot, the two embraced with a long hug. It was time well spent for the family, regardless of circumstances. Ronald Jr. then proceeded to walk his mother to her car. "I and Nadine will scoop you guys up tonight. I love you," he said as he opened her car door, letting her ease her way in.

"I love you too, son." Paula said.

Closing Paula's car door, she blew a kiss at him through her driver-side window and drove off. Ronald Jr., still in the parking lot, watched as she drove off into the distance. He began to replay their conversation from the diner in his head, and his eyes watered. He took a deep breath in and exhaled gradually. Shaking his head in disbelief, he couldn't believe the drastic change his family was experiencing. He then closed his eyes briefly, taking another deep breath in, before opening the van door and returning to work.

CHAPTER 10

GAME NIGHT
ROOSEVELT BEARS vs. HOLLYWOOD BUCKS

The Ohio night was crisp with not a cloud in sight, but only stars and a half-moon, peering just over the pinewood trees, which were a short distance from Hollywood High School. Car fumes spewed exhaust from their tailpipes on the street as old school trunks, Chevy's and Buick's alike, rattle, blaring their music at ignorant levels.

Subwoofers thumped into the night as cars pulled into the high school parking lot; It's rivalry night. And a night where you could find teenagers showing out in front of their peers. The few that were there, some were attempting doughnuts in the parking lot with their sport cars. Being obsessive *Fast and Furious* fans, it was ritual to perform tire burnouts, drawing crowds of all ages. Even the locals, not students, or alumni to the high school, were out mingling among the crowd, pregaming with blunts, brews and liquor, trying to keep the body warm in the cold. And, also, the recipe for a good night to watch a game.

The police officers were also outside, trying their best to keep the peace or, however their mood felt for the night gauged their activity. They seemed to be upbeat to the crowd's standard as they also directed traffic, guiding station wagons and minivans to the quickly filled parking lot. Fans and rivals alike made their way into the Troutman Gymnasium, named after Dorien Troutman, a dominant Hollywood Heights basketball legend. He and the team were famously known around the region in the early '90s for creating Hollywood's tough style of play that fans see on the court today.

Avoiding the chaos in the parking lot, the Roosevelt Bears arrived early at the school. They wanted to beat most of the rush as they were focused and eager to steal a victory on rival turf. Nadine was also inside the gym, who saw her husband and flagged down Ronald Jr. as he walked into the Troutman Gymnasium.

Being the gentleman, as his father raised him to be, he dropped his wife and parents off at the main entrance first before parking and walking in himself. Upon entrance, he was welcomed by the blaring music from the overhead speakers as some players shot around. He then took a glance at the court and didn't see Eric.

In typical parent fandom, Ronald Jr. had acquired every piece of school merchandise you could find, such as a Hollywood Buck antler top hat, a Bucks whistle, an Air horn, two vintage Bucks' scarves, and a *"My son is #1"* Bucks' t-shirt, which was the icing on the cake. He was a superfan of his son, and he couldn't be prouder.

Walking in Nadine's direction, he spotted his parents sitting next to her, who were happy to tag along for the night. They wouldn't miss this game for the world or time with their family. Paula smiled briefly as she saw her son approaching the bleachers. Only for a few seconds before redirecting her attention to the buttery popcorn that stole her heart at that moment. She didn't say much after the initial greeting. Ronald Sr. had his attention focused on the basketball court.

"Look at all these tall, young, Whippersnappers, Jesus."

No doubt, Ronald Sr. was looking at the future of basketball right before his eyes, all but his grandson. "Where's my little man?" Ronald Sr. blurted out, as he watched the teams go through their routine drills, consisting of layups lines, bounce pass, chest pass drills, and defensive slides, all warming up for battle.

"Eh… He's probably in the locker room, dropping a deuce," Ronald Jr. replied, only to find a look of disgust written on his father's face. "What, dad? I used to… Got me good and ready, with no backup. *BLOOP-BLOOP!*"

"Oop, not the sound effects" Nadine, chimed in not missing a beat, holding in her laugh.

Ronald Jr. continued to dig himself into a bigger hole because his father's nauseated look didn't help his case. "I mean, either that… or he's talking with his coach back there because I don't see him either, dad". Trying to save face, Ronald Jr. ended up just shaking his head over the foolishness he made, attempting to make his dad smile. Soaking in the awkward moment, Ronald Jr. decided to take his seat to get ready for the game.

Also, in the gym, cheering for Eric was his crew; Jacqueline, Angelo, and Jeremy sitting in the back section of the home team bleachers. And like most rivalry games, they were exchanging '*pleasantries*' to the opposing school's section. One popular rival chant that the school loved sounded aloud across the gymnasium:

"We da Bucks... Too Tough!... You can't handle us! Naw, naw. Not wit us!"

"We da Bucks... Too Tough!... You can't handle us! Naw, naw. Not wit us- we da BUCKS!"

As the chant recited, the entire home team section began stomping and clapping, creating an *A cappella* beat in unison and making the whole gym rattle. Even if both teams didn't win another game all year, this one was for all the marbles. They hated each other. A Hollywood Heights generational pool of talent that each school possessed made these games become a tradition.

Middle fingers and curse words were also exchanged between the two schools, not just from the rowdy students.

"Fuck that school!" Ronald Jr. yelled out, blowing his whistle fiercely, accompanying the air horn he held in his left hand. A look of surprise and embarrassment appeared on Nadine's face. "You are feeling yourself, huh?" she replied, "I can't take yo ass nowhere."

She wasn't about to kill her husband's energy by playing the more passive role and understanding the hostile environment they were in. Also, she loved his sailor mouth on the low. It gave her a spark and hoping they could make up for last night. Ronald Jr. planted a kiss on her cheek, "I love you, babe. I'll turn it down a notch, only for you."

Paula was also pleased to hear that his cussing would be at a minimum, "Thank you, Nay," smiling at Nadine before returning to her popcorn bucket. To Paula's surprise, she looked down to find her husband's hands in her bowl. She instantly slapped Ronald Sr.'s hand away, only able to grab a few kernels for himself. "If you want some, go buy your own." Paula snapped.

"Oh, you feelin' ya self, huh lady?" was all Ronald Sr. could say.

With 4 minutes left on the warm-up clock, a gradual roar of applause and cheers began to erupt. Eric and Coach Walker were walking out of the locker room together. Not letting the noise become a distraction for him, Eric held a shoebox tucked under his right arm as he raced to the bench and placed it under his seat. He then rejoined his team at the warm-up line.

"I see you with the heat, my G!" a fellow teammate responded, seeing Eric's fresh new Air Jordan 13, BRED Editions. They were everything the picture on his cellphone provided and even more. The red was deeper; the black seemed to be crisp and not dry. The white was that of snow, spotless. Eric got his shoes. The exact pair he wanted since they were talking about the release last week. Now, they were on his feet and for his team to marvel at.

"Fuck all that heat shit," another teammate interjected, "You better have come to play tonight… Those shoes better give you a triple dub, nigga! But yea… they are nice, man. And they go with our colors; sheesh! I'm in love!

"Look, I'm just as surprised as y'all," Eric uttered, receiving a pass for a warm-up shot. "I walk into the locker room, and 'boom,' there they were."

"So, what's in the other box you put by da bench?"

"Oh. That's another pair for my grandfather."

"Aye… this nigga got bread, my dude!"

"Not even," Eric replied, taking another shot inside the paint, "It's just something me and my grandfather have going on for some time now; it's nothing crazy.

"*For some time now*. Must be nice, though."

"Yea, it is," Eric shot back. He wasn't sure if his team was being supportive or salty at his relationship with his grandfather, or it could be the shoes.

Coach Walker headed to the bench with his white towel in hand, helping to manage his persistent sweating under the bright lights. He sat next to Assistant Coach Lawry on the team bench, who was busy entering players names and jersey numbers in the official game book before tip-off. Last week, according to the game officials, they failed to do it on time, resulting in technical foul shots before tip-off. Coach Walker could not afford to be that neglectful tonight.

"This game is huge! You can feel the atmosphere here. What a time!" Coach Walker said, pulling his seat closer to the court. Still looking over his assistant's shoulder, making sure he correctly entered the team's information. Taking a brief pause from writing, Assistant Coach Lawry hunched over and looked over his own shoulder, asking coach, "How are you feelin' about the kids tonight?" he was only trying to gauge the head coach's excitement given the magnitude of tonight.

"Mm, I think we gon' be ok… We just have to communicate, no ball hogging." He replied as he grabbed his towel and wiped away some pre-game sweat that started to develop on his forehead, and then continued, "Free throws too. Those are too damn critical. And let's not forget defensive stops. These fuckin kids just want to score, score, score. Play some damn, D!"

In other words, Coach Walker needed his "stars" in Eric Brewer and center, Leo Capernati, to stand out. After last week's game, he received confirmation that college basketball scouts, ranging from Division 1 to Division 3, would be present tonight. So, he took the liberty of speaking to Eric, the team captain, in the locker room before the game. Coach Walker was certain Eric might have some anxiety leading into this game. He assured him it was his time to shine. And Eric needed to know that, harness it, and control it. He couldn't afford to panic tonight. While he may be one of the main attractions in tonight's game, the Bears' were no pushovers.

Assistant Coach Lawry understood exactly what Coach Walker meant, nodding his head in agreement. As a "statistics guy," he knew exactly what an asset and a liability were in basketball and their team.

Looking under and around his seat, Coach Walker located Eric's shoe box a couple of seats down; he pointed at it, signaling to the assistant coach. "So, E, has his new shoes he's been pressed about all freakin' week. I think his parents, or his momma brought those in here a half-hour ago… Because if that boy would have risked skipping school for those damn shoes? Forget this season altogether. So, I'm glad he used that little pea brain of his." Assistant Coach Lawry laughed, pushing through his assignment to finalize the team roster. "Yea, but those shoes look damn good though".

"Hell yea!" Coach Walker, confirming as they shared a laugh.

On a personal note, both coaches didn't know how serious it meant for Eric was getting his new pair of shoes before the tip-off tonight. And It meant the world to him. There he was, warming up on the home court with them on his feet—the Air Jordan 13's.

Two minutes left on the clock to warm up. The layup line transitioned into a random shootaround, making sure their limbs were loose and warm, partly fueled by the warmup music blasting in the gym at this time. Looking at the clock, Eric passes the ball he was about to use in the layup line over to a teammate and heads to the bench to grab the shoebox under his seat.

"Shouldn't you be shooting?" Coach Walker shouted down the bench.

"Yea, just let me do this right quick, please coach," Eric replied, running off before his coach could give him the "OK."

"Uh… alright. Tip-off is about to start."

With no reply as kids tend to do, Coach Walker wasn't about to yell any more than he needed to. He needed to save his voice for the game. Not to mention, the gym was a packed house filled with fans, cheerleaders, mascots, and music. Facing the court, Coach Walker studied the Roosevelt Bears' a little more closely. "They look solid," Coach Walker mumbled to himself, grabbing his towel.

Both teams began to mean-mug one another, after taking a warm-up shot on opposite ends of the court, not letting one smile be exposed. It was the universal expression for the destruction yet to come. Conquering the opposing team and never letting them see you sweat; this was the Hollywood, Ohio way, *"The Heart of it All."* Where there is no heart for the weak, only failure and misery.

CHAPTER 11

"**O**h, look!" Nadine pointed, waving down her son, "Here comes Eric!" He quickly approached his family, who weren't too far away, sitting on the bleachers. He first greeted his mother and grandmother with a quick hug and a kiss. "Sweaty cheeks!" his grandmother, screamed. Seeing how hyped his father was for the game- and his attire- left him speechless. After taking a quick pause to look over the whole ensemble, Eric gave his father a dap and a head nod, ensuring a victory tonight.

"Dad, I think you are slightly obsessed," Eric said briefly, finally making his way to his grandfather.

"No, you're just focused on the wrong things, playa. You need to get back on the court and focus," Ronald Jr. said, as he blew his air horn for good measure.

And his father was right; this wasn't a social call. Eric was set on getting back with his team on the floor. He gave his grandfather the shoe box, wrapped in brown paper with details that resembled used grocery bags. All Eric could say to him in the short time they had was, "Here, G-Pop... We matchin' tonight, man." Eric lifted his leg to plant his right foot on the bleacher, giving his grandfather and the family a closer look at the Air Jordan shoe release on his feet.

Ronald Jr. was perplexed; he leaned over to his mother and whispered, "They look expensive."

Paula leaned back into her son and gave him a swift elbow to his gut.

"Ow! Mom," he yelled, rubbing his ribs. For tonight, it wasn't about the money. "Goddamn, momma".

"Watch ya mouth, nigga," she shot back, in a low tone only her son could catch. "And they look, so beautiful, grandson!" Paula interjects, returning to her normal octaves. All the while Ronald Jr. soothes over his stomach from the sneak jab. "I hope you kick some butt tonight!" However, all of this left her puzzled. Simultaneously, while complimenting her grandson's shoe, she wanted to know how he got them to begin with. To her own recollection, she went straight home after lunch with her son.

Even when they first encountered each other that morning at Hollywood Heights Plaza. Her own embarrassment to the entire situation and getting busted red-handed sent her home. Paula left the Feet Justice line, feeling defeated, and decided she would speak to her son next time before doing anything impulsive. So, sitting here on the bleachers, Paula wasn't sure how Eric possessed his new shoes; she just prayed her grandson didn't do anything crazy to get them. Always watching the morning news, she knew kids would go extreme for material items, which never sat right with her soul.

"Well, I have you to thank, G-Ma… Didn't think you'd 'actually' do it? This was the surprise I needed for tonight!" Paula was now more confused than ever, and her face surely revealed such skepticism because she didn't buy these shoes. But she did her best to play along with whatever was unfolding. "Uh... Yea, welcome, sweetie," she responded hesitantly, looking at her son, Ronald Jr., with surprise. Yet, in her mind, she wants to know, "What the hell is going on?"

Running back to the court, Eric knows it's time to refocus on this basketball game; not the scouts in attendance, not the friends, who are probably doing more socializing than watching the game, not the enemies, not the girls, and especially not the doubters.

"Play your game. Remember what got you here, G," Eric says to himself midcourt as he bends over to stretch his hamstrings—then swaying left to right, getting a good feel of his mobility before tip-off. The one-minute horn blew over the speakers as cheerleaders ran to their respective team benches. The Bucks' team assembled in a circle and started to clap and chant. Their repetition sped up with every double clap the team made until they couldn't anymore. Finally, with Eric yelling out,

"Bucks House! Bucks House! Who dey talkin' bout?"

The players followed suite, repeating verbatim what their passionate captain said. They felt the words recited and were ready for battle. Back on the bleachers, where Eric left his gift for his grandfather, Ronald Jr. was readjusting his Bucks' hat and asked his dad, "What's in the box, old man?" Now readjusting his Bucks scarves. Ronald Sr. couldn't help but smile from ear to ear as he held onto the box. "I'm not quite sure," he replied, "but I'm sure it's great because it's from Eric."

"I mean, he just showed you... You know what, just open the gift, daddy." Clearly, it wasn't the response Ronald Jr. was looking for from his father. The tradition is still alive, and it seemed he had no clue. After all, his grandson just displayed the gift to him on his feet. A bitter look swept over Ronald Jr. but only for a moment; however, he quickly realized this wasn't the time or place to challenge his father. So, he took it with a grain of salt and played along for once.

Nadine and Ronald Jr. lock eyes, sitting behind Ronald Sr.; they smiled because they knew what was in the box. Paula was still confused. And for obvious reasons; with not an inkling of who "set her up?" She was receiving a "Thank you" from her grandson for something she had no parts in.

"Open it up, baby," Paula said.

Ronald Sr. began to pick away at the tape binding the wrapping paper together. Opening the box, the first thing Ronald Sr. saw were two wallet-sized pictures. The first was of a middle-aged man with a boy sitting upon his lap, both giving the camera a *peace* sign. The kid's leg was extended out towards the man, who assisted in tying the kid's shoe; they were classic black and white, Chuck Taylors. The "fogginess" from Ronald Sr.'s brain began to dissipate as he glossed over the picture with his thumb. Now, he recognized the picture in full clarity. It was himself and his son, Ronald Jr. The exact occasion was still unclear to him. However, he was happy enough to recognize the faces; even it was his own, decades ago.

He found the next picture underneath the previous picture; it was himself and his grandson on his 13th birthday. They were both standing side by side again, giving the peace sign. Old memories, locked away, started to unfold of the brighter days. The younger days. And as to why he was so adamant about giving the peace sign in the first place, the Vietnam War. After his tour ended, returning to America in one piece, he had a different outlook on life and its purpose, as well as the war itself. So, from that point forward, the peace sign was the only sign Ronald Sr. was willing to give, especially after the war. Flipping the picture over, there was a caption on its face written by Eric that read, "*It's always deeper than basketball. It's always deeper than the shoes. I love you. –Eric."*

"Oh, wow...this is nice," Ronald Sr. said in awe. The background noise had no impact in the gym and completely drained out his verbal excitement. But it was written all over his face. Finally removing the white tissue paper from the box, they were a pair of Jordan 13 Retro, BRED, and the same pair Eric had on for tonight's game.

"His shoes! My Shoes!... Ok, grandson!"

"Duh, daddy," Ronald Jr. said jokingly as he popped himself in the head. Once again, it was a bittersweet feeling for a son to see the decline of someone who's always been around.

"Is this what he meant by, '*it's always deeper than basketball*,'" Ronald Sr. said, thinking to himself. He smiled, taking a nice, long look at his gift. Was it because Eric is slowly losing his grandfather, or could it be Ronald Sr. feeling like he's on borrowed time? Regardless, they both knew what *this* time meant to one another.

"Sheesh! how the heck did that boy buy those shoes for you!?" Ronald Jr. said, "Man, that's a good grandson there," glancing over to his wife, who also was all smiles; Ronald Sr. and Eric weren't the only ones in sync. "He'll do anything to make you happy, Pop-Pop," Nadine said to Ronald Sr.

And it's true; parents will do just about anything to make sure their kids are happy; it's embedded in their parental DNA. Nadine and Ronald Jr. always did what they had to do behind the scenes to keep the bond strong and nurtured within the Brewer family, and tonight was no exception.

That morning, at Hollywood Heights Plaza after seeing his mother sacrifice her morning, standing in the winter cold over some shoes for her spoiled yet, deserving grandson. Ronald Jr. felt horrible once he drove off, leaving his mom there. So, he made an executive decision on the way to work and called the wife to give her a play-by-play on what just unfolded. She was sold.

However, it wasn't until after lunch with his mother that he decided to pull the trigger and use his network around Hollywood Heights. After a rough lunch with his mother, he spoke to Nadine again and informed Nadine of his next steps. Yet, over the phone, they couldn't help but make light of the situation- for their own sake. "The shoe dilemma," as Ronald Jr. described it, he chuckled on the phone, reminding Nadine that she "Looked out of place in a line full of teenagers and shoe geeks." Smoothing the plan over with his wife, who was still at work herself, he proceeded to call the owner of Feet Justice shoe store.

Unbeknownst to Paula, her son and the owner of the Feet Justice store were high school teammates at Hollywood, class of 1990; two years before the reign of Dorien Troutman, who the gym is named after.

While their high school team didn't go too far in the state and barely made it out of regionals, their relationship did and flourished throughout college to this day. So, it was nothing for the owner and friend to look after a fellow Buck alumnus. The owner also knew Ronald Jr.'s father personally. As a freshman and sophomore, he would often catch rides back to their neighborhood after practice. Just to avoid waiting on the after-school bus, which was always tardy. On a personal note, the Feet Justice owner also has been a fan of Eric and his game on the floor which made Ronald Jr.'s "hookup" all the better. The icing on the cake was the shoe discount Ronald Jr. got for two pairs.

After Nadine and Ronald Jr made it home from their respective positions at work, they weren't done for the day, and the clock was winding down until game time. With "packages" in hand and wrapped, the couple pressed on. It was no more than a 15-minute drive to get Ronald Sr. and Paula, who were already dressed when they arrived. Pulling up to the school, Ronald Jr. dropped the family off at the Troutman Gymnasium's front entrance. Nadine got out of the van and escorted Ronald Sr. and Paula inside. She was carrying Eric's green duffle bag that she found when going through his room. Inside were two pairs of shoes.

Finally getting Ronald Sr. and Paula to their seat, Nadine had to construct a lie, saying, "I'll be right back, you two… Eric needs his clothes for after the game! Be back!" She sprinted in the direction of the locker room- where- she bumped in his head coach, Shawn Walker.

"Hey! Mrs. Brewer… how are you doing, ma'am?"

"Thank God! I thought I was going to have run in there myself."

Nadine hands over the duffle bag to Coach Walker, "Make sure Eric get these, please. It's from his grandparents."

"Say less. I got you. Damn! … he got those new shoes?"

"Yes," Nadine replied, "he was pressed… it's deeper for him, though. So, we bit the bullet."

"Aye, I understand. I may start doing this with my daughter. I like that connection."

"Just make sure he gets this, please… Thanks"

Relieved, she completed her "secret mission," and it is now out of her hands. Nadine made her way back to the bleachers awaiting her husband, who was parking the van; it was all in a day's work for a pair of loving parents. They decided to have some fun with the "surprise" and leave the curiosity of how the shoes came to fruition; it's up to Eric and Ronald Sr. In his own selfish act, Ronald Jr. just wanted to see his father smile. Even though if he didn't receive the credit, the smile was enough. This moment was solely for Eric and his grandfather, and Ronald Jr. was content.

"…You should try these on, baby," Paula said, grabbing one of the shoes out of the shoebox to loosen up the shoestrings. However, in a euphoric state of mind, Ronald Sr. was caught looking at his grandson warming up on the court. It was a proud and loving moment they shared, despite the large crowd in the gym. Eric looked back to the stands at his family, and with a quick head nod, he smirked, knowing the energy tonight is special. He then refaced his team back on the floor to form a pre-game huddle middle court, reciting their chant:

"Bucks' house… Bucks' house… What dey talkin' bout!?!" as the final buzzer has sounded- It's game time.

CHAPTER 12

Angelo is boosted with excitement by the rival atmosphere across the bleachers. The chants, the 'Boos,' the explicit language loosely flung around the gym, and the cheerleaders; the high school boys couldn't resist parading on the sideline. Angelo was soaking it in so much that he couldn't help but dance every time the cheerleaders would recite a chant, stomping their feet and clapping their hands. Or when the gymnasium played songs all the kids loved.

The spiritual booster, "Swag Surfin," by F.L.Y, (Fast Life Youngstaz). The, I'm locked in song, "Get Paid," by Young Dolph. And for the adults and kids in attendance, "Who let the dogs out," considered, *played out,* amongst the youth. Ronald Jr. was secretly obsessed with it, however. But undoubtedly, the Hollywood High School gym anthem was "Put on" by Young Jeezy featuring Kayne West. The gym would erupt on demand when the beat dropped. Parents also enjoyed the track; they just preferred more edited version. The school disc jockey, a house party favorite in Hollywood, clearly didn't care, nor the school itself, at least not for this game.

"Damn it, Gelo, Watch it! You're stepping on my shoe!" Jacqueline shouted, already irritated by his actions. Angelo, flailing his arms, unintentionally smacks Jeremy in the face and almost hits a few onlookers near him on the bleachers. Jeremy, also annoyed by Angelo's actions, stared at him and pierced his soul as if he would get payback for the cheap shot to his face. If Angelo didn't sit down and act like he had some sense in a public setting, Jeremy for sure was going to set him straight. He wanted Angelo to be more like him; cool, calm, and collected. He took pride in always trying to remain calm and play it cool. That wasn't Angelo's character and would never be. Jeremy ultimately knew this. He was asking for a lot from someone, so opposite to his character.

During game nights at Hollywood High School, Jeremy loved to sit high up so that he could see everyone. Even the rival opponents were sitting on the visiting bleachers. Being an adolescent from a rougher side of town, his father schooled him to scope out all "exit" signs. Just in case something pops off in the middle or end of the game. You could never be too sure with Hollywood High School, especially a rival game. If Angelo continued to act in his typical immature way around this crowd, in Jeremy's eyes, something would surely pop off, either home team or visitor.

Jeremy knew that this night was different. He felt the crowd was different once he walked into the gymnasium; he saw new faces. Focusing his sights on freshmen, he'd never seen before. The atmosphere was different, and it hit him like a brick wall "Holy shit! We are really Seniors, y'all."

Jeremy, now sitting upright from his natural slouch position, continued, "Like... This is it. This is over after this year." His look of irritation over Angelo's goofiness quickly switched over to a cold, blank stare of anxiety and uneasiness. Jeremy was currently coming to terms with his own reality as he stared off into the crowd amazingly. Jacqueline sought to provide some comforting support, the best way she could as a friend by being a smart ass.

"I mean, duh, nigga. But keep ya head up! That's what happens after 12th grade. College, I guess- except for Angelo. He has comedic dreams, so schools are out of the discussion for the *white boy*.

In his humble opinion, Angelo felt the need to respond. He felt, again, he wasn't being heard. He wasn't being understood, by his own friends. He needed to speak up, and it was something he found himself doing often. He hated feeling like he was misunderstood regarding the path he chose to take for the future- his future.

"Ok? ... and?" he said, holding their attention, "Hell, Eric has shoestring dreams with basketball. Jeremy has model dreams with his pretty boy stuff. As asinine as it is."

"Aye, fuck you, dog!" Jeremy shot back, laughing at himself in the process, trying to kick Angelo with his foot.

"Ha! Didn't think I knew that word huh. White privilege, I guess. But I'm just saying, man…even with Jacci. She has her, 'Get out of Ohio cornfield dreams,'…Fuck it, we all got'em. So, let's execute it! You feel me? Oh, I'm not a white boy, jerk…"

"Aw, come here, Gelo," Jacqueline said, wrapping her arms around the two as she continued, "We are going to be fine; we have each other. Even if we attend different schools, nothing should ever keep us apart; we've been through too damn much." After a brief group embrace on the bleachers, they were alerted by the same final minute horn that Eric's family heard as Ronald Sr. began trying on his new shows gifted to him.

Preparing for the game at the scores table, the game announcer, Slicky J, local radio host- and Buck's alumni, began to call the starting roster for both teams over the microphone. Far from an athlete, Slicky J, like Angelo, had the gift of gab. However, unlike Angelo, many of the people in attendance on both sides of the gym were absolute fans of his. He is a short and chubby, dark-skinned man, known for putting words together so "slick," the name stuck, Slicky J.

Not only were his words slick off the tongue, but his style of dress complimented his witty pizzazz that nobody in the city could compare, especially in a city such as the heights, a commercial city full of blue-collared workers. He arrived to announce the game in his signature black bucket hat, with the initials "HH," stitched in red on the front. He was dressed in all-black attire and wore his Cuban gold chain with a pendant that read, "Slick."

Earlier in the week, on his morning radio show, "Slick-N-DA-Morning," he said he was asked to announce the rival game against the Bears, and he accepted. Pushing the envelope, like his viewers around the state of Ohio knew him to do, he went on to say he was going to wear "all black," as he was going to attend Roosevelt's funeral Friday night. And as Hollywood High School alumni himself, Slicky J expected the Bucks to deliver and back up his 'slick talk.' Nevertheless, he wanted to see a great game.

After hearing the horn sound, Jeremy glanced down the bleachers to his left to see Eric's parents at a distance in the front row, near the home team bench. "Hey, look! There goes E's folks," Jeremy squinting with a little more focus, scoping out the scene more he recognized Ronald Sr. and Paula, "Oh shit! His grand folks are here too. Y'all wanna go over there? - sit with them?" Angelo, hesitant at first, shrugged his shoulders and decided to lead the pack and take the first steps down the bleachers, and leaving their high vantage point for the taking.

"I just hope they laugh at my jokes this time," Angelo said, "They hate me, G."

Jeremy replied, "Naw, they just hate your corny ass jokes. But we told you already, stop acting surprised. You aren't funny, man." He attempted to playfully slap Angelo's neck, striking his skin harder than he expected, sending a shooting echo around the vicinity of the fans. The slap even sent Angelo buckling his knees; Jeremy would deliver a blow that heavy unaware. And as typical high schoolers do, they instigated the situation.

"Damn!"

"Hell naw, that's wild! I would never…"

"Nigga, you gonna take that?"

The slap made Angelo stop in his tracks. He was slightly embarrassed as he began to rub his red neck. He turned around to face Jeremy, who stood there in fighting positions, thanks to the instigators. But nothing happened; Angelo *did* take that. Picking and choosing his battles was something Angelo took pride in. He was, by no means, considered a pushover. He just loved living and enjoyed the risks he took in life thus far. So, something like a whimsical yet, heavy-handed slap amongst friends he can live with. If anything, he oddly enjoyed the attention that the slap brought. "The people got to see a show" in his unique train of thought. But In everyone else's mind, he was "extra" and just "doing too much at the wrong time." So, he took the playful slap with a grain of salt, ignoring the peanut gallery.

As they resumed their short journey down to the bleachers, they greeted Eric's family and sat amongst them. They found their seats just in time to hear the home team starters announced. Being one of the starters on the bench, Eric patiently waited for his name to be called. In the home color attire, the Buck cheerleaders are equipped with burgundy, white pompoms, and white hair ties to complete the ensemble. They proceeded to the court, forming their traditional tunnel for the starters to run through and greet Coach Walker, who was standing and clapping alongside the rest of the team. As the announcer, Slicky J, called each starter, Eric got into a relaxed mental state. Knowing his name is the last to be called, it always gave him enough time to recite his traditional game-day prayer:

"My Savior, my Lord. Another one for the road. Asking for wisdom, making the right decisions on the court. Knowing when not to attack and when to depend on my teammates, as they depend on me. Please, strengthen any weaknesses that I may have on the court tonight, God. And that I can overcome any obstacle on my way. My support system is here—family and homies, to where my homies are my family. I thank them, love them, and pray their support ignites my fight because yea, it's a big game, God. Amen."

Hunched over, taking a deep breath in, Eric lifts his head from underneath his palms, just in time to hear Slicky J's smooth and dramatic style of delivery as he announced the starting guard.

"And now… get on ya feet, baby. Y'all… this playa came to ball… here to kill it all—the shooting guard, bang, bang, and the big senor dog. The team captain- you know what happenin'… Eric Brewer!"

Eric, still seated, unfastened his sweaty hands, then smacked the hardwood floor with tremendous vigor. He jumps out of his seat to let out a roar, clapping his hands and feeding off the energy of the crowd. Even the "boos" from the rival fans made him smile. The Bucks' cheerleaders started to wave their pom-poms as Eric ran through their man-made tunnel. The cheerleaders screamed at the top of their lungs with pride, followed by his teammates and Coach Walker waiting on the opposite end of the tunnel. Oddly enough, neither team greeted the opposing starters after reading the roster coaches, too. As tacky and unprofessional as it was, they absolutely were ok with it. They rather just stare each other down, setting the mood.

The concession stands line grew smaller by the second. Many painfully decided to leave once they heard the final buzzer go off, not trying to miss a single second of the game. "The popcorn will always be there at the second half." The atmosphere around this game was contagious, as roars and screams reminded a lot of the onlooking college scouts watching the game of where they were. This is Hollywood Heights, Ohio.

Amid the exhilarating feeling that grasped the gym, Ronald Sr. was there, looking at the new shoes Eric gave him—reminding him of a simpler time when Eric was just a child. More specifically, the days when he used to gift his grandson with basketball shoes every birthday since he was 13 years old. Granted, tonight it wasn't his birthday and not for a few more months, but the thought of the love coming back tenfold to Ronald Sr. spoke volumes. It was his turn to receive some shoes.

CHAPTER 13

Suddenly, it clicked for Ronald Sr.; he knew why Eric got him those shoes. And not the other way around, as it has been for years. He could now comprehend why his grandson has been by his side for the last 3 years—practically attached to his hip. The days that Eric spent over in his house, spending the night studying film. Just the two of them- nobody else created an unbreakable bond built on love, blossomed by an uncanny shoe crazy between the two vastly different age groups. But the shoes themself had a unique way of showing their "love." And it was unique to them because they understood the reason for all this back and forth. It simply started with love and will end in that as well.

Recently, there have been times where Ronald Sr. had to be reminded by his grandson to take his medication. Subtle reminders. Yes, but reminders, nonetheless. Eric looked up to his grandfather and adored him. Even when he felt pushed to the limit due to his grandfather's adjustments to his prescribed medications. It has been a trying couple of years for Eric to finally accept what his grandfather was going through. Before that, Eric refused to express a look of worry around his grandfather.

"The kid knows, doesn't he? He knows..." Ronald Sr. uttered. It was a sober realization that not just Eric, but "everyone" dear to him knew of his Alzheimer's condition. A fiery wave rushed through his whole body, starting from his toes, traveling through to his spine, and extending to his arms and neck. He was embarrassed and overwhelmed with guilt.

Like Eric, Ronald Sr.'s palms began to sweat sufficiently after his prayer ritual. The detriment could serve his sacred relationship with his grandson, in his opinion. If he does know, it wasn't an ordeal that Ronald Sr. was not prepared to tackle. Yet, this was how he found out.

In hindsight, he's had a decent week mentally. He hasn't had any "serious" issues or lapses to cause too much concern. Just the usual slip-ups and wrong names being called out. However, this predicament stung his ego. Ronald Sr. found himself trying to wipe away his sweaty hands against his dark grey khakis. Immediately, he stood up, shouting to Eric, who was walking on the court preparing for tip-off.

"Eric!"

It was all Ronald Sr. could muster up after succumbing to a fury of emotion and understanding- all under a couple of minutes. He still knew where he was at. Through the intense noise in the gymnasium and the cheerleader's cheerfulness, the mascots revving up their fans; Eric still heard him and made it known as they both made eye contact. Eric gave a wink to his grandfather and a chest pound. He assured his grandfather that he did hear his name called. The bond and the memories they shared throughout the years, even with his grandfather battling Alzheimer's, was still something worthwhile and worth the sacrifice. And for only a moment, it felt as if it was only those two in the gym.

Angelo, Jacqueline, and Jeremy also tried to show Eric some love and a few words of encouragement. In the short time they had, they stole the intimate moment from his grandfather.

"Aye, Go E!"

"Kick that ass, mane!" exclaimed Jeremy.

"Let them know who the big dog is! Who the big buck is!"

The gang, alongside his family, were clearly in game-time mode, hoping their words would provide Eric with a boost of inspiration. Angelo started thrusting his hips and waving his arms in every direction physically possible. And once again, almost smacking everyone around him. This time, he didn't give a damn. He always embraced the moment for what it was, soaking it all up with the possibility of delivering a laugh or two to the stands.

"You literally have no home training, dude," Jacqueline said, trying to keep her distance from Angelo's misguided hands. "Move around; you're embarrassing me." She had no choice but to scoot closer to Jeremy, who didn't particularly mind as her hair brushed against his cheek.

Hearing the crew about to revolt against Angelo, Nadine signals to him, "Angelo, you come over here and take my spot." She was sitting next to her husband, Ronald Jr., and someone who didn't want to be childish antics around him.

"What are you doing?" Ronald Jr interjected as he blew his air horn once more.

"Hush," Nadine fired back, "Come here, baby. Y'all two can turn up together."

"Don't do this to me... please."

"Boy, hush. He doesn't mean you any harm". Nadine just figured Ronald Jr. would finally have someone who was just as ecstatic about tonight's game as he was. Not that she wasn't but jumping up and down and screaming all game wasn't her forte.

"Thank you, Mrs. Brewer," Angelo replied, sending a Hail Mary prayer up, hoping it was a good idea.

"Relax… he ain't gonna kill you. You're more than welcome. Y'all have fun."

Swapping seats with Angelo, Nadine found herself sitting next to Jacqueline. There she found the comparison between the two as night and day being more reserved than Angelo. To be honest, Jacqueline even resembled her personality as a teenager in high school.

So, Nadine felt confident in the new seating arrangement, as her husband glared at her from a distance. Even Jeremy was nothing like Angelo and someone the Brewer's knew on a family-type level; being childhood friends with Eric, he was a well, mild-mannered young man. They all were the complete opposite to Angelo, even her own son. It made Nadine ponder the question, "*Why and how are all these kids became friends?*" She began to reminisce about her days in high school, and a look of humorous confusion masked her true question prodding through her mind; she could relate.

On the other hand, Ronald Jr. was consumed with the high intensity from watching the teams' warm-up. With the music amplified and his father still admiring his new kicks as a secret gift of sorts. He just wanted his father's smile to remain for as long as it could. As Angelo approached him to sit, he didn't really give a damn about Eric's friends. "Hey, man. Just don't distract me from the game," he said sternly to Angelo, who sat gingerly next to him.

Between he, himself, and I, Ronald Jr. was thrilled to at least have one person there who was just as excited as he was; he just couldn't let him know. That was the mystique of being a parent. "They better kick their ass. Let's go, Bucks!!"

Ronald Jr. screamed from the top of his lungs. His display of comradery and hate for the opposing team sparked a flame in Angelo's timid eyes. He was pleased to see the amount of passion displayed for the upcoming tip-off. The gaze Angelo had on Ronald Jr. was almost that of a father seeing his child take his first steps.

"Mr. Brewer," Angelo paused for a second, "You actually might be my brother from another mother. I love yo spirit, man!" The unorthodox interaction left a sour note in Ronald Jr.'s mouth as he began to wince at the remarks. And quite the opposite reaction Angelo was expecting. Ronald Jr., repulsed, looked Angelo up and down and bluntly replied, "Boy, what the hell? Are you high!?"

Music is silenced as heads take a bow. Some had their hands placed over their hearts as the *Star-Spangled Banner* was played aloud instrumentally over the loudspeaker. Everyone, but mostly players and coaches, take this final moment to get their emotions, anxiety, and nerves in order. After the ending notes played for the national anthem, Coach Walker found enough time to squeeze in a few last words while the game officials get ready. "Beat… dat… ass. Enough said. Bring it in, men". A short but to-the-point message, and it was enough words to get the team's blood pumping. As the team captain closed it out, Eric brought the players' hands in, "1-2-3- Bucks!" They all shouted.

Both teams got situated at center court. An angry Bucks' head logo, with red-bloodshot eyes, and air shooting out of its flared nostrils, was the decorative half-court emblem representing Hollywood High School. And to them, the picture suited their style of play. The teams eye each other as they lick their chops. Their moist hands were used to wipe off any residue left beneath their shoes; the court wasn't in the best of conditions. So, each team was looking for a sizeable first advantage to start the game. The lead official approached the scores table, where the official game ball had been placed before warm-ups. Grabbing it, he held it in the air parallel to his eyes and dropped it. It bounced back up in the air, striking his elbow at the midsection to his body; this was an acceptable ball for regulation play.

Fans in the stands continued to scream and stomp on the bleachers, making it virtually impossible to understand what anyone was saying close by. "Alright, gentlemen, let's play some ball!" the lead official said. Approaching the jump ball zone was Bucks' starting center, Leo Capernati, and Bears' starting center, Cecil Tremont, both shuffling their feet.

"Ok... I want a clean game, you two. Don't make this a long night." The official said.

"What?" Leo said, pointing to his ear.

"I said... don't make this a long night!!

"Huh!?! I didn't catch that," Cecil said, squinting his eyes as if he was trying to make out the words. But missing the message a second time.

"...Ok. We have some comedians in the house. I get it." He quickly caught onto their mischief.

"Yes, Sir!" they responded in unison, smirking at each other. It was a telling sign of things to come. The lead official tosses the ball with both hands directly in the air to start the game. The jump ball barely misses the tips of Leo's fingers, ultimately letting the Bears receive the ball first and putting the Bucks on defense start of the game. The fans roar as the game starts, and the Bears bring the ball up the court.

"Ugh," Angelo's eyes roll to the back of his head in disgust, "We need that tip!!"

"That's what 'she' said," Jeremy snickered, "It was too easy; I was here all day, and I don't know how I'm better at you in this joking thing."

However, Jacqueline gave him some food for thought as she overheard Angelo's early bickering. "Zip-it over there! It's literally the first play, and it's only the tip-off. Not all hope is lost... so relax." Unconsciously, she began to slouch back in her seat, folding her arms, intensely focused on the game and hoping her words would reign true. "If anything, they could use Jeremy's height. But that's right; he wanna be cute for the camera and model," Jacqueline said in her attempt to crack a joke. Which warranted an abrupt head turn from Jeremy sitting next to her. He was greeted by Jacqueline's playful eyes, a gesture that wasn't working this go-round.

"Whomp-whomp... if you would like to make another joke, please press '1,'" Jeremy shot back. "And trust, I'm going to make it aight. Anyway, Eric isn't new to this game, so the team will be fine. Plus, I know I'd be a dog out there. We played for years, before senior year... I just don't know. Kinda fell out of love with the game... He's way more passionate than I was ever." Finishing his statement, Jeremy quickly stands to his feet, urging the Bucks to turn up the intensity on the court. As Jeremy stood up, cheering, and watching the Bucks' attempt to stop the oncoming offense, he kind of wishes he could be in the game tonight. But it was only a passing thought for the night.

CHAPTER 14

The Bears' first offensive attempt resulted in a short shot, falling off the front of the rim, and rebounded by Bucks Center, Leo Capernati. "Oh snap, Jack! A missed shot! If you have any more bricks, we'll take'em... you see how this school look," game announcer, Slicky J, reported as the home team laughed, "But nice rebound by the big man-big nasty, Capernati."

The announcer couldn't afford to miss a beat of the game. His passion for highlighting plays or calling out the weaker players is what drew half of the crowd in the stands tonight. Fans need their validation card stamped with their "at-home" basketball expertise on game nights. Majority of the fans thought they were the "Einstein of basketball," especially when their thought process aligned with Slicky J's game announcing. Some parents that attended the games were selfishly trying to relive their youth through the players. Parents would reminisce their golden days with their peers, seeing flashes of their ball days on the same court they once played, 10, 20, or even 30 years ago.

Two minutes into the first quarter, the score was (0-6). A three-possession tear left the Bears on their heels and some of their fans quiet, early. As all the points put up was that of Eric Brewer. An outlet pass was made to Eric, making the Bucks' defense-to-offensive transition effortless. Exactly how Coach Walker and Assistant Coach Lawry envisioned. Regardless of it almost being stripped away by the defense, Eric found the strength and balance to recover the ball. With his head up and eyes seeking an open man, he spots shooting guard, #21, Tareek Baxter, flashing his hands in the corner. He was wide open, welcoming the incoming pass.

A slinky 6 foot 2 inches Tareek Baxter was still finding his place on the Bucks' varsity team. Nonetheless, he was labeled a serious competitor by most of the players this season. Knowing that Eric is graduating after this season, there was a high probability that he would be the newest team captain. Tareek always found a way to step up and make his presence known. Over the years, from freshman to junior varsity, Coach Walker has kept an eye on his growth, realizing he can become a reliable asset on the floor. Now, as a varsity player, they expect nothing less.

As Eric passed him the outlet, Tareek caught it by the corner above the three-point line. He pump-faked the corner three, long enough to draw the defender's oncoming movement out of his visual. With the coast clear, he drove in with urgency to the paint for an easy left-handed layup and two more points for the Bucks'. (0-8).

The Bucks' coaches applauded the team; he loved the strong start and teamwork thus far. Grabbing his white patent towel, Coach Walker screamed for a "Double Team!" and "Trap!" wiping away the sweat from his forehead. He encouraged the made baskets but still wanted to ensure that the ball has seen at least three passes before a shot attempt is made. The majority most listened.

Assistant Coach Lawry's primary job kept him at bay in most games. Focused more on data consumption than applauding the players' every made basket. He tallied away at every statistic the scouts in the bleachers would analyze, such as Shot selection vs. passing opportunities, rebounds, defensive stops, even offensive time of possessions. So, his hands were full, and the players never took it to heart.

On the flipside, Coach Walker's countless looks of anguish and disgust over silly turnovers or a missed shot far from the rim always made the team quiver and often become defensive with their head coach. "Y'all don't communicate through those damn incoming screens?" Coach Walker blurted out his typical ice breaker into a prevalent tirade amongst his team and the officials.

Back on the hardwood, the Bucks are still in the lead, but the Bears eventually get in the swing of things amidst the hostile crowd and their own emotions. Finally putting some points on the board and slow down the bleeding. (6-10). The Bears started to catch on to the Bucks' 4-minutes into action, "pic-and-roll," calls and got back on defense, stopping some fast-break transition plays. However, it still wasn't enough. They needed some muscle.

As the Bears bring the ball up the court, Eric gets blindsided by a pick stonewalled, knocking him flat on the dusty, hard Maplewood floor. Surely it was a dirty shot, as the offender protruded his elbows outward, connecting his elbow directly into Eric's chest. His attempt to let Eric know who was "Top dog," on the play and possibly the remainder of the game. The echo of Eric's body hitting the floor made a thunderous noise, making even the rivals in the stands turn their faces away in misery.

"*Damn!*" Slicky J shouted, confirming the other explicit undertones that rang throughout the gym. Eric's family and friends couldn't help but look alongside, disturbed by the play. A burning look of anger swept over the home crowd's face when they didn't hear a single whistle blown. And with the ball still in play, the Bears then transitioned the cheap shot into a two-point play. (8-10). A host of roars followed the basket; all were screaming, "*Boo!!*" from the home stands. Coach Walker had to contain himself from catching an early technical foul.

Shaken up but not hurt, Eric quickly bounced back on his two feet. There wasn't any time to complain about a cheap shot. He just couldn't believe that not one referee witnessed this "shitty excuse" of a screen. All for the rivalry, I guess.

It wasn't just the players jawing at one another. The fans and parents also had their moments. Even the high school rival mascots, a Buck and a Bear, were caught seen in a brief tussle, expressing a multitude of emotions with what they had seen so early in the game. However, when Bucks got away with a few cheap shots of their own, not one Bucks' fan complained. Some on the other side would point out the obvious fouls, as the remaining would clap their hands, saying, "Good call, ref!" Some still weren't pleased and rather pissed about a few other missed calls that the officials disregarded earlier in the quarter.

"Well damn... Look at that... Finally, we get a call," one Buck fan yelled.

"Guess they know where they at now!"

As the 1st quarter closes out, the Bears took mid-range shots and long-distance 3's, trying to bring the point margin closer. Young athletic legs provided a small highlight of slam dunks on both sides of the court. Also, in defense, both sides were up to par. More than usual given the atmosphere the environment provided. Seeing good defensive stops on the court was something many of the older fans and scouts could appreciate. Yet, if they weren't already disengaged from the game, most of the kids in the gym, chit-chatting with their peers, wanted to see "flash" on the court. Today, they want to see "jelly-like" drives to the hoop and "silky," smooth threes, as if they were raindrops falling from the heavens. This is the new art of basketball. Besides, these kids today, other than physicality, are far more athletic than what the '80s and '90s produced, and their raw skills showed it.

On the other hand, the scouts in attendance, sitting amongst the fans and family members, saw dollar signs. Blended in with the crowd so that they weren't sticking out like sore thumbs. Most of them watched the game from a different lens, and not one of fandom but one of business. The average man will look at star players and think, "He/she is unique." Whereas a scout's train of mind is, "I see unique… potential for our establishment."

Many- are unaware that scouts on a collegiate level take these college tours because it's their profession. Players are viewed as dollar signs, running up and down the court. "What can you produce for me?" is the primary question formulating in their minds, eyes, and notepads. And from a financial standpoint, that's all that really matters, *'quid pro quo."* Scouts get paid a nice chunk of change for their knowledge and expertise. So, can you really blame their train of thought?

As the clock ticks down, sweat drops down a Bears' player's chin with the ball in his hand, looking to score the last-second shot attempt. Eric guarded him at the top of the key. Thankfully, the Bucks' stopped the shot attempt as the first quarter ended and the horn sounded. (Bears: 19-Bucks: 23) The Bucks were up by 4; as physical as the play was, they weren't out of the woods.

After their 3-minute water break and Coach Walker's quick pep-talk, he encouraged his players to keep fighting through the no-calls. "Yes, Coach!" was resounded as they got off the bench to start the 2nd quarter.

One minute into action, two officials had to break up a scuffle between three players- a Bucks' bench player, shooting guard, Anton Fuller, and two Bears' players. Eric started to bring the ball up the court after the Bears' made possession. To his surprise, he witnessed a Bears' defender, elbowing Anton in the chest, fighting for position on the right-wing. Having a short fuse and refusing to be used as a doormat, Anton fought back. He grabbed the Bears' defender by the back of his jersey, and he flung the defender's body completely to the ground using his weight that was resting on Anton's leg. Anton then proceeded to step over the fallen defender, taunting him and leaving a fellow Bears' defender to run up and push Anton from his taunting position directly to the floor.

The hostile aggression ignited both team benches to clear simultaneously, leaving the crowd in a frenzy, yelling profanities across the court at the rival visitors. Hollywood Heights police who were watching the game, more than policing the gymnasium, needed to act fast. They were posted at the stations near the home team and visitor team section. They hustled over to the benches to simmer down the players who were ready for a "free-for-all rumble," as the announcer, Slicky J, so elegantly stated. "Y'all in the stands… Watch ya pockets, fellas! This is when those dollars start pickin' up legs and taking strolls into other folk' pockets! If ya get, ya get it!!"

If this game is disqualified, the referees will have much more to worry about other than who called or didn't call a foul. However, these were seasoned officials accustomed to these intense territories. They were hip to the game with over 35 years of knowledge about the rulebook under their belts.

After a couple of minutes, the officials and the police officers were able to restore some order. The lead official gave both teams a double technical foul and a warning. However, not too much was adjusted after that regarding the physicality of the game. "If there are no deliberate punches or kicks thrown," the referees said, "Play on," letting the tough play resume and ignoring the complaints from the stands and coaches. After a fast-paced second quarter, with more issues than the first, both head coaches could live with the halftime score. They both wanted blood as they eyed each other after the second quarter horn sounds, leaving for their respective halftime locker room.

Headed to the doors, Coach Walker stops and looks back at the game clock, squinting to make out the score. He pats his head one last time before heading into the locker room; he wasn't impressed. After an emotional first half, the Bucks' have maintained the lead, but not by many. (41-49).

And despite the lead, Eric's numbers were on the low side, compared to other games this season. He knew it and wasn't happy. After the horn went off, Eric stormed straight into the locker room, shoving the double doors with force walking down the hallway. He didn't even bother to acknowledge the fans or his family.

Eric Brewer: 8 points, 1-2, on the free-throw line, 1 rebound, and 4 assists in the first half. Something surely the scouts weren't going to seem interested in, especially given his resume, which each scout received before the game. The scouts were looking to see Eric's more "aggressive, assertive, and wise" style of play. Again, in a high-octane environment such as this one, when the stakes are high, "If you can't perform on this level, do you think the collegiate level will be any more forgiving?"

CHAPTER 15

During halftime, cell phones were immediately ripped from pockets and purses and into their thirsty hands. Aside from the calls being made, people were catching up with what they had missed during game time. Twitter timelines and Instagram feeds- seeing what's trending in tonight's juicy topic section and scrolling over celebrity pictures- tracking their every move. The scouts were also busy making calls of their own during halftime, updating college recruiter's and athletic front offices, ranging from historically black colleges and universities to *prestigious* top-name universities.

The extended 10-minute halftime show was also accompanied by a set from the school's dance team, *Hollywood Buck Nazty Step-Team*, and a sophomore high school magician for the younger crowd. It was enough entertainment for the fans to enjoy the company around them while the teams regrouped for the second half. That also went for the forgotten ones, who missed out on the first-half concession snacks and could finally redeem their goodies. Some even went back to the parking lot to finish off the rest of the liquor they brought with them, knowing would they have their seat when they returned. Many of the other concession goers just needed their refreshments refilled, trying not to ruin dinner for the night. While others attending the game with relatively weak bladders relieved themselves in the bathrooms after being glued to their seats for a long time.

Coach Walker and Assistant Coach Lawry are upbeat in the locker room, despite the energy their team Captain is portraying. They didn't want to discourage the other boys too much. With that said, Coach Walker still wasn't convinced they came to play and give it their best effort- not yet. The Bears still had a lot of life in them. And they still felt good about their first-half performance despite being down eight points. Most importantly, they were able to shut down Eric.

Assistant Coach Lawry began to read the stats for the 1st half, followed by the strongest and weakest players of the half, finishing off with the players in potential foul trouble, even turnovers. The Bucks could sense that it could potentially pay off in the final seconds by playing hard and staying aggressive against the Bears' offense. Yet, it may come at a cost the team will have to bear. Some of the Bucks' players have fallen into early foul trouble and now must smarten up if they want to maintain this lead. Basketball IQ is always critical in these specific moments. The mind is usually the last to go as the body weakens out, with no will to use brute strength. Coach Walker just prays their age won't start to show when their will is tested. Age and maturity can hinder a lot.

Closing the locker room door behind him, "Alright, fellas, we're in the trenches now. Up eight, and playing your asses off," Coach Walker said as he patted his head down with his white towel. He takes a deep breath, regaining his composure to continue his heartened speech, "John, Tareek,

Isiah, Eric, and Leo; you guys are my starters. I need you to finish these fools off! Get them outa here. This is our gym!"

"Yes, coach!"

Coach Walker proceeded to race back and forth in the locker room. Every step he made would cause an echo to travel throughout the locker room as he continued his plea.

"And you, Anton." Coach Walker continued.

"Look, coach. My fault,"

"No! I love that energy, boy! They are in our house!" Coach Walker exclaimed, surprising all the players with his remarks and Assistant Coach Lawry.

"Yea- Uh… That's what I meant!" Anton said as he smiled, dapping up some of the closet players near him in the locker room, as Coach Walker picked back up.

"How dare they try and clear the benches thinking they can beat us?" Coach Walker added. The look of determination began to rekindle in their eyes, touching their soul. Coach painted a valid point in the players' minds. "How can they come in here and start a fight? And start a fight on the wrong side of the tracks, too? Then try to bully us?"

The Bucks' come to grips with the reality; they could lose the lead they've sustained in the 1st half. The Bucks' wanted victory more than ever now. "Eric, you're the leader," Coach Walker said, pointing to his distressed team captain. He was looking defeated mentally, more than physically. Sitting on the locker room bench, looking down, and sulking. Eric was seen gripping his gym towel with all his might, made visible by his knuckles turning a pale white.

"Aye! Head up, man!" Coach Walker yelled at Eric, "We all know who you are! So, turn it up, man!"

"Yea," the players said, chiming in, "you know you got this, E."

"Stop letting those men punk you," Coach Walker continued, "They not even big." Eric's eyes shifted, cutting like a razor pinpointed at Coach Walker and saying in his mind, "You got the wrong one. Punk who!? Who's a punk?" Instead, Eric said something much worse and in front of the entire team.

"Coach, you got me fucked up!"

There was about 5 seconds of silence. For once, the players were in utter shock. Some were caught holding their mouths open, stunned. Others covered their mouths with their hands, and some snickered, wondering what coach was going to do next. But, hell, even the coaches were shocked, leaving themselves wondering, "What had gotten into this young man?"

Eric didn't really speak like that to anyone, let alone his coach. And a coach who has his future basketball career in his hands, trying to guide him to the next level. Assistant Coach Lawry halted the work he was computing on his calculator for the 1st half. He was saddened by the harsh response Eric gave his coach; it wasn't like him. He then turned, looking at Coach Walker, wondering what the counter would be, as did the players.

To everyone's surprise, Coach Walker only stood there, raising his eyebrows, and a snarly smirk was given back to Eric. Coach Walker looked at Eric as if to say, "No sir, No- 'You' have me fucked up." As the tension grew, players started to squirm in their seats, wondering what would occur next. However, instead of risking his job and possible jail time for assault. Coach Walker rearranges his face and fixes his hands, placing them on his hips. "Excuse you, boy?" he said as he stood there, waiting for a better rebuttal. At this point, it's not about the game anymore; this is respect, and time has no limit.

Eric, whose spirits were already brittle, had his anger been misguided towards his coach. In which, to the benefit of Coach Walker, he didn't know. Still tightly grasping the gym towel, Eric began clenching his jaw, trying to bite his tongue. Eric would attempt to restate his claim. Taking a deep breath, he readdressed his sentiment on the subject, "I'm just saying, Coach… I'm trying, man."

As the "captain" of the team, that individual should always remain calm or at least seem that way. And tonight, Eric was battling in that role. Struggling to keep his composure around his team and not to "rock the boat" amongst the coaching staff and players. As senior and team captain, his teammates did look for his direction and guidance on the floor. He was their veteran on the team. And with trust, the coaches depended on him to make sure the game plan was executed on the floor- on a superior level. The scouts want to see all that was mentioned, and then some more. But the fans just wanted a win at all cost.

Frustrated and at a loss for words, Eric forcefully elbows the locker behind him.

"Oh, E-boogie on one today," one teammate said under his towel to a fellow teammate. Everyone has the same thoughts about what is unfolding before their eyes. It was the first visible sign he was unable to contain his anger and pain inside him. He got up from his seat swiftly, clenching his fist, not even rubbing his battered elbow, and said to the team, "Goddamn! Look y'all- It was just a bad first half for me." He paused and then continued, "Listen, fellas, we got it. It's my job to make sure we see it through. Everybody is playing great, besides me, right now. And I get it. But 'we' need to put more points up on the board and stay on their necks."

As the team took a few seconds, looking around the locker room, gauging one another's reaction to Eric's apologetic speech. They all began to nod their heads in agreement. And was good news for a beaten-down captain, which inspired him to go on, "And that's my bad for my horrible ass playing, man. But we got two quarters to go, and I won't let y'all down; I promise."

Tareek Baxter studied Eric's body language. Over the years, he grew to know Eric, learning a lot about the team and their aggressive coaching style. He also knew Eric was a person who did his best to keep his word. So, he believed him and accepted his challenge. "Aight, cuzzo. Let's do this…" Tareek said, reaching out to exchange handshakes. And once Tareek accepted, it didn't take much for the rest of the team to fall in line. Everyone seemed to be locked back in. But with only two quarters left, time will tell.

The locker room doors open as the team's water boy walks in, informing Coach Walker that the magic show had just ended. He gets the team to huddle up in the locker room for a team chat before exiting. At this moment, he was looking for any boost he could get to keep the kids motivated in the fight and engaged. "Get out there and warm up… let's finish this."

"Yes, coach!" Keeping in mind that these are high schoolers, Coach Walker wished they understood that no coach should ever need to motivate a player to do their job. Granted, we all need a push from time to time. But the *will* to be better should be internal, going back to the passion of "why" you do it in the first place. One thing he knew was that the Bears weren't going to let off the gas. And as they were now well rested; they will surely come out the gates swinging. However, he couldn't take his eye off his star player, who was the last one to join the huddle. Something was up with Eric- but what was it?

Eric still zoned out, had his grandfather constantly on his mind, and was emotionally drained. His plans for a future after high school seemed irrelevant. Flashbacks from the morning slip-up his grandfather called him flickered in his brain. Right now, he wasn't concerned about the game or what the scouts were thinking. He was beaten, and Coach Walker could tell.

Clapping his hands, Coach Walker instructed the remaining players out of the locker room, giving them enough time to get warmed up for the second half.

"Coach, make sure they start with lay-ups," Coach Walker instructed his assistant, who was washing his hands in the locker room sink after a bathroom break, "Have them get those legs loose."

"Yes, sir… Let's go, guys!"

Once the locker room was ready to exit, Assistant Coach Lawry opened the door, releasing the team to warm up for the remainder of the halftime. The players were jumping, clapping, and shouting. They were hyped-up as they slapped the white brick walls parading down the hallway reentering the gymnasium. Fueling off the energy of the screaming fans as happy to see their faces return from the locker room. This also gave Coach Walker a few minutes to figure out why Eric is so distraught. His instincts told him it had to be deeper than the game tonight.

Clearing off the bench full of gym towels left by the players once in the locker room. Coach Walker invites Eric over. "Eric, come sit down with me, please."

Hesitant at first, Eric welcomed the invite, clearing his throat and stepping in the coach's direction. He understood that this was his head coach. He was damn near obligated to address him if he wanted to play any more minutes tonight. "Yes, coach?" Eric gingerly sat back down next to his coach, wondering what he would say next. Was it more about his sporadic play on the floor? Or his erratic behavior in the locker room during halftime? Coach Walker gauges Eric up and down one more time as he took his seat. Trying to read his attitude, it wasn't often he had to wonder if his star player would be able to "get it gear" for the second half. Eric still looked out of it, unmotivated.

CHAPTER 16

Unfortunately, Eric has had a rough look at reality lately, a somber and early lesson about how this world operates-unforgiving. Outside of the game of basketball, he felt life was "unfair" at this stage in his life. And he wanted to be selfish with the things he loved. Especially when he feels it's being taken away. He often used basketball as an escape, like most athletes tend to do with sports. Or a bookworm, devouring its next genre of literature. It's as if God granted us a ticket to freedom with these tools to escape life's hardships if you utilize them. However, the way he played tonight had Eric feeling as if he was enclosed within four tightly spaced walls, and the sky was falling. "The sky," being Eric's grandfather. "The walls," being life in his current state. And nowhere to run. Hence, the breakdown at the half in front of the entire team.

"What's going on with you, young man?" Coach Walker reached his arm around Eric's shoulder, hoping to ease any tension they may have manifested in the locker room minutes earlier. Eric was still sulking, with his head down. Coach Walker empathetically began to rub his back, encouraging his team captain.

"Hey man... I need you, brother," Coach Walker expressed, "I need you to finish strong for me. Hell, we know the team needs ya. Shoot... I need ya. You're the 'real' leader, E."

Usually, these phrases of empowerment and empathy from Coach Walker helped in situations like these. He could be a hard ass on his players, but he also cared deeply about them; it showed in serious situations like these. He continued to soothe Eric's back until he finally broke down into tears right in from of him. Coach Walker was caught off guard by the temperament swing in Eric. He suddenly retracted his own emotion of frustration, to more of compassion, for a grieving teenager.

"He won't remember much after this year," Eric uttered, fighting back the tears, "He won't- He isn't gonna remember a damn thing, man. Why me, though!?"

Coach Walker's mouth slowly opened in shock, ceasing the rubbing of Eric's back. Silent still, he was ready to catch any remaining words Eric had left in his tank. He was now fully engaged, listening as a struggling teen carried on about his personal struggles. "Why, Coach? This is my year. It was gonna be something I won't forget. But he will. And I just can't *deal* with that right now... Shit, this is one of the best weeks he's had in a minute, given everything that's really been going on in the past few months. It's just always something new in our house, man."

Tears continued to pour out of Eric's red puffy eyes, which unfortunately drowned out some of the words he was trying to get across. But Coach Walker understood. Not necessarily Eric's personal battle- for that, he can only sympathize with, but as his coach and a man. He made it his mission long ago to console a player or student in a time of grief. No matter the circumstance. And as a man of faith, this was second nature to him. "Ball is life," as the people say, but nothing compared to day-to-day life circumstances. It just hits different.

Wiping away at his nose and getting the tears cleared from his face, Eric looked at Coach Walker and quietly said, "He has Alzheimer's coach, my grandfather... He doesn't remember a damn thing at most times. This week just happened to be a good week... Hell, a great week, but whatever. Two weeks ago, he asked me to help him find a girl's name to write a letter to her. It was crazy as hell! I'm just glad my grandma wasn't there." He started to chuckle slightly at the dark humor of it all, even though it was still very traumatic.

He once again succumbed to the tears. Each word he says reprocesses that he was going to lose his grandfather. Coach Walker was amazed. Not only was this kid one of the local basketball stars in Hollywood Heights, but only in high school.

Eric felt he had the weight of his own personal battles wrapped around his neck, trying to suffocate him. All the while still trying to boost his GPA up to a 3.0 for college. The citizens of Hollywood Heights, who knew of Eric Brewer, could testify that "He was the true definition of a student-athlete."

"Ah, come here, son."

The two embraced for a few seconds, still seated in the locker room. Coach Walker now understood the pain Eric was feeling, a breakdown at such a critical time. "Eric, listen, man. Don't worry about the scouts," he said, "Don't worry about the fans... Just be a kid tonight, go have some fun." Assuring Eric, they both dapped each other up and smiled.

"Aye, we gotta go. First, wipe those tears, boy... you know how the team is," Coach Walker jokingly said, easing the tense moment in the locker room.

Eric smiled again and wiped his face with his jersey as Coach consoled him by rubbing his back a few more seconds. It seemed as if that brief exhale of pinned up emotions freed Eric's mind to rally back after a personal bad first half. That and the uptight remark from Coach Walker followed, regarding Eric's shoe choice for the game, while readjusting his tie in the mirror before departing.

"I don't think those 'cute' throwback shoes gave you the spark you wanted, big man. But there is always the second half," Coach Walker laughed.

But Eric's mind starts racing, "Maybe, these new shoes ain't cutting it, tonight." He was looking for anything to start the second half without the 3rd quarter jitters. Suddenly, an idea immediately enters his head, "Why not my old practice shoes?"

They were half-a-size smaller than Eric's new game shoes. Yet, he figured they'd be worth a shot. The shoes were stealth black, Air Jordan 10's. They had been worn so much- half-a-size down or not- it had found a way to mold well to Eric's growing, teenage feet. He also saw the personal value in these shoes as well. For his grandfather gifted it to him a few years back, on his 14th birthday.

"Eric!" Coach Walker yelled, "Get out of here and get ready to start this 2nd half strong," he finished off as he was exiting the locker room.

He was completing his personal grooming in the mirror. "And the 3rd quarter is about to start! Move ya ass!!" Coach Walker quickly pops his head back in the locker room, "Please!" giving Eric a quick stare before popping back out of view. Eric couldn't help but smile back at his coach. He wasn't himself if he didn't yell.

With a minute or two to spare, Eric darts to his designated team locker, responding to his coach's demand,

"Ok, Coach… one second!!" He quickly enters his locker combination on borrowed time just as he hears the team warm-up music faintly in the background and then ceased playing. Upon opening his locker to grab his old shoes, Eric stumbled across an old picture. Amongst the collage of photo memorabilia plastered onto the inside of his locker door. With the likes of Kobe Bryant and Allen Iverson, wedged in between, was a picture of his 14th birthday with his grandfather. Standing side-by-side, wearing the same shoes he's ironically about to put on his feet. Eric smiled, taking it as a sign from the basketball Gods above, grabbing his old pair of Jordan's out of the locker. With each tightening pull of his shoelaces, he knew he was ready to lay it all on the line as the horn gave off its last warning.

"Alright, Buck's fans! Makes some noise!"

Slicky J began addressing the crowd in his casual patent flair, which was always a crowd-pleaser, given by the uproar of screams from the eager fans, ready for the second half to start. As the horn sounded, it never accounted for much during halftime events on rivalry games. Compared to the game announcer, especially "Hollywood's own," as he was known, Slicky J- it was simply inadequate.

To the fans, the game clock's only job was to keep the score and make sure you don't cheat the game by shaving playing minutes off the clock. Hearing Slicky J on the microphone, welcoming everyone back to their seats for the second act- was theatrical, in a sense. His uniquely smooth tone and style of delivery in his words and the vernacular was one of a kind. He enunciated every word on purpose with crisp precision, keeping all fans glued to the action. And it took work.

Slicky J pulled his black *Kangol* bucket hat down. Barely exposing his cool, light-brown eyes, ready for action. "The second half of this colossal, pivotal, astronomical, rival game. That's right… You heard me, baby, Rivalry!! The Bucks', 49… Looking to keep that energy going." He flipped the stat page over and proceeded to read for the courtesy of the Roosevelt guest. "Now, those baby bears," he paused for a moment. He lifted his head to look around, giving the home team crowd a chance to "Boo," rant and rave- pissing the visitors off… "Sadly, they only have at 41… Po' thing. That's an 8-piece difference, baby, and hold those fries!!"

Slicky J covered his mouth as if he was awaiting a cliffhanger from a movie to reveal itself, an overdramatic reaction for mocking the Bears. However, the home team loved it, as they laughed and cheered, "Bucks' House… Bucks' House!!" Waiting for the start of the 3rd quarter. The visiting Bears' fans didn't find much to cheer about. Some of the Bears' players warming up on the court stopped their dribbling, just to "flick off" Slick J. And those in the visiting bleachers, who disapproved also chose to respond to the announcer with flagrant hand gestures of their own. "Hey, don't shoot the messenger, baby. How will they, except they bounce back? Let's get it! Makes some noise, Buck's fans!"

Fans started to refill the gymnasium, rushing back to their seats. Players made their way back to their bench, the only group that seriously acknowledged the halftime buzzer. In the crowd, Eric's friends were worried about his performance and whether he would come out more assertive. "Boy, he suckin' today," Angelo said, comfortably sitting in his bleacher seat and shoving popcorn in his mouth, "At least we up thought! Now- that announcer- Slicky J, my idol!! That dude is great!!"

Angelo devoured the popcorn in a barbaric fashion, leaving pieces flying all around him. Safe to say, he embarrassed his peers in another attempt at being him. Not only did they not appreciate Angelo's sloppy eating. They no longer wanted to tolerate his "care-free" dialogue about their friend and the family nearby. His "tact" usually resulted in a mixed bag of sour faces. However, Angelo wasn't done, as he proceeded with his pessimistic rant. It made no difference to him whether they listened or not. And that is what mostly bothered them.

Licking his greasy fingers and cleaning of the buttery residue, he said slowly, "But here's the thing. The team is playin' great. They passin… all that. And 'actually' playin' some defense. I just think he's nervous, or something. Y'all here, too".

Angelo then looked passively to Ronald Sr. and said, "Y'all, being 'you,' grandpops." Then smiling casually at him for a few seconds, just before diving back into his remaining popcorn bucket. As he took a kernel and popped it in his mouth, he said to Paula, "Grandma Brewer, you were right… This is popcorn, fire," winking playfully.

Ronald Sr. looked at Angelo with conviction and some offense. Starring at Angelo, he thought, "You little shit!" But then thought, "What if he's right?" Then he turned to his wife, Paula, and said, "Maybe we should go home and let the boy focus."

Angelo, already feeling like the jerk in the group, intervened and corrected his miscalculated approach; after all, he was only joking. "Nonsense, old man- I mean, Sir!" quickly, correcting his laxed lingo around his elders, which was unintentional this time. Ronald Jr., watching it all unfold, now regretted the seat change his wife made in the first half. He could not stand how Angelo spoke around everyone. Ronald Jr. stared on, piercing his eyes into Angelo's soul. But only a simple on-looker at this point. However, no disrespect shall be taken with his family, and Eric's friends were no exception.

Angelo just loved to test the waters. It was almost as if he saw Ronald Jr. too or a figure of some sort. So, to reassure the family that he was on the same page with them, Angelo made a compelling argument, "Look, I personally know this is a battle for him- because he's been stressing all week, honestly. And for only God knows. But he's built Ford tough, man. And y'all know… Y'all raised him well, Right? Win or lose."

Jacqueline and Jeremy figured Angelo had already shot himself in the foot with his mouth. They tried to mitigate the issue and find the silver lining to "whatever" Angelo said. In which, there wasn't much to go on, leaving the two stuck to improvise. They just wanted to uplift Eric's parents, if they were down at all by their son's performance. It was just an assumption though. His parents didn't need it. Little did they know, they were just as competitive as their son. Now, as responsible parents, their responsibilities have changed. And in turn, they dialed back their "competitive" juices a significant amount. However, being a competitor at heart isn't something you can just shake off like a common cold.

Ronald Jr. and Nadine were both All-State ranked athletes in high school. Today, Nadine sits back quietly, observing all the moves her son does on the court, hoping he makes the right decisions as a guard to ensure a victory. Ronald Jr. wants his son to win, too. He just views it differently from his wife. Personally, he felt he was blessed when his son showed attraction to the same sport that found his heart as a kid. Now, as a dad, he can be a true fan and enjoy the game for what it is, a game.

"Ms. Brewer, your son is going to be fine," Jeremy said, trying to assure her. He then pointed across the court, parallel to the bleachers, "Those scouts up there are only here to see your son. They tried to blend in, but I saw the one reaching for a notepad, jotting down their thoughts. I think some even made some phone calls. I'm more than certain they know what E, can do.

A blank stare occupied Nadine's face as she looked at Jeremy. The sympathy route was never her cup of tea, especially in sports. And Jeremy got a clear understanding of that just by the hint by her gaze. He then sharply turns back to the court and continues, "I just want these boys to win."

Nadine snapped back in good fashion, "You must have forgotten I also played ball. I probably could still do a number on you. We know how scouts work, boy, so sit down. We don't need your pity; it's not *me* on the floor."

Befuddled by her sharp response and tone, Jeremy was left looking for a way out from the unexpected tongue lashing. However, all he could do was sit down and say, "Yes, ma'am." As the nearby fans caught wind of their exchange, a slight snicker started to develop around them.

Ronald Sr., also like Nadine and his son, wasn't worried about Eric. After going over the film this week with his grandson, he was confident he would fight, no matter what. "Eric will be fine everyone," Ronald Sr. said, "But I'm not going to let you keep talking down on my grandson. Like I'm not sitting right here. You're his friends, right?" His stern question was more of a rhetorical one for the group but was something Ronald Sr. needed to address. Specifically, with Angelo, since that was who he was eyeing at the time.

Being the best friend of Eric, Jeremy tried his best to clear the hostile air for the second time. The second half was set to begin, plus people were starting to look at the escapades the Brewers were stirring up in the front row. From Angelo's popcorn munchies to the jokes fired at each other aimlessly and with no remorse, and their overall loudness. They could draw attention.

"Forgive his ignorance, Grandpop," Jeremy said, reaching over and planting his hand on Ronald Sr.'s leg, "Sometimes, he just doesn't know how to act in public; he ate batteries." He then turned to Angelo and said, "Where ya manners at, man? Fool."

"In 7th-period wit yo momma, and I wasn't tardy either." He proceeded to give Jeremy a fake smile, who was now pissed that Angelo had brought his mother into the session. A foul play to make in front of the parents.

Ronald Jr. turned to face Angelo sitting next to him and slapped him in the back of the head, shutting down all the chaos in their section with one swoop of his hand. "Y'all are doing entirely too much shit over there. Sit the hell down- shut the hell up!" He then turned to his father and said, "Sorry, dad."

But finally, there was silence amongst the group. Leaving Ronald Jr. to drive his point home to everyone while he still had the opportunity. "Can we please watch the game, please!?"

"I guess," Angelo said, rubbing his throbbing head.

Sitting on the edge of the group was Nadine, positioned on the bleachers, hunched over. Flustered at her own family, she could only utter a few words during such a screwy period, "God, I know you see us. But I hope those scouts aren't looking at us, Amen." As the quarter was set to resume, her head continued to sink in shame after her quick prayer.

CHAPTER 17

Most of the players were warmed up and ready for the second half action except Eric. He was seen racing out of the locker room with only 30 seconds left on the clock to join in a short shoot-around with the team. The game officials rested and returned to the floor from their own designated resting area, tucked away in Troutman Gymnasium.

"Yikes! Look at this late ass dude here," one of Eric's teammate said, pointing, seeing Eric, sprinting to the court. They were all curious why Eric missed majority of the halftime in the locker room and, "Why in the hell are his eyes so damn red? "Aye! You been crying fool?"

"I'm good, I'm good."

"…. Did Coach 'do' something to ya… ya know… *do* something?"

"What the fuck!? Aye, come on, fool. Don't play me," Eric shot back.

"Ah, lighting up, we just bullshitting!" He gave Eric a friendly nudge, easing the tension, and awkwardness, "Ok. Aight, I'm just checking. You can never be too sure out here, playboy."

"Right, we don't need a Jerry Sandusky on our hands," another one of his teammates said, chiming in on an already childish conversation.

"Now you know you foul for that one," Leo Capernati said, laughing as he passed by, walking to the bench.

"He knows he's wrong. He knows what he doin…" Eric said, pleading his case to Leo.

As the players place their practice basketballs on the rack, they all approach their head coach. He understood why Eric's eyes were slightly red but didn't bother ragging on him. It wasn't the place or time, or situation; they had a game to close out.

None of Eric's teammates noticed the shoe change that Eric made during the half; they were too busy cracking jokes at his red, puffy face. The only one who could tell, surprisingly, was his grandfather, who was in the stands. Carelessly leaving his glasses at home, he had squint to make out what they even were. With the team standing in front, positioned directly in his view, he couldn't tell what kind they were, but he knew. Ronald Sr. smirked. Regardless of what shoes his grandson had on his feet or if he played well or not, he was just happy to see his grandson upbeat—a complete opposite from the end of the 1st half.

With no time to spare, the officials were not letting another minute pass. Eric got the team together for a quick pep talk. "Yo, Fellas. My bad for the bullshit in the locker room. That won't ever happen again. I got y'all back. I just need some help to carry ya boy this game. So, let's tear their fucking hearts out."

Nodding their heads and looking around, the team agreed. "Hell yea!!" It was pleasing to Eric's ears as he finished it off, "I won't have a sloppy second half. We comin' for 'em. This is our house!"

The team spirit began to reignite with each word their team captain spoke. They could taste blood again. And Eric needed to redeem himself.

As a team, they brought their hands in for a quick, "1-2-3- Bucks!!" count. But not before Eric's teammate, Tareek Baxter, chimed in. He couldn't resist the urge to point out the elephant in the room now with the whole team around.

"You know coach was holding 'everything' within his power not to slap the shit out of you in the locker room." And on cue, the entire team busted out in laughter, even Eric.

"Yea. Aight. What did you expect me to do?"

"Coach!! ... you got me fucked up!" Tareek said, imitating Eric's shaky, high-pitched voice, as the team laughed some more at Eric's expense.

"Naw, for real though! You were talkin' crazy to that man, cussing and shit. I loved it! But we better win, or practice gonna be hell". Everyone on the team agreed with Tareek's assessment. Eric had to make sure as the leader not to fail. "Well, let's go to work then. Bucks on me, Bucks on 3."

Eric had no time to warm up, unlike his teammates at halftime. His energy was spent sobbing and collecting his thoughts in the locker room, trying to pick up the pieces. He needed to refocus. The officials were standing by the scorer's table and ready to begin the second half. Before the start, they had a conversation amongst themselves; they wanted to ensure a good flow to the 2nd half. Nobody could afford to have any further hold-ups, given everything that happened in the first half.

Coach Walker also wanted to share some quick words for the team. Eric was fully engaged, opposite of his previous attitude in the locker room. But back there, those two had a moment. Moments that can shape many young, adolescent boys' minds around the world and how they perceive conflicts. How one can be receptive to empathy without having judgment cast onto them. A resounding "Yes, Coach!" was all that anyone in the gymnasium could hear.

The cheerleaders encouraged the crowd to stomp their feet. The metal and wood bleacher started to produce a thunderous noise, filling the gym. On the other side of the scorer's table, the away team screamed together, "1-2-3-Bears!" The lead official blew his whistle, signaling for both teams to prepare for the ball to be checked inbounds at the baseline he was facing. With the 3rd quarter beginning, it's the Bucks' possession.

The referee hands over the ball to Bucks' center, Leo Capernati, and is passed into play as Eric receives it, and the referee chops down his hand, starting the quarter. With a new mindset and attitude and his old pair of Air Jordan 10's on his feet. A more confident and less hesitant Eric dribbled up the open backcourt. As the defenders set up in a zone, choosing not to press at the start of the quarter like Coach Walker assumed. Eric took his time up the court, waited for Leo to sprint back down, and take his position in the paint.

However, seeing how lackadaisical the Bears' defense was, he had other plans. He stops just 4 feet shy of the red three-point line. With a quick trigger, he jumped, shoulders squared and released his shot. Following through with his shot, using his shooting hand, it was nothing but net. He looked up to the sky briefly, praying that his shot motivated the team to play tighter defense; and score more points. Tareek ran back up the court with his hands still poised for a pass he thought Eric would make. "Oh, that's how you feelin' now!? Ok!" he said jokingly, "It's gonna be a long night when he gets going!". He gave Eric a quick high-five in passing, now ready to play defense. Eric was also backpedaling to get on defense. His eyes were glued to the Bears' offense, stream rolling quickly back up the court.

Unaware that Eric would take such a bold shot and make it, Coach Walker leaps out of his seat, pointing to the ball and screaming for a full-court press. "Don't let them breathe!" Coach Walker yelled. But regretfully, due to Eric's ill-advised shot mixed in with the Bucks' excitement, the defense found themselves unprepared and collapsing late on the Bears' transition offense. Their fast-break play resulted in an easy transition lay-up to the basket for two points. (score: 43-52).

"Damn- Damn, Damn-it!" Coach Walker said, stomping his foot against the hardwood, "What are you all doing out there!?" He pointed to the court, "You press! You press!" then turned to face the bench, pleading with them to learn from the mistakes that they see on the court before substituting. Coach Walker was furious again, and only two possessions into the quarter, he plopped back into his seat and looked over at Assistant Coach Lawry and said, "Man, you go coach these boys. Their asses clearly don't want to listen to me!" His cry for help was more so a stress reliever than him resigning. So, Coach Walker said this in good faith, knowing his assistant understood.

The Bucks quickly inbounded the basketball. But just as quickly as they received it, the Bears' stole it back. With the ball again in their possession, they gave a swift outlet pass, traveling to the top of the key, finding an open Bears' player. Fortunately, with the length the Bucks' provided, one of their players was able to hustle back and defend the ball before shooting. The Bears' player pump-faked the shot from the top of the key, but it didn't work. Plan B was to drive past him. The Bucks' defense was too flat-footed to keep up with the Bears' top ball handler. He stutter-stepped with his left foot. Then with one hard dribble with his left, he took it behind his back, over to his right hand.

Finding the defender on his heels, he drives into the paint, drawing the defenders to him. Only to fool the Bucks', as he dished the basketball back out. There, he found a Bears' small forward, standing at the right-wing. Catching the pass in motion, he shoots and drains the three-pointer, then points at Eric. And at his is expense, Eric was the closest defender to him at the time. The small forward snarled his lips, growling at Eric, saying, "You can't see us. Fuck what chu' thought," flexing his arms to the stands. Leaving the Roosevelt fans wanting more.

The Roosevelt Bears were not threatened by what the Hollywood Bucks brought to the table. In their mind, "We are better than this Bucks' team." And It seems like Eric's three-pointer at the beginning of the 3rd quarter had little to no damage on the Bear's spirit. The bright side for the Hollywood Bucks was that the referees on the floor saw the taunting and jawing in Eric's direction after the made shot. The lead official issued the Bears' a taunting warning, written down at the scores table instead of a technical foul, resulting in a free throw shot.

The officials wanted a competitive game, like the old days. But a game that also flowed, and with not many hiccups. Majority of the home team Bucks' fans didn't appreciate the pointing and cursing at their star player. And with no flagrant foul distributed, they felt short-sided.

Eric started experiencing Deja's Vu, and found himself slowly becoming frustrated with the change of events. Yet, he hasn't given up hope. And still adamant about finding the *will* to win and staying victorious in the match-up. The

Bucks were still winning but less than comfortable about their lead. In the home bleachers, those same sentiments rang, "Do they have the momentum?" A popular question they usually asked themselves. Maybe their star player was, "In over his head?" "Maybe his eyes were bigger than the plate?"

Shaking off the last play, which was a debacle, Eric wiped his hands on his jersey and received the inbound pass without first looking down the court. "Man? Or Zone?" should have been the first thing to pop in his mind as a guard before bringing the ball in. But to his surprise, it was neither. It was worse; a full court press directly in his face. The Bears defense wanted to initiate a counter to the Bucks' failed attempt at executing a full-court press; something Coach Walker was still furious about. The thought process for the Bears was simple, "Kick them while they down and suck the life out of this place. We may be down for now, but we are never out." The fans cringe at the sight of another turnover. And Eric was mad that his team failed to let him know what was behind him before inbounding the ball.

Finding the full-court press to succeed, the Bears' steal the possession from Eric's hands before doing anything. He wanted to attempt a cross-court pass, wanting to keep them on their toes. However, the Bears without reserve, toss the ball to the goal, attempting to score two easy points. Eric, defending now, deflects the attempt, sending the ball to an open area on the wing but picked up by a Bears' player. On the opposite end of the court, the remaining Bucks also high tail it back, trying to prevent the easy score. But with no help from the team, the Bears' pump-faked the ball, leaving the Bucks' player in the air as he drove to the basket. Eric fouled the shooter hard, attempting to stop the easy lay-up.

"Fuck man!" Eric shrieked with emotion. His eyes slowly rolled over to his bench, and he saw some of his teammates shaking their heads. Some were clapping, urging him, "Don't get down." He took this moment to place his hands over his head, trying to catch his breath. Eric also hoped the official would let his emotional outburst slide, just this time. Coach Walker, standing on the sideline, gritting his teeth, uttered, "Damn… Do y'all 'really,' want this? What you doin', Man!?" He slapped his hands together with tremendous vigor. It instantly turned his palms a bright red as the sound traveled throughout the gym. But the official wasn't done with his foul call announcement to the scores table as he ran closer to them. They couldn't quite make it out due to the overall noise and cheering in the gym.

"Count the basket! Red #22. Hit! One-shot remaining!" Eric couldn't help but laugh. To his surprise, he didn't even realize that "lucky" shot went in, a sign he didn't foul him hard enough.

Coach Walker grabbed his towel and told the tableside official he wanted a timeout if the free throw attempt is made. If not, the Bucks will play on and learn how to adjust and communicate as a team. The free throw attempt went up, it was made, and the official granted a timeout. (49-52).

Then Coach Walker grabs Assistant Coach Lawry's clipboard. Eric approached the team bench and noticed the sweat beads quickly forming on his forehead. His sweat beads produced little "sweat creeks," running past his ears, down to his chin. But he wasn't worried about that as much as the kids were. The only thing on Coach Walker's mind was finding a way to score more baskets before they catch up. The Bucks' lead was slowly dwindling.

CHAPTER 18

"Guys, guys, guys, come on! It's almost the end of the 3rd, and we've only put 3 points. Now, we are only up by 3. Someone should explain this to me!" Coach Walker said.

The team went silent. Some even began to hang their heads, not wanting to look directly into his raging eyes. And taking it as disrespect, Coach Walker felt it was best to scorn the team, as white foam began to form at the corners of his mouth. "So, we just silent!? Just like that play out there, huh?! Silent! This is their quarter- must be... One basket this whole quarter. Thanks, Eric."

Coach Walker looked directly at Eric, who was sitting down catching his breath during the timeout. He stared back, but he was wise enough not to answer him with enough years under his varsity basketball resume as this wasn't a compliment. Some players, though, did eventually resurface their heads from the disappointment and shame that they had. They knew they still had another quarter to make amends.

Coach Walker started to pace, trying to find the right words and cool off, but something that would light a fire under them. Something stern, brief, but to the point some lecture. And he found nothing. "Do you, men, wanna lose a crucial game? In our house?" he said, revving back up, "We have no talking... Y'all pressed, maybe 4 times this whole game with no damn defense! Oh! Our passes are getting sloppy! We are home, for God's sake!"

"Yes, coach!" They all replied.

"So, play like it! Smarten up!" he said, pointing to his head, "Or this bench will be your home base!" pointing to the bench. Some bench players would also like some burn with their parents here and all..."

"Yes, coach!" was their only reply. And a smart one. As the players broke the huddle, they made their way back to the court with a heightened sense of urgency to turn the tide. Coach Walker chucks the useless clipboard to the bench. Almost hitting Assistant Coach Lawry, forgetting it was his clipboard he borrowed him in the first place. "Oh damn! My bad brother," Coach Walker said, not to misdirect his anger towards his co-host, "It's these kid's, man, they are makin me wanna scream!!"

"Ahh, blame it on the kids," Assistant Coach Lawry responded, jokingly, "Yea, no worries... Just relax a little." Flustered, he picked up his clipboard from the bench seat. And his pen, that rolled onto the floor- ready to enter more 3rd quarter data.

Eric, who hasn't taken a seat all game, besides timeouts, felt his energy getting low. With his hands on his hips and head hanging low. He reverted his drained eyes from the hardwood court to his old shoes. It was a brief euphoric moment that came over him. Despite a dismal performance on his behalf, he knew his family was going to support his efforts, at whatever the cost.

He had a sudden flashback to when he was younger. And with his grandfather teaching him the basics of shooting free throws. These childhood sessions were often held in Ronald Sr.'s backyard. Usually, when he was out of school in the summertime, his parents would drop him off for the day instead of daycare. Cracked cement and loose gravel filled the driveway leading up to his backyard.

The basketball hoop was more secure than it looked slightly loose from the wear and tear. It was accompanied by a half-rust eaten pole. The layout of the land wasn't the greatest. But as a kid, it was everything to Eric. And one of the reasons why he plays the game today. Looking down at his shoes reminded him of that. There's still joy in basketball

"Big E!"

"AYYYYE, E!"

Eric quickly looked to the stands as he heard his name being yelled. Competing with the other various noises in the gym, and within a few seconds, he noticed his mom, followed by Jacqueline, first waving in his direction. And not a second passed when he had his vision of his mom and Jacqueline, compromised by Angelo and his father. Once they locked eyes with Eric, they began waving their hands erratically. Ronald Jr. then blew his air horn for the 12th time tonight, piercing Angelo's ear drum.

"That's my son! Go get'em, boy!"

Eric only seems to acknowledge his mother and Jacqueline at the time. After being chewed out, he needed to focus on the task at hand. But now, he was slightly embarrassed at the attention he was getting and how his father was acting. His family could do that to him. Glaring at the game clock on the wall, it read 3:47 left in the 3rd quarter. "Let's go, fellas!" Eric said as he wiped the excess dust off his shoes before the basketball was inbounded, wanting to finish this quarter on a high note.

Throughout the 3rd quarter, the Bears continued to wreak havoc on the Bucks'. Relentlessly pressing the offense, which resulted in key turnovers for the Bucks'. Life-threatening? No. But enough to keep the Bears in the fight. With each basket, they scored off turnovers, and it added fuel in their heart not to quit. In fact, the Bears took the lead towards the last two minutes of the 3rd quarter. (55-54).

One of their star players, #12, Shila Rook, was a monster on both sides of the court. Standing at 6'4, 180 pounds. Despite his wiry frame and weight, he could deliver shot after shot for the Bears. Not only were the scouts looking at Eric, but they also had Shila Rook's name on their recruit list. In college, Division 2 at least, they would surely place him as a 2- shooting guard, maybe a small forward, especially once he puts weight on him. With that said, it doesn't mean Division 1 schools weren't interested as well.

Everyone in Hollywood Heights knew Shila was going "somewhere" after high school. Even though Eric was noted as the "highlight player" of the night, Shila played low to the ground with his crafty maneuvers to the basket despite being tall. He. His low style of play provided his explosive attack to the rim whenever needed. He was also a left-handed guy, which was a rarity. Overall, he dominated the game. And a slight advantage to most when it came to shooting, blocking shots, and attacking the bucket.

Eric knew he needed to step it up, or his limelight tonight could be snatched. Fully aware that his shot was not falling as he wanted. And despite being the only player to hit a three-pointer before timeout. He took the initiative to step up his defense, as a team captain should. He was also very comfortable with turnovers leads to points, but Eric still needed to play smart or risk foul trouble. Starter or not, with a coach like Walker, benching was a high possibility.

Foolishly, and without regard to the overall outcome, Eric yelled to the team, "Press them!! Press!!" It was an error in command. In his train of thought, "If we press them full court, leaving the guards to depend on their speed, maybe we can put this game away for good."

A key highlight on tonight's scout's sheet about the Bucks' team was their length. Their ability to deny passes, clog passing lanes, and crowd a court with only 5 people. It was fascinating to the scouts but terrifying for the opponents. One thing was for certain; the Bears didn't want to risk any cross-court passes against a long and agile team, like the Bucks'. Nevertheless, just as risky as it was for Eric yelling out, "Press!!" The Bears' felt the odds were still in their favor and attempted away.

Eric depended heavily on his center, Leo Capernati, to clean the shots, set "hard" screens, and attack the hole, especially since Eric has been off tonight. For Leo, this resulted in easy rebounds for the big man. He always struggled with the put-back attempts, but he never quit. However, when he would find his "groove," It would be nothing short of amazing; the way he snagged missed shots from the air, retrieving it, kissing the basketball off the glass for an easy put-back lay-up or two. Leo Capernati was a 6'8, country-fed boy. And in his offseason, he would help his father with the cattle on their farmer, located just on the city's outskirts. He was one of the few white kids on the team, but he was as cool as the rest of them. And the players loved him for it.

A graduating senior himself, he only played basketball to work on his footwork, football field, and keep his conditioning up to speed. Last year he committed to the

University of Alabama before his junior football season. With basketball, he just loved the game. And his friends, with who he became tight over the years he's played.

Eric always tried to find a way to reward his center for the dirty work he put in throughout the game tonight was no exception. "Give me the damn ball!!" Leo screamed as he fought for his position. Eric, seeing him, fed Leo the ball in the paint. Whenever Leo had his defender sealed in, with no hope of stopping him, he would get the ball, and he would simply tower them with one dribble, using his body weight. Or over anyone foolish enough to attempt a blocked shot. After making a basket, Leo would often shout, from his lungs, "They too small for me, man!! Let's Go!!!" he said as he ran back down the court. His teammates loved the energy he brought. It made Coach Walker shake his head in disgust.

The home team also began to feel rejuvenated. What once seemed like a slight scare midway in the 3rd quarter ended with an astonishing roar from the home bleachers. By finding other ways to be effective on the court. instead of scoring, Eric willed his team to remain on top by the sound of the 3rd quarter horn. (59-64).

The Bucks' cheerleaders rushed to the floor to do their last cheer routine for the night. The Bucks' team, exhausted, on the bench, collecting their thoughts. Some players were hunched over, grasping for air. Some chose not to sit down, only taking squirts from their water bottles in between breaths. It was clear that the 3rd quarter was more of a challenge than they anticipated. Even though they were up with five-point, Coach Walker and Assistant Coach Lawry exchanged looks. Uneasy with what they see on the bench, heading into the 4th quarter. "Maybe the basketball Gods are not on our side tonight," Coach Walker said, entertaining the thought in his head. Whatever the case may be, they didn't like it, and their non-verbal exchanges expressed that.

On the opposing end, the Bears' head coach happened to glance over to their bench, seeing what their hard work did to the Bucks'. He saw the look of panic consuming the faces of the coaching staff and the team, encouraging his boy to "Finish the fight."

CHAPTER 19

On the home team bench, Coach Walker needed to find another way to encourage his boys. His old ways were wearing thin on the players' morale. With phrases like…

"Boy, sit up!"

"Anton, stop hunching over like that…"

"Come on, Eric! Stop chugging down that water so fast!"

"Y'all want cramps, Jesus!"

It was safe to say that Coach Walker had a challenge of his own. Coming to grips with his own hard-nosed style of coaching, but it wasn't working. Wiping his hands over his face, he took a deep inhale, trying to understand how aggressive his language and body language can be with the kids. At the end of the day, that's what they were, kids. So, Coach Walker exhaled slowly and tried again. "Fellas… We are up. Ok? 'We' just need to keep it up and finish this thing out. Y'all are playing hard, and I love it; I just need more of it. In the first half of the 4th quarter, I want to initiate a full-court press. Let's try that, please."

A large exhale escaped the lungs of the players, paired with some eye rolls and grunts. They were letting their coach know exactly what the players thought of the idea. Also, what they thought of him at that moment.

"Coach, we are tired, man," Tareek said, objecting to the idea and speaking for the majority of the team.

Coach Walker wasn't trying to hear their "cop-out," laughing off the team's desire to quit in front of his eyes. However, entertaining it for a few seconds, he gave them what their ears so desperately wanted to hear. "So, what? Y'all tired now? Y'all want to pack up and go home?" Surveying the bench, he continued, "Shit, I can call the game right now if ya want. But *I'm* the coach, remember that men."

As head coach, Walker was secretly hoping his reverse psychology would play to his favor. Taking an old page from his college coach in his playing days; something that did wonders for his squad when they were in a downward spiral. But it did not work for the Hollywood Bucks', a high school team. "Ok, Coach," was what their eyes said, keeping the words inside. And nothing can hurt a coach more than seeing their team quit on them right before their eyes amid battle.

A silver lining, the Bucks had other options for when strategies, or the coaching gets misguided. And that option was Assistant Coach Lawry. As he quickly stepped in, alleviating a player revolt, some were starting to form. Not even Eric, the team captain, could coddle the damper spirits. He has defeated himself, still from the 1st half. The last thing this team needed was more fighting amongst each other as they go into the 4th quarter. They weren't as focused on closing out this rivalry game as they should have. And with the Bears continuing to breathe down their necks, they needed to devise a new scheme to close out the game. Being the more reserved individual than Coach Walker, Assistant

Coach Lawry felt he could reach the team in a way Walker couldn't. This was their second option and the last.

As mentioned, Assistant Coach Lawry was well-liked around the team. More so because he didn't chew the team out as Coach Walker did. This helped provide a new line of communication for the players and those too scared to address Coach Walker directly. With that said, Assistant Coach Lawry had an idea to help preserve the team's energy. And giving them a shot to keep the lead, beefing up their school record. So, they needed to take heed to every word he said. Assistant Coach Lawry was always welcomed in the huddle by the players. Taking Coach Walker's position in the huddle, he got down on one knee, making sure they heard every word he said and had only 2 minutes to spare.

"Ok, guys. Quick! Come in…" Assistant Coach Lawry starts, "You're tired, I see it. And when you're tired, that's your mind drifting away from its rational thinking on the court. Not like y'all have any…" He smiled as he looked at the team, then turned to Coach Walker and smirked.

The players still found his energy inviting and began to chuckle, breaking the ice. "It's ok, though!" Assistant Coach Lawry continued, "It can happen to anyone." He pointed towards the visiting team bench, "They aren't excluded over there! The key is to remain calm in these situations, you understand?" The team sipping their water understood what Coach Lawry was trying to get across. They received his words with good intentions as he carried on, "Pay attention. We're up by 5, gentlemen." He then points to Eric, "Sorry, playboy. Your shot just ain't falling, man."

"Tell me something I don't know," Eric snapped back.

"The good news is…" Assistant Coach Lawry continued, "You're finding your teammates, and that spreads out the floor. Anton, Tareek, John, everyone, I need you guys to shoot!! Eric, keep finding them. Naturally, the defense is looking to collapse on you- good night or bad."

Eric wasn't too thrilled he was given the "red light" to stop shooting but took a sigh as he understood his place in tonight's game. He was only one man in a game where he needed four others to compete alongside. And to depend on when things go south.

"Leo, keep snagging those boards. And Fellas, keep feeding that man down there!" He pointed to the Bucks' center, "Look at that big ass boy! Feed him the rock. He's hungry, Ok?" Assistant Coach Lawry concluded.

The players all smiled, including Eric, setting some of their nerves to the side and agreeing with their assistant coach.

Assistant Coach Lawry was such a relief to have on the team for the players. And unbeknownst to head Coach Walker, he probably saved his job from a team that was ready to quit on him. Principal Teely was also in attendance for the night's game. Along with her son, Jacob, the Hollywood High School's morning and afternoon news announcer. He was there jotting down notes from the game, critical information needed for Monday's morning announcements, especially if they win. But, to the principal's surprise, Teely was not expecting to see Coach Walker's conduct in such disarray and in front of hundreds of "her" guests and his fans.

Rivalry game or not, she wasn't pleased. Even in her worst days at Hollywood High School, she wouldn't dare use "this" type of verbatim with school kids. It was something she made sure to keep a mental note of and his assistant's performance.

Leo Capernati, laughing at himself, took no offense to the joke Assistant Coach Lawry flung his way. He was aware of his size and how much folks spoke about it. He took nothing but pride in it. Even Coach Walker, standing on the outside of the huddle, arms folded, also couldn't help but snicker. He was a "hard-ass," to the players, but he tried his best to better acknowledge the humor in things and in life.

Eric, looking at Leo, daps him up. The two seniors believe they have just enough to seal the deal tonight.

Coach Walker wanted to briefly chime in passively, agreeing with the new tactics his assistant outlined. "Yea, sure… I think the press does have you guys gassed; why not?" However, giving up his reigns to allow his assistant to lead, he was at discord. Personally, he still felt the kids were making an excuse not to run a full-court press defense. But no longer being "option A," at this point, it was out of his hands and into his assistant's. Or without at least trying to sneak the last word in. "Also! Men, just…"

"Coach! Please!" "Let me handle this!" Assistant Coach Lawry sternly addressed him.

Being a head coach, Walker always wanted the last word. Tonight, he didn't get it. Feeling courageous, and with the "silent" support of the players. He even directed Coach Walker to a place by the bench where he could sit and cool off. Head coach or assistant, neither one liked having their toes stepped on.

With an uneasy look written on the players' faces, Coach Walker felt it was best to take a seat.

To everyone's surprise, he obliged. And Assistant Coach Lawry continued speaking before the start of the last quarter. "Ok, instead of running a full court press," he said, thinking aloud, "Let's move to Zone, at half court. 1-3-1. And keep the paint full and Clog it up!" The team nodded in agreement. "Force them suckas to shoot. I don't think they have it in them to do it on our court.".

"Suckas?" Leo chimed in.

"Yea, Suckas. What do I say?"

"You are old, G. I'm sorry- *sucka*.

"Oh, thank God!" Tareek shouted, looking up pointing to the ceiling. They were relieved to know they could reserve some of their energy by switching to a zone defense. And for Tareek, his energy could be reserved for shooting.

"Just remember," Assistant Coach Lawry closed, "Put pressure on your man until that damn ball crosses half court. Then shift to 1-3-1. Put pressure on that ball-handler and get me some turnovers!" Still on one knee, he glanced between the tall players in the huddle, seeing if Coach Walker had any input to give. Coach Walker was listening but staring off. He was clearly still trying to calm down from an overreaction he felt was on his assistant's behalf.

"Anything you want to add over there, Coach!?"

Coach Walker casually looked over and smiled carelessly, shrugging his shoulders. "Just have fun and finish strong, boys," was all he could manage to say. In his mind, he felt most of the boys had already given up the fight. So, he really had nothing to contribute to the course.

As the officials blow their whistles, preparing for the 4th quarter, the Bucks bring it in, arms raised was led by Eric. "Bucks on me, Bucks on 3!!!"

With no jump ball possessions in the 3rd quarter, the Bears' quarter started with the basketball. Walking back onto the floor, Eric was curious to know where his "foul count" lied. He figured the last foul call put him in some sort of foul trouble, which would restructure how Eric applied his own defensive pressure. He was a tough defender and loved it before he learned how to score consistently. But since his shot wasn't falling, defensive stops seem to be the only thing going his way tonight until his recent foul, which still rang a salty taste in his mouth.

Asking the assistant coach, Lawry looked down at his notepad and signaled a "3" with three fingers.

"Damn!" uttered Eric. He was perplexed; he even put himself in this situation, to begin with. Two more fouls and he's out of the game for good. He wiped his feet with his hands once again to gain traction. Hearing the crowd in the background, he takes another deep, slow breath. And for a few seconds, he glanced over to his grandfather, who he saw holding hands with Paula.

Ronald Sr. eyes were locked onto his grandson's as he smiled at Eric. Ronald Sr. mouthed, "Go get'em!" Laying it on softly with a warming smile and his smooth wink, "Go!"

Then Eric nodded, making the words out the best he could, confirming their quick interaction. But his eyes and brain are now focused on the incoming offensive possession by the Bears as the 4th quarter begins.

CHAPTER 20

"What'd you say to him, baby?" Paula asked as she turned, facing Ronald Sr., and continued to hold his hand, caressing it over with her thumb. "I just told him, 'Go get'em'. Play your game." Ronald Sr. replied, then grabbed his free hand and placed it over her grazing thumb, giving his wife a small peck on the lips.

"Aw, old love!"

Angelo, spotting the "PDA," with an exaggerated grin on his face, "It's so cute."

"My G, why are you so damn creepy?" Jeremy said, eyeing Angelo gazing at the kissing couple, "And those dolphin teeth don't help either- ugly, boy!" Childishly, he busted out in laughter. It was an "off-putting," corky laugh; mixed in with a yelp for good measure.

People around him who witnessed it wonder. "Was it an animal or an actual human that was hurt?" And Jeremy sometimes didn't know if it was the jokes he cracked or the "one of a kind" laugh he had that people found amusing. Regardless, on cue with his unique laugh, laughter soon started to spread throughout his bleacher section.

Jacqueline was included in the group laughter and still trying to be the voice of reason. "I'm sorry, Gelo. I just never heard him snap back like that. I think Eric is rubbing off on him. Dolphin teeth!? Like what?!" She was in an uncontrollable ball of laughter, but it was ceased by Ronald Sr. sitting in front of the two. He turned around to Jeremy, trying to tone done his amusement, and said, "And don't you start that God-awful whimper that you call a 'laugh.' Were you 'actually' born with that? You sound like a lawnmower, and what kind of woman want that?"

He was finally getting his issue off his chest. A stare down began with uncomfortable Jeremy and Ronald Sr. As he turned back around, looking at Paula. He then closed them, relaxing his face as he bit his lip, trying not to bust out laughing, but Paula decided to do the laughing for him.

"Yea! And I'm 'Cuban,' you ass," a delayed but grateful Angelo shouted. He then shook his head, portraying to be hurt and trying to receive some sympathy points, but he failed.

Even Ronald Jr. primarily focused on the court and not their shenanigans. He couldn't help but overheard the joking segment and snickered. Laughing at his father, "Please don't get my dad started, I beg you…" he stated.

In the 4th quarter, the intensity progressed rapidly, so did that of the coach's hunger to lead their teams to victory. Both coaches were yelling aloud different offensive schemes, trying to counter one another. It became a grueling mental game of chess, and as the battle carried on, the players would soon find out how much Ball IQ they possessed—and not just relying on pure athletic muscle. The "muscle of the mind" can be a fierce weapon on the court. Once you mastered the basics of the game. And as high schoolers, they were far from masters of "this" craft no matter what they may believe. They still wanted to hang at the mall, eat junk food, and go to amusement parks to see girls. However, on display tonight, they laid it out on the line. The "will" and determination to perform at a high level were clear as day. And they all wanted to leave an imprint on the game.

Wiping sweat from his face using his half-tucked jersey, Eric hears Coach Walker shouting for them to tighten up their defense because "Once the Bears' cross that half court line!" It was war. The Bucks' made sure they imposed a strong 1-3-1 defense as instructed by Assistant Coach Lawry. Using the length they have on the team, they could force over turnovers from miscalculated passes. And easy rebounds from the lack of drives to the hoop, being in zone.

It seems simple enough. They were fully aware of Bears' hot hand, Shila Rooks. And understand that the Bears' will look for him to score majority of their 4th quarter points. So, it was critical the Bucks "deny" him the ball or any entry pass. If he does get it, deny him the basket through the numerous lines of defense. The first line of defense was Eric, at the top of the key. His main assignment is to guide the ball whichever way it should go, not letting him through the middle, and hoping the rest of the team follows suit.

In the first two minutes of action, the Bucks were successful defensively. They denied any cross-court passes or any bounce pass they tried to wedge into the 1-3-1 defense. The Bucks' created a "defensive forcefield" around the basket. The only downside to their dominating performance was that they still struggled to put points on the board. They couldn't take advantage of the countless turnovers the Bears' offense gave. As the first line defender, Eric also became the "first choice" on offense when a steal would occur.

As good as the outlet passes were, call it nerves or just being too eager to score. But Eric missed countless wide-open layups. Shoe change and all. On the very next steal, he stopped just above the three-point line and delivered an airball to the crowd. He tried to swallow his pride, shaking off the miss after miss. But to him, it felt as if a golf ball was lodged in his throat, not allowing him to breathe. "Was the 'pressure' getting the best of him?" Eric felt exposed and frustrated at the airball and his own carelessness. He neglectfully forgot to follow his own show and missed a key opportunity to recover his own shot.

Instead, a Bears' defender ran underneath the rim to save the airball before bouncing out of bounds. It drew a roar of excitement from the visitor bleachers. Not trying to kill any momentum they have gained by not inbounding the Bears at the baseline start the transition down the court. Eric, humiliated, now playing defense again, ran aggressively to the ball without any rationale. Swiping right and left, trying to free the ball from the Bears'. He slapped the ball carrier on the left forearm, picking up his 4th foul.

Gasps sweep the gym as Coach Walker stomps his foot on the sideline. Pleading with his star player to get it together. "Eric... Relax!!" He insinuated as he clapped his hands repeatedly, getting Eric's attention. "We are still up... we're in this- Hey, you have 4 fouls!!" Coach Walker pointed to his own head with his index finger, reminding Eric to "Play smart." One more foul, and he's done for the night. The pressure to perform and succeed now seemed to mount on his shoulders more than ever.

"Well, there goes the 'fun,'" Eric said, shaking his head in disgust. He then turned around to get a glimpse of the scoreboard. A red and white antique Jumbotron was always missing a few yellow light bulbs that illuminated the score, time, foul count, possession, and period. However, many of the locals in attendance were used to the old device; and could make out the score just fine. And Eric was no exception, as he saw they were still up, but only by three now. (65-68).

To add insult to injury for the Bucks', Eric's foul has put them in the foul bonus, meaning from this point forward, the Bears get a "1 and 1" free throw attempt. If the player makes the first shot, they get the pleasure of attempting another free shot. It also provides a "vital" opportunity for the Bears to turn the score around in their favor. If the Bucks' reach the maximum bonus foul count, which is 10, the Bears will have the luxury of shooting two free throws, free of charge.

Eric, electing to move past his horrific airball, runs over to Tareek while the players lined up for the first free throw attempt. The pair huddled together, with their hands on their knees, keeping the conversation close. At the top of the key were two Bears' players, discussing strategy amongst themselves.

"You got some of that energy, now, Reek?" Eric mumbled to Tareek.

And with no hesitation, Tareek stood up with his hands positioned on his hips, "Hell yea, man- what you think?" he said, chewing his *Big Red* gum, "Let's go, dog!" The first free throw attempt was made. (66-68).

He was pissed at the sight of seeing the basketball going through the hoop; Eric doubles back to Tareek, "Aye, man. We ain't losing this shit; let's ball out!" re-wiping his Air Jordan 10's with spit from his hands.

"Say less," Tareek replied.

The players line up again on the free-throw line, anticipating the second shot and waiting for the referee to pass the ball to the free-throw shooter. Before the shot, Eric screamed out to Leo, "Leo- box out! We movin' man!!" Leaving the Bears' players at the top of the key wondering, "What are they up to?" Hearing it loud and clear, Leo nodded his head and proceeded to spread the message to his teammates on the line, "Get ready."

The referee, twirling the basketball with his hands, passes the ball to the shooter for his second attempt.

In the designated coach's box, Coach Walker had his arms at his sides and tried to keep his composure. He calculated and yelled out to his team just as the shooter attempted his shot. "Watch for the press!" As any basketball veteran knows, Coach Walker knew it was coming in a tight game situation such as this.

Notwithstanding the unexpected outburst from Coach Walker, the Bears' shooter swished the second shot anyway. And as emotions rose in rival games such as these. The shooter turned to his left and gawked at Coach Walker, sizing him up and down as he sprinted back up the court. He placed his index finger over his lips, telling him and the home fans, "Shh." (67-68). And the Bears' just as Coach Walker predicted, began to press the Bucks' full court.

Leo grabbed the ball directly from the net, not giving it time to bounce on the floor; he quickly inbounds to Eric and sprints down the court. He was hoping to be a "last-ditch" relief if the full-court press is too overbearing for the ballhandlers. However, to their own surprise and the Bears', the Bucks were able to break the press with ease this time, as Eric dribbled up the court. He found Leo in the paint with a defender who is no fit for him. There he was, flashing his hands, and welcomed the pass. Eric fed the ball to Leo, and in transition, he took one dribble to regain his footing and delivered an easy lay-up off the glass and into the basket. (67-70). "Let's Go!!!" Leo yelled in excitement.

On a high from finally making a legit basket. Unconsciously, they took Eric's lead and began an "ill-advised," full-court press of their own, trying to score an easy bucket. Something Assistant Coach Lawry strongly discouraged from them at the start of the 4th quarter. Arms stretched out to the heavens. Coach Walker's rage was set to a new level. "What in the damned hell are they doing? Call a timeout, Eric!!" He shouted.

Thankfully, Eric didn't hear the irate command from his coach. He was focused on the oncoming offense. However, if Eric attempted to call a timeout without having possession first, or at least a dead ball, the result ends in a technical foul shot, which is another chance for the Bears to trim the lead even more.

Also, Assistant Coach Lawry was there to correct the head coach's mistakes. "Uh- we're on defense now!!" he said, rolling his eyes. As the seconds passed, he was irritated by Coach Walker's aloof direction and forgetfulness, yet it was a very common feeling.

"Well then, on the next made basket! And who are you yelling at?" Coach Walker fired back, trying to refocus his time back on the court. "Get back down to half court!! Hustle!! What are y'all doing!? You guys are killing me!!"

"Oh, shit!!" A look of urgency consumed Eric as he remembered the instructions given to him by Assistant Coach Lawry. He races back down the court, hoping the offense doesn't execute a play with their ill-prepared defensive, trying to form a 1-3-1 zone. He was already playing it risky as it was with four fouls. And he surely would have picked up his last, even attempting to get a steal by playing full-court press. Thankfully for the Bucks and Coach Walker's heart, from a near breakdown on the sidelines. They made it back to half-court and assembled their defense just as the ball crossed the half-court line.

As the ball made it to the front court, Eric was still feeling lucky, seeing the basketball bounce like a piece of candy in front of him. The Bears' point guard started to direct traffic. "I think I got some time…" Eric said to himself.

As they tried to draw up a play, Eric took a quick swipe at the ball, missing by an inch. Seeing how exposed the ball was made it extremely, tempting. Especially with no guard hand or body protecting it. "No. No. No- He wants me to swipe and foul or, does he?" It was still a big risk. Yet, Eric tried again and missed. However, he could feel the soft leather graze against his fingertips; he was close yet, still a risk.

This didn't discourage him. He knew he could steal it, but just under better conditions. Still, Eric licked his lips like a dog seeing a meal prepared just for him. "No! 'You' have 4 fouls, E, don't chance it. Just play it out," talking himself off a ledge. Which he did, sticking to the defense instructed by the assistant coach. Instead, Eric forced the Bears' point guard to the left corner of the court, forcing him to make risky cross-court pass or get trapped at the wing. Taking the first option, he tossed it with the ball floating in the air, way longer than the guard intended. It became a "free-for-all." And Leo, with his height, outreached over 3 Bear's defenders nearby and intercepted the ball. He saw his teammates, John and Tareek, at first glance.

Ultimately, kicking it out to a sprinting Tareek, who was running down the court, he caught his overhead pass in transition for a corner 3-pointer. "Swish." (67-73).

"That's the young bull- Ty, Ty- #21, Tareek Baxter!" Slicky J announced over the microphone. Now, standing to his feet, encouraging the rest of the fans to stand and cheer also. "Make some noise, Bucks' fans!!!"

Eric fist-pumping, excited, Tareek made a clutch three for the team. Acknowledging him as he pointed in his direction, back-peddling down the court. Simultaneously, he rechecks the game clock, and it read 3:35 left to play if this doesn't go to overtime. After Tareek's three-pointer, the Bucks' felt they were beginning to pull away from this tight game; and it was theirs for the taking.

Making it back to the top of the key, Eric pounds the hardwood floor with his hands, welcoming any defender who comes his way. As the home fans gradually start rising to their feet, adhering to Slick J's request, they make a thunderous noise as they stomp on the wooden bleachers, hollering, "Bucks!! Bucks!! They don't want it with us!!!"

"Alright now! That's what I like to hear, baby," Slicky J responded.

The Bears were unphased by the noise coming from the home section as they inbound the ball. Because of their own hearing pleasure, their side of the gym also began to scream just as loud for them, "Knock'em dead, Knock'em dead. Cuz we ain't neva scared!!!" A popular chant Roosevelt High School would recite when they knew they had a chance at victory.

CHAPTER 21

At half court, in their 1-3-1 zone, the Bucks are feeling little pressure now, as their body language reflected it. Primarily due to it being a home game and accompanied by the cheerleaders and mascot jumping up and down and fan screaming at the top of their lungs. If the Bucks are victorious, they would have bragging rights until they meet again. But the Bears' shooting guard, Shila Rooks, had a different outlook on the game. And welcomed the pressure just like Eric; he fed off it.

Locked-in and intensely focused. In his low patent stance, Shila dribbled the basketball, looking for an outlet from which to score. He then locked eyes with Eric, who refused to let the offense drive to the lane. However, the joke's on Eric.

In two, hard dribbles with his left hand, he had Eric, the eager defender, off-balance as he tried to swipe at the ball. Eric, staggering to hold his position in the battle, gets left by Shila. He gave Eric a quick crossover dribble, switching the ball to his right hand and driving to the paint. Passing Eric, he ended his move with a left-handed floater to the rim, all in a blur. Leo had no choice but to foul him as he was the last line of defense. As he swung his hands down, forcing his weight on Shila's arms, he torso. Leo always had a theory about fouls, especially with his knowledge in football, "If ya gotta hit'em- make' em feel it."

Shila let out a grunt on contact, trying to sell the foul call. As he rolled on the ground for a second, soaking the pain in. Shila felt all of it and still made good on the basket attempt as the ball circled the rim before dropping in.

"Jesus Christ!" Leo shouted, "Damn good shot, boy!" Reaching down to help up Shila, he snatched his hand away in disgust, correcting Leo's word choice. "Who the hell you callin' a boy, Bitch?" In passing, Leo passively gets bumped by two Bears' players as they run to help up their star player.

"Relax, man... Nobody meant anything by that," Leo implied.

"Ok. Bet. Well, less talk, more hoopin," Shila responded, shaking off the contact as he high-fived his teammates, who helped him to his feet. He headed to the line for a free shot. And giving Leo his fourth fouls of the game. "Punk ass," Leo mumbled, walking to the free-throw line.

"They're tired, coach!" Assistant Coach Lawry started to plea with Coach Walker, "I don't think they're gonna last till the end of the game- Call a timeout."

"Well, how many timeouts do I have remaining?" Coach Walker asks, not sure of his own timeout count.

He depended greatly on his assistant to feed him this vital information. It was of true importance when the game was on the line and the clock was winding down. "You only have one remaining," Assistant Coach Lawry answered.

"Ok, then," Coach Walker said, looking at his assistant, irritated, "So, If I only have one left, do you expect me to take it now? You're the clipboard, man. What do you expect me to do?"

Choosing to laugh off the blatant disrespect and chalking it up to simple miscommunication, Assistant Coach Lawry swiftly lifts his head from his notes. Taking a quick inhale, keeping it as blunt as possible without losing his job. "I expect you not to kill these kids," he uttered, looking back into the stands, "Who's gonna fight those parents up there when one of the kids passes out?"

All the while, during this engagement, Shila sinks the extra free throw point. (70-73). Taking his assistant's advice, Coach Walker alerts the table side official, who blows his whistle. "Final timeout, Bucks- Full!"

A once, raving Bucks' crowd, suddenly felt a wave of alarm and anxiety come over them. Including the players on the Bucks' bench as they hear the whistle blow, frustrated.

Shaking his head, Eric asked Coach Walker, "Why did you call that?" Only to be swiftly corrected by him, "Don't you question me. Y'all just sit down and get some air. This is our final timeout, fellas- Ok? We got to give it our all."

Trying to step up in other ways besides shooting. Being the leader of the team, Eric wanted to stand his ground. "I just think it wasn't smart to call our last one- is all I'm saying. It's 2:41 left, Coach. That's a lot of balls."

"Yea," his teammates concurred with his sentiment on the subject. They felt they needed to just play smarter and be coached better.

"Okay, and if I needed your opinion, I'd ask for it. If this timeout was a mistake, blame Coach Lawry and me. But don't you ever argue with me on my decisions with this team."

Eric stayed silent, sitting on the bench for the duration of the timeout, resting his legs as he took another swig of his water bottle. It was silence on the bench, with not much said. Only minds were contemplating how the game would end.

"Bring it in," Coach Walker said, "Let's finish strong, fellas." And as the team broke off onto the court, Coach Walker glared at his assistant, hoping this timeout wasn't a bad idea because the gym's emotions didn't align with the coach's judgment.

Watching the 4th quarter unfold from the home team bleachers, Jacqueline and Jeremy begin to "Boo" alongside the crowd. Expressing their issues with Coach Walker, as he waves off the crowd unprofessionally before taking his seat, grabbing his white towel.

"This doesn't look good at all," Jacqueline said, looking back between the scoreboard and the action on the court.

"Nah, you ain't lying," Jeremy replied, "Like, who calls their last timeout with damn near 3 minutes to go."

"Right."

"Well, if they lose this game tonight, we know who to blame this one on."

At the same time, Jaqueline and Jeremy looked at each other in agreeance, "Coach!". Sitting next to Ronald Jr., Angelo was alerted of the two's conversation by his sensitive ears. Sipping on his refreshment drink, leaning back in his bleacher seat. He fixed his eyes on the two, who were finally coming to grips with his early synopsis. "Damn, I guess… I wasn't 'too' wrong earlier, huh? But let me not be the *Debbie Downer*- That's y'all, now!" Angelo said as he chuckled.

As Angelo took another sip of his drink, the pair rolled their eyes, reverting to the game. "Why do we tolerate this man, again?" Jeremy said, turning to Jacqueline. She shrugged her shoulders; it wasn't a big deal right now. The game was still too close to call.

As the final two minutes rears its ugly head, pushing players to step it up another notch. Both teams are in full motion, as the scores are close. After their final timeout, the Buck will have the task of inbounding the ball from the backcourt baseline. They know that a full-court press from the Bears is set to materialize soon as the ball is put into play, and they need to be ready.

Grabbing his white towel once more, Coach Walker patted himself dry as he sat down. Reminded the team of the oncoming press so that they are aware. By this point, late in the game, Coach Walker is drenched in sweat. It was remarkable to his players, given he didn't play a single second; he just yelled and stomped from the sidelines. But for coaches, shouting at their highest decibel level, they considered this a "calorie burner." Removing himself from his suit jacket. He then loosened his tie and rolled his sleeves up, locked in.

On offense, the Bucks inbound the ball, finding their guard, John, first. And in one quick-fire pass up the court, it found Anton. He took two easy dribbles, not rushing as he transitioned his motion into a bounce pass, right up the court's sideline. There, it found Eric safely. Now, with the ball in his hands, Eric started surveying his surroundings. And fortunately for him, he saw only one player, a Bears' center, as the only defender within his vicinity. He also noticed the center wasn't positioned where he should be if he wanted to make a decent stop against Eric.

Being too fast and too savvy for the center, Eric pump-faked the corner shot, leaving the approaching big man with his arms swinging mid-air, trying to block the attempt. The Bears' center found himself out of control, off-balance, and now at an extreme disadvantage. And with the center completely out of view, Eric pushed the ball with urgency to the paint. As the "runway" cleared him for takeoff, he exploded to the sky in two power dibbles. It was "Jordanesque," for the fans knew this wasn't going to be a layup. As he continued to elevate, his forearms met with the side of the rim, leaving him no other option but to dunk the ball with all his might. Upon landing he finally let out a resounding howl as he pounded his chest. Even the Bears' fans couldn't help but say, "Well, Damn!!". (70-75).

Good game or bad, Eric could always find a way to score. It was a well sought-after commodity as well as a gift that many people admired seeing him do. And some envied it, too. Granted, his shot wasn't falling tonight. Eric was still known to give you at least 6 points on his worst days. But his dunking was a spectacle everyone loved to watch when he was airborne. The way his body would float and contort in the air, adjusting to whatever obstacle comes his way. According to the fans, some swore it was as if he was "levitating," the way it seemed he climbed an inch by the second. And once Eric reached his apex altitude, he brought the sheer force of "aggression and pain" down on the rim. It was as if the basketball rim did something to him.

Leaving the backboard rattled, the fans erupted, just as Eric did, letting out that ferocious yell. Helping him to release all the pent-up feelings that recently plagued him. Besides letting his tears flow in the locker room, his dunk felt just as good, if not better. However, his emotions were still in the balance with his struggles within his family, as he didn't want to think too much of that during game time. He still wanted to secure a victory against their great rival team, accompanied by referees, who call tonight's basketball game like it's 1997.

Nevertheless, the freedom he felt dunking that ball was just an escape. Looking into the stands, Eric found his grandfather, and he pointed out to him, confirming he saw the dunk. And he did. Who could miss it? The entire Brewer family and friends were all standing on their feet, screaming at the top of their lungs. This was the Eric they wanted to see. The one that will finish the game strong, no matter what the score is. The Bears' center instantaneously grabs the basketball amid the celebration. And with no time to spare, inbounds it with the swiftness.

The Bears' center throws the ball overhead, clearing the Bucks' outreached fingertips. Being overwhelmed with excitement and caught off guard again, the Bucks failed to rush back down the court to get on defense. Regardless of Eric's phenomenal dunk, the game was still in play. And the Bears knew they had them on their heels, still. The quick pass from the Bears' center found the hot man, Shila Rooks. He popped out from the paint area, below, tipping the ball to himself. As he caught the tip in motion, he was located just below the 3-point line on the right-wing.

The Bucks, trying to quickly adjust to the fast pace offensive transition from the Bears'. The Bucks couldn't even set up their 1-3-1 in time. It led to Eric making an executive decision as he screamed, "Go, man! Call out your man!" It seemed to be the best option for a defensive improv.

Realizing the Bucks are no longer in their zone, Shila receives a screen on the right-wing. The defender, unable to fight through it, and his teammates failing to call it out for him, gets burned. Shila, using the screen to his advantage, went left, dribbling away from his defender. He stopped on a dime. Now, above the three-point line, creating more space for an open shot and sinks it. (73-75). "Man, let's go!! We endin' this shit!" Shila said, as he kissed his finger and pointed it to the sky. A tradition he did when he made any shot behind the arc. And with every shot made, Eric's anxiety about the game grew as the seconds dwindled. But seeing the Bears' make that three was gut-wrenching. Even though they were still up, the Roosevelt Bears just didn't seem tired.

After another minute of back-to-back highlight defensive stops, the scores were still the same. Opposite the first half, the younger crowd started to appreciate the "rough and grungy" play they saw on the floor. Many of them weren't accustomed to this style. It wasn't the same feeling as seeing someone dunking, like Eric. But seeing someone's shot get rejected, thrown out of play into the stands, or spiked back in someone's face and causing a nosebleed was cinematic to the kids. Instead of scrolling their cellphones, they recorded footage from the stands and on the court, sharing it with the social media world. Yet, in the last 1:30 of play, it was a slugfest. The Bears still had a timeout remaining. But, instructed by their head coach, only as a "Need basis." And currently, this game is about heart, will, and pride; at this point, *who* wants it?

CHAPTER 22

Eric wants it. Hell, he wants to "end" it right now if he can; even with four fouls and tired, the fight in him hasn't wavered. He felt he still had more to give his team. Plus, he had to push himself more with the scouts looking on and taking notes on his performance and Shila's. He was the team captain of the Hollywood Bucks'. And as a team leader, you must show the pack who their "rock" is. Their foundation, for when things get weary, as they tend to do in games. Yet, over the years, game after game, he has made it known to the team who the Alpha was by sacrificing his body—going after loose basketballs on the floor—diving and wrestling for balls against the defenders for possession.

Given the hype around this game and what the officials spoke about before the start of the second half. "For any aggressive tussle between players," they blew their whistles for "Jump Ball," slightly faster than usual but rightfully so. In a late 4th quarter "skirmish" between Eric and Bears' center, Cecil Tremont, a stocky, 6'6, center, who was "only" known to rough up players. Cecil was simply the muscle. And irritated anyone he played against, often being the fastest one to foul out of a game. Most importantly, he wanted his revenge for the shifty pump-fake Eric gave him before his highlight dunk. It was personal.

As the play went, Anton Fuller saw the basketball being knocked loose out of the hands of Tareek. Seeing he was too far to grab the ball, Anton froze as the ball rolled on the floor, leaving it open for anyone to take. That was Eric, being the closest one to the ball. But nearby was also Cecil Tremont, diving for the ball simultaneously with Eric. Wrestling for the ball in the Bears' backcourt. Eric received a cheap shot from Cecil Tremont, clocking him in the mouth with his elbow.

Within two seconds of the tie-up, whistles immediately began to blow. However, it was too late; Cecil got to him. Getting up, he left the basketball where it rested, and Eric was in pain, lying on the court. Quickly, he reached inside his mouth, using his index finger, and felt a burning sensation, only easing the discomfort by swishing his tongue around his cut.

As much as the pain shot through his mouth, the cut was minor. Cecil ended up splitting the inside of Eric's cheek. His teammates or the home fans appreciated that childish act. Yet, they all expected it from him. Rubbing his cheek to soothe the pain, he sat upright, waiting for his teammate's assistance. "Man, you sucka ass, boy," Eric said, "For real, dog," snarling at Cecil. He really didn't care what Eric had to say as he just smiled back at him. He soon walked back to his teammates, huddled on the floor, giving out "high fives" for a job well done. To add insult to injury, no foul was called, only a jump ball. Beaten up but not out of the game, Eric wasn't discouraged, as he received help to his feet by Tareek.

"You good, my G?" Tareek said, grabbing Eric's hand, pulling him up.

"Yea, man, thanks," Eric replied.

"You sure? I can kick his ass!" Tareek suggested.

"You're a buck 40, soaking wet... No," Eric responded, confused.

"I'm skinny strong, don't play... Get up, man."

Eric appreciated the gesture of his "young buck," in Tareek. But felt he was doing too much to prove himself, especially tonight. "Bucks' Ball!" the official shouts as he points his finger in the direction of the possession.

With the possession arrow reading, "Bucks," The fans shriek with excitement, jumping up and down, knowing they can possibly seal the deal and win this game. Given where the infraction occurred, the Bucks' will inbound the ball at the half-court marker. And something the Roosevelt fans and coach weren't too thrilled about. Both teams are now equally exhausted. Still, the Bears' refused to call their final timeout, giving their players a hard-earned break. "No," they prefer to run their opponent into the ground first before taking a timeout. They wanted the Bucks to have no shot at regaining their composure.

Tareek, with the ball on the sideline, inbounded it to Eric in the backcourt. Wiping his shoes for traction, he kept the ball in play, then dribbled up the court, avoiding the 10-second violation. Exhausting their players, the Bears' defense opted to go "Man-to-Man" instead of committing to a zone defense. But this is what the Roosevelt Bears' have practiced, night-in, night-out. And Shila was at the top of the key, awaiting battle with Eric.

Eric takes his time as he dribbles the ball up court. Understanding that he now has control over the pace of the game play and the game clock as it ticked down. There was no time for any foolishness; as reckless as he played at times, his basketball IQ was still higher than most high schoolers. Eric understood there was also no shot clock counting down, according to the county rule book. Only the official referee can begin a chop count when a defender chooses to play up close, which they weren't. They wouldn't dare foul him on purpose. He spent too much time practicing his free throws for that to happen, and they knew he could hit them. As Eric dribbled further up the court, the crowd noise amplified with anticipation, wondering how this game would end. However, to most of the players on the court, the crowd was just "white noise." Sounds, on top of sounds, form as one. And it was apparent, the Bucks' needed to score.

Dribbling with his dominant right hand, Eric noticed the Bears playing a "tight" man-to-man coverage. He saw Leo on the block, battling for position with the Bears' center, Cecil. Eric waved him off, not willing to risk the option of feeding him the basketball and turning it over to the defense. Cecil was a "bully" defender, no doubt, and Eric couldn't afford a late-game error to piss his coach off even more. Even if he fed the basketball to Leo, he wasn't the best free-throw shooter. On the team, he was below average.

So, instead of a "risky" pass, Eric signals for Leo to set a backscreen pick on Shila, hoping Leo's huge mass would stop Shila like a brick wall. If Eric could break free of Shila's restricting defense, he might have an option to shoot or possibly drive to the hole. The other "last resort option" is a "give and go," play to Leo. Once he sets the screen, breaking Eric free of the defense, Leo rolls back down to the paint for a layup. Hopefully, uncontested. If they score- just maybe- it would force the Bears to call their final timeout. The options weren't endless, but they were much, making Eric feel more in control.

Eric Signaled for a screen-like clockwork, and Leo frees himself up from the paint, leaving his man with the option to chase him or guard the paint. He chose the latter, following Leo. As Leo runs to the top of the key, where Eric was, he sets the backscreen perfectly, shielding Shila from stopping Eric's attack.

Now free from a defender, Eric drove to the basket. But takes a sudden "step-back," giving a slight hesitation, keeping the Bears' defense at bay by not computing his plan of attack and briefly observing the court. Eric knew he didn't have to shoot the ball if the lane was open. And to all the glory, it was, and he attacked. It seemed like the basketball Gods were going to answer his prayers, after all. It was another clear lane provided for another making of a highlight dunk.

"Oh shit!" Jeremy yelps as his eyes widen. He proceeded to grip Jacqueline's arm, "He's gonna yam that thang!"

As Jeremy rose to his feet, it seemed everyone in the stands followed suit, preparing themselves to see more poetry in motion. Ronald Sr. was also standing, smiling, and watching the play for his grandson, unfold. "You can do it," he said to himself.

Ronald Jr. and Angelo, who were once at odds because of the forced sitting arrangement, both had their hands planted on top of their heads, anticipating the aftermath "Booming" sound the rim gives. Nadine had another prayer to send up to the heavens.

Putting the basketball to the floor, Eric gains traction and makes a run for it to the rim. As he gathered his control to jump, extending himself to the rim, his eyes suddenly widened. He realized his attack was somehow too late and not fast enough to get to the hoop. It was either "youthfulness in mobility" or having a better basketball IQ than Eric. But Shila Rooks rolled smoothly off the backscreen set by Leo, and with a slight "push-off," not seen by the officials, he countered the widebody screen; and caught up to Eric in a split second. Heroically, he used his own length and small frame, sacrificing his body for the play.

And just before Eric could take flight. He collided with Shila, planting his knee directly in his stomach. The air swiftly left Shila's lungs as he let out a nauseating grunt before hitting the floor, then looking at the referees for a call. The tableside official, with the best view possible, blew his whistle. He had no choice but to make the obvious call.

"Red #22!! Offensive foul! Bears' ball!" The tableside official signaled "charge." Then pointed to the Bears' spot of possession, where the baseline official will insert the basketball back into play.

"Now you can go rest, nigga," Shila whispered under his breath to Eric.

"Hell, you say!??"

They both quickly get up, approaching one another, face-to-face and completely disregarding the heavy impact each one took. Once the adrenaline kicks in, small nicks become numb.

"Tsk, Tsk. 'You,' heard me, go sit down."

"Man, Fuck you!!" Eric replied, returning the favor.

Whistles blew from all directions as the officials hastily put this bickering to bed. Players on the court tried to help the referees. For the risk of getting a technical was in high demand, as their patience trying to control the game was wearing thin.

Pulling them apart, Eric yelled out, "Keep that same energy!! With that mouth witcho' bitch ass, boy!!" Wanting to do far more than words could describe. He didn't, and they ceased the confrontation with the help of his team. Personally, Eric hated stooping to that level of immaturity and in front of college scouts. After school was one thing, but during the game, that was "tacky." And tonight, he did it in front of his own family. They looked on in embarrassment. Honestly, Eric had nothing left in the tank. And to make matters worse, he was now out of fouls to give. All Shila could do was continue to clap, with pride, as Eric took his long walk to the bench.

The scores table blew the horn, temporarily stopping play before the basketball was put back onto the floor. Putting up five fingers, the table signaled to the officials there was a "foul out." "Oh no! What do we have here? Easy E out of the game!? Hecky, naw?" Slicky J said on the microphone. He was shocked to see the sudden dramatic end of Eric Brewer's night on the floor. As a matter of fact, the entire home crowd was in complete shock. "Keep ya' head held high, young G… You got them again," he added.

Fouling out of the game with a minute to go and being only up by two, was not how Eric envisioned this game going. *"God always laughs at our plans."* And the way the Bears are playing, a minute was enough for the game to take a change drastically. Now, with Eric on the bench, there was nothing he could really do to help but cheer. The Bears' use their final timeout. With the Bucks' best player off the floor, it was time for them to gather their wind and strategize on how to pull off the upset.

Still heated, Eric continued to eye Shila as he was escorted to the bench by his team. Yet, once he looked away from him, he knew he was done for the night each step he took. And a fleet of flooding emotions ran over him like a semi-truck. His teammates were looking at each other, at a loss for words. His family and friends are all amazed with a range of looks from sad to embarrassed.

Eric rarely fouls out of a game. "Holy cow," Nadine said as she covered her mouth, sitting back down. "Aw, baby," Paula said, who was never a big sports fan but knew what being "fouled out" meant and could still empathize with her grandson.

"Maybe the pressure got too much for him, or maybe it was just a bad day," Paula suggested to everyone.

"Yea, mom... I've 'never' seen him stink up the joint like this," proclaimed Ronald Jr., "Wow!!"

For once, Eric's friends were in total silence. While the crowd still grapples with the "saltiness" of seeing their best player leave the court for Shila Rooks. The Bears' fans, in good fashion, gave Eric applause for his performance, and after a few seconds of soaking in the bad news, the home team gave Eric a standing ovation.

Struggling to hold his head high, Eric is greeted with a firm handshake from Coach Walker and a soft tap to the back of his head as he continues walking onto the bench, seeing Assistant Coach Lawry as well as the players. Before finally collapsing on the team bench, resting his feet; he's done for the night. He grabbed a white towel that he saw hanging on one of the seats, threw it over his head, needing to let out some tears of frustration.

Everyone in the gym knew what he was doing, and he didn't care. He didn't want to see anyone. He'd rather sulk in his own miseries and alone. Eric knew the game was over. The Bucks had a solid team, but they were an exceptional team with Eric on the floor. Now, it was certain the Bears would finish them off. All Eric could do was replay his last drive to the basket in his head, and that put him on the bench. Lifting his head from the towels, the first person that came in his line of sight was Shila, with the ball in hand about to drive. So, Eric emotionally put his head back down and started to think about how the scouts will give Shila Rooks a better review than him. He was devastated with his play tonight. Even more, he was pissed, and his assumptions were right regarding the Bucks'; the lead began to collapse as the Bears' crowd roared in the last minute of play.

Two fast possessions later, and only 30 seconds have burnt off the game clock. With sad news, the Bucks' all-star center, Leo Capernati, fouled out as well, following Eric's lead. The game quickly started becoming one-sided once Leo's physical presence left the floor. The Bucks' relied on him heavily to clog up the lane.

Leo's backup power forward, Tahj Rickles, would only play center on a "need to" basis. And this was one of those times. Being a power forward, he was a lot smaller than Leo and didn't have the needed experience to finish out this game, being a sophomore.

CHAPTER 23

The pair, Eric and Leo, are now watching from the sideline. Seeing Tareek and the rest of the players scratch to stay alive. But with each Buck's possession and any attempt to regain the lead. It would result in costly, steal, turnover, or blocked shot. Bears' center, Cecil Tremont, can now move more freely as Leo sits, staring blankly. Shila continued to persevere in his role offensively, knocking any of his choosing shots from mid-range to an easy layup. He was able to weed in-and-out of defensive traffic, with ease to find the basket.

Eric could only start to get teary-eyed again. He was sick of hearing the Bears' fans go crazy with each possession they had. But Bucks' fans were just looking at Eric. Wondering, "Why is he so emotional?" they couldn't compute the toll life had on him outside of basketball. This was simply as a release, mixed in with a bad game. Tonight's loss against their rival was just icing on the cake. Many in the stands didn't know the "strain" the past few weeks had on him, including today. Trying to win a key matchup where scouts were present, making sure his grades were legit for college, and spending as much time as he could with his ailing grandfather. Eric felt the time was running out for the two like the game clock on the wall; time was dwindling. And tonight, it all came full circle for him.

The final score is (83-79)—Bears' win.

The game horn sounded as the clock reached zero seconds, and the scoreboard reflected "The Bears'" as the victor. The Roosevelt fans stormed down to the court, Instantaneously, leaving their drinks, popcorn, and coats. Some even kept their kids in the stands, not to get stepped on, on the floor. Not in disrespect to the Hollywood Bucks', but they were ecstatic. They traveled to Hollywood High School and beat the Bucks on their own floor as rivals.

"Bears- Bears!! Step to us. You dare- You dare!!" It was all the Bears' fans could recite once they got to the court. Fans were grabbing and tugging at the players of Roosevelt's jerseys, just hoping to grasp a piece of Hollywood Heights fandom. But these were high schoolers and didn't own a piece of merch they wore besides their shoes. A couple of Bears' fans picked up the lightweight Shila Rooks. They placed him on their shoulders for a moment and chanted their rival cheer over again.

Fans stampeding to the court to celebrate with their winning team was something not even the police could halt. As the home crowd continued to overlook on the bleachers, arms crossed, silent. Some began to pack up their belongings and head to the exit, not wanting to get caught in the traffic let out. Others grabbed their cellphones, making calls, describing the game in a few words, "You just had to be here, man." Some just stood there, holding their hungry kids in their arms or over their shoulders, not moving an inch since the horn sounded. Still in shock by the wild turn of events.

"Honestly," they couldn't afford to be too mad at the Bears. They beat them fair and square. And it was what made for an exciting game. "Rivals?" Yes. But Roosevelt

High School was just on the other side of town, 20-minutes from Hollywood High School. And some of these people saw each other daily; some were neighbors, some were coworkers, some attended church together, and some played little league baseball together as kids before going to different schools. Most of them even placed bet on the game. In a sense, Roosevelt High School and Hollywood High School are "deeply rooted," rivals that are also distant cousins.

Slicky J, sitting at the scores table, was choked up. Swallowing his pride, he humbly said, "Good game, Bears-I'll give you that." He proceeded to cut the microphone off, readjust his bucket hat, and fold his arms as he sat back in his chair. He wanted to take a moment and collect his thoughts for the night. Perhaps, even figure out a way to spin this on his radio show, Slick-N-DA-Morning Monday. He was appalled, just like the rest of the Bucks' fans, wondering, "How did this even happen?" and on their home turf. Slicky J knew he was going to have to plead his case to his loyal fans who listened. He already knew that first thing Monday morning, the callers were going to be "extremely" hostile with him being a Hollywood High School alumnus.

Eric was on the bench, continuing to sulk in his own team's defeat. Watching the Bears' parade on their floor, he was mad at the world. Some of his teammates saw Eric, still sitting on the bench, as they were walking out to the locker room. They circled back to check on him, assisting him to his feet. Regardless of him missing the dunk or playing subpar, this man was still their team captain. Their friend, and brother, on the battlefield.

"Keep ya head up, G," Tareek said, pulling Eric up, "I gotcha, my nigga. Come on."

The devastating feeling of a loss never sits right with a competitor, and the white towel still draped over his head made that statement clear. After finally getting to his feet, Eric heads back to the locker room to freshen up and greet his family. He already assumes they will have a lot to say about his performance and near "Fisticuffs" during the game. Eric wasn't in the mood to hear it. Even though this game was filled with championship-caliber play and stunning highlights, it was still the regular season, and there were plenty of battles left in the school year. Tonight's game just "stung" differently. But redemption. And that was something Eric had to remind himself and the team as he walked down the dark hallway leading to the team locker room.

"It's not over y'all!" Eric blurted out in the echoing hallway, "We'll see them again- Trust!" Finally, removing the white towel from his head.

Half an hour had passed by since the game clock hit zero. Which still illuminated on the wall. The Roosevelt Bears', now on their away bus, were headed back to their school. The bus ride back was a rowdy one, as the team and Roosevelt's coaching staff were still on a high from the victory. They played music the whole ride home, and the explicit version, another friendly bet, was lost by the head coach.

The game officials were long gone. They took the backdoor exit of the school, making sure nobody followed them to their cars. They left in no time flat. Not even giving their car's engine a chance to wake out of their cold sleep. But with how the fans felt the game was officiated, it was best for them to just leave promptly after the game.

Now making their rounds through the bleachers, the janitors are trying to clean up any leftover popcorn buckets and soft drinks cups. There was plenty of sports paraphernalia left. Abandoned on the ground after the game by a sad Bucks fan who felt it wasn't worth taking home. At the cost of $2.00 for a pair of Hollywood Bucks' noise clappers, they were fine where they were.

Sports can do that to you, exposing one's true emotions when things don't go your way. But it also makes any sport a "beautiful" concept and an abstract to life. "You win some, you lose some, but there's always redemption sooner or later if you keep pushing."

After a fresh change of clothes, the team prepares to leave the locker room. Deflated by the obvious loss, they managed to keep a smile on their faces and prance around as they walked out of the double grey doors, greeted by their family and friends. Game banners made by the Bucks' Pep Club were still raised in the air as they came out, and to a few roars and applauses.

'Bucky the Mascot' was also there. The team spotted him on the baseline alongside the cheerleaders ruffling their pom-poms and cheering with the fans. Some spectators stayed on the bleachers, passing the time and catching up with one another as they for the team. The majority were just kids from class and people from the surrounding neighborhood. Girls who had "school-day crushes" for some of the players on the team also stayed back after the game. They convened where the Roosevelt visitors were once sitting. They would constantly check their cellphones, mainly for text messages planning out the move for a Friday evening. And hopefully, cheer up their crushes after their loss.

One of the last ones out was Eric. He was holding a gym bag in one hand and his backpack hanging over his right shoulder. He was also pleased to hear the fans' and cheerleaders' cheer as he reentered the gym. It felt good to his heart, seeing the smiles come his way. The "Thank you" for a hard-fought battle was laid out on the floor.

Nevertheless, tired, he continued scanning the crowd to see who all stuck around after the game. And after a couple of minutes of socializing with his peers, he finally noticed his family sitting by the scores table. They were relaxing and in no hurry positioned in the middle section of the bleachers, a few seats up from the front row.

The Brewer family and company wanted to participate in congratulating Eric and his team on the court. However, the crowd size deterred them from going over there and socializing. More specifically, his grandparents, Ronald Sr. and Paula. It was a little past 9:30 p.m., which was considered "late" to them. Ronald Sr. yawned, stretching out his hands. To keep his energy up, he chose to joke amongst the kids, Jeremy and Angelo, and his son, Ronald Jr. Even Paula engaged in a wisecrack or two. But only so she wouldn't drift off to sleep.

Jacqueline and Nadine were having a conversation of their own, a sincere one. This free time allotted them a chance to catch up on each other's lives, or as much as a teenager and a grown woman could engage in. Nevertheless, the dialogue grew deeper than neither one of them expected it to get. At first, they were simply chatting, waiting for Eric to come out of the locker room. But Jacqueline was the mature one in the group. She always sought wisdom from the older crowd. She would instantly "light up," hearing a story from "back in the days" from an old head. Intrigue, engagement, and thought-provoking were her "keys" to understanding "life" and the purpose of it all. Besides being the only girl in the group, her curiosity always made her feel like an outsider. Even though she knew she could handle her own, she didn't mind being a loner at times.

Jacqueline told Nadine how she wanted to leave Ohio and, "for good," once school is over. She always hated Hollywood Heights, especially at this time of year. Being indoors inside a gymnasium, she still had to wear her silver bubble coat and red knitted hat. "This" was not her idea of "comfort." Cold air still seeped through the white chipped brick walls, which erected the gym. Many people, students and staff alike, pointed out the cause of the ongoing issues directly in the school system. For 5 years, the Montgomery Public School System has failed to reinstall insulation for the Troutman Gymnasium, amongst other burdens. The gymnasium only produced heat when hundreds of bodies were stuffed in there on game nights, jumping around-burning off energy. Overall, the gym was too unbearable to look at. But they weren't the only schools in the county going through the same situations.

Some months back, in a newsletter, Hollywood High School leaked a story, saying the "real" issue was related to an ongoing dispute with the Ohio School's Budgeting Board and the Montgomery County Public School system. Neither one of them decided to comment, but either way, Jacqueline was over it. She wanted to move south, anywhere south. Like Angelo, she felt like the "true" oddball in the clique. She stated to Nadine, Mrs. Brewer, how she feels the group may lose the strong connection they have built over the years.

Even after her sappy speech in the bleachers with Jeremy, and Angelo, they were her "brothers." She always wanted to voice this opinion to the fellas but was too intimidated to mention it no matter how close they were. Jaqueline also, briefly, snuck in how she had a "special interest" in someone, which received the "eyebrow raise" from Nadine. To Jacqueline, it was more than a "crush," at least, in her eyes. She didn't know how to go about the complex situation because it's not every day she "liked" someone; she needed advice. So, without mentioning a name, she let it be known.

Nadine loved Jaqueline's free spirit and wished she was more like her at her age. To be such a young woman and wise beyond her years, she knew Jacqueline was destined for greatness. Especially hearing her speak and with such confidence over her own future for years to come. Nadine also had the opportunity to get some stress off her chest, venting to Jacqueline. Nadine expressed how mad she was that the car's heater went out today regarding the home front. So, they took the family van to tonight's game. Ohio's winters were very brutal around this time of year. She also mentioned how it'd been a trying week for her and the Brewer family in a few words and further addressed which Jacqueline empathized with. But it brought Nadine back to their previous conversation about the future. She also inquired about Jacqueline's own career path. Being a young black woman in America, "What was in store for her?"

Easing her own mind of her issues at home, Nadine provided Jacqueline with some dating advice of her own. Recently celebrating her 17-year anniversary, maybe her counsel could be of some resolve for the young queen. Nadine's goal was now, so don't get held down. This city can be a tough place if you let it. I've seen, firsthand, folks getting sucked in by temptations we don't necessarily need."

"True," Jacqueline chimed in, making sure she paid attention.

"It's infested here," Nadine continued. Trying her best to be sensitive to the topic at hand, "Drugs and crime are all around us, everywhere. Because 'we' aren't in it; I guess we choose to ignore it… Life is full of options, baby girl. Like movin' south."

Being the wise girl Jacqueline was, she knew what Nadine was alluding to.

Placing her hand on Jacqueline's leg, Nadine continued, "You have the vision that thousands wished they had here, so move, girl!" They both started to snicker, covering their mouths with their hands trying not to cause a scene. The gym was far less noisy compared to an hour ago. A casual conversation would echo throughout the gym, bouncing from wall to wall. "Go to school in the south, Jacci," Nadine persuaded, "Find you a southern gentleman. Shit, I did. And never looked back." Nadine concluded as they giggled again.

Jacqueline laughing off the comment in good taste remembered who she was still talking to. And they weren't "friends" per se; they were just shooting the breeze until Eric resurfaced from the locker room. But Nadine's comments struck a nerve in Jacqueline as she glanced over to see Angelo and Jeremy, still cracking jokes. And in perfect timing like a scene from a rom-com, Jeremy happens to look up, catching eyes with Jacqueline, and flirtatiously smiles her way. Just long enough to cause a pause in the banter he was currently engaged with on the bleachers. Jeremy, looking back down, dove right back into the roasting session. All Jacqueline could say to Nadine, as she rolled her eyes, was, "Men are such boys."

CHAPTER 24

Fighting through the crowd on the court after all the fans' daps, handshakes, and hugs, Eric was finally able to flag down his family on the bleachers as they responded. Lugging his bags to the bleachers, he sat them down beside him and sat next to his grandfather. Eric was greeted with a lax, one-armed side hug and a kiss on the forehead, "Good game, grandson." Ronald Sr. proceeded to pat Eric's leg and winked at him.

"Dang, not 'Great'?" Eric, wanting clarity.

"You'll get'em next time," Ronald Sr. replied, clearing it up.

The Brewer family, minus Eric, continued to carry on in the gym. Ronald Sr., hearing jokes being hurled around, still went back to engaging in the jawing with Eric's friends. He was happy to receive a brief embrace from his grandfather, but he didn't care for their charades at the time. Eric took a deep breath in and exhaled, stretching his lanky arms over his head before folding them behind his head as he leaned back.

Staring up at the ceiling, Eric was trying to get lost in the gym ceiling lights. He then closed his eyes, hoping the darkness would help blind out his horrible game flashbacks, but unsuccessful. Taking a deep breath, he was relieved the game was over. Quite frankly, the week altogether was too much. In hindsight, Eric felt like he let his emotions get in the way of his gameplay. He failed to play to his own standards, not to mention his academics.

Uncomfortable, Eric repositioned his posture, already feeling the impacts of the game. He sat hunched over, folding himself into a ball. Now, staring at the ground, looking at his shoes. He began to think to himself as he heard his family talking among themselves. "Not even my old shoes could've helped; I played like ass."

The history behind these pair; and the moment he opened the box on his 15th birthday. He instantly remembered the smell of charcoal burning on the grill, music on blast while couples two-stepped. Despite finishing off that school year with a "C" average, his grandfather looked out for him anyway. However, he made sure he quizzed him religiously on math problems, as well as critical thinking. Ronald Jr. didn't necessarily approve of the gift but understood. Honestly, that could be said for his birthdays, 13 through 17. Eric wasn't sure if his parents knew their relationship. Or how "tight" they have become over the years. Yet, they did. They were the "super-heroes" behind the super-hero, who purchased the new pairs of shoes for Eric and Ronald Sr.

However, these shoes, which he received on his 15th birthday, didn't produce any magic. Something so sentimental to Eric and so materialistic to the world. Not even 'those' could have saved the day. These were the same Air Jordan 10's that had won him multiple overtime games in high school and AAU. His first "in-game" high school dunk, an indescribable experience. And even a 47-point game, which was his career-high, and a new Hollywood

High School Men's Basketball game record. Yet, like his grandfather's life, he thought, "Nothing lasts forever." And it was a telling sign because, as a basketball player, it's common knowledge that you don't wear your game shoes outside of gameplay. And there Eric was, on the bleachers with his old pair of black Jordan 10's on his feet.

"What's wrong, Eric?" Ronald Sr. asked, nudging him gently to grab his attention and pulling him out of the cocoon he created for himself. Irritated and now sore, Eric lifted his head slowly, turning to his family and completely ignoring his grandfather, "Y'all ready to go? I need to shower, and I want to finish this homework so I can practice this weekend."

Ronald Sr. let it slide this time. "Yea, we're getting ready now, son," Nadine replied, wrapping up her enlightening conversation with Jacqueline.

Eric turned his head, looking forward. A raspy voice with a heavy, southern drawl was heard interrupting the Brewers' session on the bleachers. "After a game like that, ya might want to ice ya body and take that weekend off." The voice was followed by a tall, slender gentleman, not taller than 6'6, with dark Caesar fade and a peppered goatee. As he approached the Brewers, he placed his foot on the first step of the bleachers, using the length of his arms to extend his hand to Eric as a greeting; Eric was now sitting at attention, thanks to the nudge from his grandfather. Eric looked at the oncoming guest perplexed and still taken aback by his shrewd comment. Eric's face said it all. But the gentleman continued, "Good game, sir. My name is Derrick Clements. I'm the head coach and scout recruiter for Sojourner Truth University, a pleasure to meet you."

Finally shaking Coach Derrick Clements' hand, Eric was curious and said, "Sojourner Truth?" feeding for more answers.

"Yes, sir. We're an HBCU, a historically black college, and university," Coach Clements explained. "Located in Marietta, Georgia, just outside of Atlanta."

"Ahh, I see," still bothered by Coach Clements' earlier remarks, Eric was in the mood to ruffle his feathers. So, shaking the table, he shot back at the coach. "I know what an 'HBCU' is, thanks. And 'you're' the head coach and a recruiter? Y'all must be on a budget or something?" he said as he pointed to the ceiling, "Like this place? Don't they separate those two positions?"

As his eyes widened with embarrassment, Ronald Sr. nudged Eric with a little more force in his ribs, all the while maintaining eye contact with the optimistic head coach standing in front of them. "Ouch! Hey!" Eric said, wincing in pain from the rib shot.

"Act like you got some damn sense…" Ronald Sr. whispered in his ear, trying not to make a scene. But for Eric, combining that rib shot with the rough game he just played, he was in pain as he rubbed his ribcage. However, taking heed to the warning, he tried to play it cool, refocusing his attention on Coach Clements.

Coach Clements chuckled, taking Eric's "snooty" comment with a grain of salt, and proceeded with the sell. "I know you had a rough game, brother. Hell, we all saw it, but 'we,' me included, have heard some great things about your play, which was probably why the gym was so packed. And with the approval of the university, I took the liberty of checking you out for myself. And you didn't disappoint me, sir!"

Fixing his once perplexed look from disturbed to surprised. At this point, Eric welcomed any good news he could get. Unlike the typical sympathy, he would receive from his friends and family, who he knew would always be in his corner. Never has anyone approached Eric with their own personal high regards to his basketball play, and coming from a college coach, it seemed as if a whole new level of basketball had been unlocked, a new level to his *shoestring dreams*.

"Thank you, sir!" Eric replied gratefully, "Even though you had to witness a loss tonight. Hence, my rude introduction. My bad." Eric tried to save face in front of the coach as he went on. "But don't be wrong. This season isn't over. We'll see them again." Eric turned to his grandfather and continued, "It just sucks I lost this big game in front of my old man, right here," he then reaching over, grabbing Ronald Sr. for a hug.

Coach Clements could quickly gather that the bond between this teenager and his grandfather was an organic one. The two spoke for a few more minutes, just getting familiar. He continued to discuss with Eric possible future endeavors with his university if he chooses to come. "That was also something I wanted to share with you… The way you took the initiative on the floor tonight. And you didn't quit! That is exactly what I'm looking for at STU. People like you. You win some; you lose some. Everything else is a practice but, but you can't practice heart."

"Well said," Ronald Sr. concurred.

Ronald Sr. couldn't believe what he witnessed with his own eyes; what a time to be alive. The jokes in the distance between Jeremy and Angelo came to a cease when they also overheard Ronald Sr. clapping his hands, singing praise.

There was some "life-changing" chatter taking place in their background.

Jacqueline, Paula, Nadine, and Ronald Jr. were already being nosey in the back. Glued to the good rhetoric between their son and the coach, they figured their son would handle it if it got serious. Future conversations will be set up, but this was special for Ronald Sr. for many reasons. His grandson could possibly get to play for a college and secure his education for free on a scholarship.

Ronald Sr. interjects gleefully, "Yes! My grandson is great. And I mean, a 'Great' player! He learned a thing or two from me. Today wasn't an example of that, though," as he busted out laughing.

"Come on, Grandpop, chill," Eric pleaded. He had enough of the hostile remarks he endured tonight. Not to mention the giggling from the peanut gallery he called "family." However, Eric still played along, laughing off Ronald Sr.'s sly remark and keeping his composure.

Upon opening his thick, black binder, Coach Derrick Clements slid out a blue and gold business card and a brochure and gave it to Eric. Enclosed in the brochure was the information surrounding the background of Sojourner Truth University and a summary of their history and the athletic programs they provide, from baseball to lacrosse, which were all Division 1 programs.

"Thanks for the info, sir," Eric said, grabbing the brochure, "If I have any questions, I'll give you a call." He skimmed over the new material a litter harder. "STU, huh? It does have a little ring to it."

As some of the overhead gym lights slowly cut off, one by one. It was a "warning" from the custodial crew, telling everyone to "Wrap it up!"

Getting late, Coach Clements thanked them for their time before parting ways. "I'll be looking for your call personally," he added, pointing to Eric, "Goodnight, everyone!" He ended the conversation the same way he walked in, with another firm handshake between the two.

But before it completely ended and the gym closed for the night, Eric was stopped by his head coach, opening the door from his office. He quickly looked around the gym and spotted him walking out with his family and friends.

"Mr. Brewer! Thought you would have run out of the building by now," Coach Walker joked. "Yea… Well, they wanted to chit-chat, and then some head coach….

From Sojourner? We talked for a lil'. He seemed cool." Coach Walker cut him off.

"Oh, nice! Good, glad I caught you!" Assistant Coach Lawry also stepped out of the office, joining in on the conversation.

"Check this man out, Marco," Coach Walker said, "He's getting a lil 'buzz' now- think he hot suff. Don't get big-headed, though. We still have more season left."

"Yes, coach- What up, Coach Lawry?" Eric replied.

"Congrats on the news, Eric!" Assistant Coach Lawry said, giving Eric a pound. In his other hand were 3 business cards. "You may want to research and follow up on these as well as STU. They were also in attendance tonight." The assistant coach smiled at Eric as he handed over the business cards.

Eric smiled too, but only briefly. He was happy, but "Why didn't they take the time to stay and talk? If I mattered" That was his way of rationalizing the intent someone had with how they interacted with him. And they just didn't care to chat.

"Dang!" Jeremy shouted, "Check my boy out!!"

"One more thing, Eric, before you leave," Coach Walker said, pulling from his back pocket an enclosed envelope marked "Letter of Recommendation." "Now, it's a basic one, meaning you can use it for multiple schools, but I hit on some key things you have done, on and off the court."

Eric's eyes froze, wondering if the coach included anything related to his grandfather, but was quickly relieved when Coach Walker followed up with, "No, not that," looking only at Eric.

Eric was in shock, the good kind this time as his family smiled on for him.

Before handing the letter off to Eric, Coach Walker had this to share. "I want that GPA to a 3.0 by the end of this year, sir," always reminding the kids of what comes first before any basket is made. Because, after basketball is all said and done, and you hang your shoes up in the closet, collecting dust. When the "real" life hits you at 35, what will be your part 2? Not saying you even need college, but trade and education can get you far. Even when your body breaks down, the mental is there.

Eric quickly responded with joy, "Yes, Coach! Thank both of you so much!" He graciously took the letter of recommendation and dapped his head coach up, hugging him. "Read the letter on your own time, just get those grades up, Family! Y'all have a great night!"

"Goodnight, everyone. Good game, playa," Assistant Coach Lawry responded. He and Coach Walker wave goodbye to the Brewers and company. Walking back into their office, they had a lot of film from tonight to study, preparing for next week's battle against the Resident High Boilers, who were 3-4 this season thus far.

It was a bittersweet night for the young talent turn prospect from Hollywood Heights, Ohio. He fouled out of a rivalry game, played like garbage, and lost. However, with the news he got from coach Walker. He felt he was headed in the right direction and that coach introducing himself also made that clear. As the final lights cut off in the gymnasium, Eric glances once more at the business cards from the college recruiters, and none were HBCU's. And none of them were head coaches.

Parting ways with his friends for the night, Eric was happy they came out to show him love and support. Regardless of where his future was headed, he knew he would never come across a group of friends like this again. It could just be a moment of "euphoria," consuming him, or maybe when you know you just know. Eric knew he was blessed. He made sure to surround himself with overall good people. The type of people with positive energy and genuine souls.

Ronald Sr. and Paula locked arms with their grandson as they walked to the family van departing the Troutman Gymnasium, out in the cold blunder, once again. Ronald Jr. being the proactive man and a winter warrior, was four minutes ahead of them, already warming up the van. Eric first opened the door for his grandmother. Then, the other door for his grandfather. He gave them both a kiss on the cheek, thanking them for braving the cold, just to see him stink up the joint. But caught in the moment, Ronald Sr. grabbed Eric's hand tightly, not letting go and directing his eyes to his grandson, and vice versa. Ronald Sr., seeing his once "little partner in crime" becoming a man, he knew this moment would come. And he wanted to bask in it.

No matter what came next. No matter how cold it was outside. And no matter how long it would be, Ronald Sr. wanted to stay in this moment forever. Eric, feeling his grandfather's grip around his wrist, made him instantly fight back the tears. Not only did Eric know that this bond was at its demise. He also knew this moment would only be remembered by himself, not his grandfather. If lucky, Ronald Sr. may remember this moment for a week. And just the thought of that predicament. The thought of him not knowing "this" moment happened.

As they looked at each other, Eric's mind was sent into a whirlwind, and tears began to flow at a rapid pace. He softly placed his head in his grandfather's chest and whispered, "I just wanted to get you a win. Didn't want you to forget it, grandpop. I'm sorry". Hearing the child-like whimper Eric uttered, it almost made Ronald Sr.'s heartbreak. He pulled Eric into the idling van.

Ronald Sr. may have been exhausted from the day's events. But he will always support his grandson in a time of need as sensitive subjects were still "hard" to digest in the Brewer family. Ronald Sr. made a light-hearted joke as he whispered back in Eric's ear. "Boy, as bad as you played tonight, I will 'never' forget this, ya hear? Now stop crying... Well, unless you have to."

Eric, eyes opened, not expecting that response. And laughed, as snot flew from his nose, "Man, you play too much," he replied. But bringing it back home, Ronald Sr. finished with "I love you, Eric," caressing his bad. "I love you, too, grandpop, always, man." They squeezed each other harder, not wanting to let the other go. The entire van was able to digest, first-hand, a moment between a boy and his grandfather—two people who would risk it all for one other with no questions asked.

CHAPTER 25

It's been a long time since Ronald Jr. saw his son exposed. Naked. He was caught in the moment. He knew their relationship was strong, but not to this degree. He couldn't help but shed a tear at the sincerity of it. And for Ronald Jr., he was glad to see his father so open with his emotions today. A vast difference for his own youth. But all he could do was smile; it wasn't about him. Eric was always transparent in his love for his grandfather. It was all any father could ask for. Nadine, in the passenger seat, was an emotional wreck. She opened the glove box, grabbing tissues for herself and Ronald Jr., trying not to cause a disturbance with her own sobbing. She loves love and loved expressing it. As she patted her eyes dry, Nadine knew she raised her son right. Turning to her husband giving him a tissue, her spirit rejoiced, "Ron, I love your Southern charm, baby. Don't ever change."

"Huh?? What?" Ronald Jr. said, sniffling his nose. His tears were interrupted by the confusion up front."

"Yea, baby. I'm just glad you have mattered. Good manners. That's all", Nadine said as she wiped the tears from her eyes. Ronald Jr. leans in, kissing her on the tip of her nose, then her lips. "I'm the lucky one, girl. What are you talking about?" he replied. They kissed one more time while Eric and Ronald Sr. embraced a little longer. Paula, by this time, was exhausted, had fallen fast asleep in the van with the door still ajar- missing all the action.

As the moment forcefully came to an end from fear of freezing outside. Eric was forced to let go of their embrace and finally close his grandfather's passenger door. Wiping away his tears against the cold air, still sniffling and fighting back the urge to cry. Eric opens the van's backdoor to hop in, leaving his friends, who were socializing in the parking lot for the night. He chucked the peach sign at them, promising to catch up with them over the weekend. Tonight, was a family night and these types of moments were "timeless."

An hour later, the family picked up some dinner in the drive-thru and dropped off Ronald Sr. and a sleepy Paula to their house. The Brewers finally arrive safely at home and ready to escape the blustery wind "Old Man Winter," welcomed. Stuffed from a burrito bowl, a hot shower, and his bed were the only thing on Eric's mind once his father opened the front door. After the game, Eric and the players refuse to shower at the schools. With fears of lead contamination from old, rusted pipes not changed in decades, people understood. Their definition of "freshen up" revolved around "tons" of body spray and sink water until they got home. So, his house shower was the best option.

Ronald Jr. walked back outside, collecting the mail and grabbing the trash can from the morning pick up. Nadine spent a few minutes tidying up in the family room, then the kitchen. Eric began his walk up the creaking wooden steps that directed him to his bedroom. He passed old family photos on the way up, mostly from family reunions, graduations, and holidays, like this recent Christmas. A classic and Brewer's favorite was at the top of the steps. It featured everyone, and from a few years back. Paula and Ronald Sr. sat up front as Eric, smiling from ear to ear, was placed in the middle of the two. Ronald Jr. and Nadine were standing directly behind them, with one hand on Paula's shoulder and one on Ronald Sr.'s. They were dressed in their best. And wearing the color of navy blue. It was Ronald Sr.'s favorite color.

Opening his cracked door, Eric takes a deep breath as he walks into his room. It was the tranquility of it, his oasis when things went south. Often laying on his bed, he would watch "ceiling fan." Thinking of what he could have done better in the hours passed through the day, whether school, life, girls, or sports. It was all on the drawing board for him. A green lava lamp stood about 5 feet away from his bed, illuminating his mahogany dresser. Next to it was an iconic poster of Michael Jordan and Michael Jackson playing basketball. And being a relatively young kid who didn't get to see either one in their heyday, it was such a peculiar picture. He had to have it when he saw it in a store at Hollywood Heights Plaza.

Somebody that was known for basketball. Playing against someone who just sang for a living. Eric knew they were celebrities, thanks to his parents. Ronald Jr. would shout at the television when Kobe Bryant took his patent fade-away shot. "Pssh, This MJ wanna-be. Who this nigga think he is?" And as a child, he would always enjoy the melodies of the Jackson 5 Christmas album when it played during the holidays.

So, with that said, it was soothing to Eric. And that picture always brought him delight, with a certain amount of mystique in the mix. Because "Why?" With a full stomach and clean body, Eric stared at the poster as the green light from his lamp bounced off Comfy in his bed; he slowly drifted off to sleep. He was spent.

Months pass as the snow and ice begin to melt away, and bird chirps are more prevalent. Complimenting the rising and setting sun. Springtime was near, and the weather reflected it. More basketball games are played, too. Some were won, and some were lost. Coach Walker, as many head coaches do, stays true to his form. He continued to lose his mind after "amateur moves" resulted in turnovers and points for their adversary. It was safe to say, the talk he had with Principal Teely didn't work out. However, she let it be known he was on a "very short leash."

Principal Teely also gave Assistant Coach Lawry his props for saving the team in a crunch-time crisis. Even with a loss. He continued to be the extra strength, *Tylenol,* the team needs.

However, the Bucks' finished the season strong, having a record of (13-4), and punched their ticket into the district finals. They had to face a strong (15-2) Bears' team, again- but winning. Not to mention, this time, it was on Roosevelt's home court- leaving their fans silenced for once. The Bucks' made it to the Ohio State Championship. But out skilled and riddled with injuries into the second half of the game, they fell short by 4 points. They fought tooth and nail, against a monstrous team, in the Cleveland Gardens High School. The final score (62-58).

With most things in life, there was a silver lining in that championship loss. Eric was free to finish out his school year strong. He chose to focus on his academics more, even requesting "extra credit" to boost his grades. Which helped improve his GPA to a 3.1, respectively, from a 2.9. And it was extremely pleasing to his physics teacher, Mr. Holloway.

Without a commitment made to any college or university, Eric still had offers arriving in the mail. He also began to receive more phone calls from schools interested in his talents on the basketball court. Unfortunately for the Brewer household, this also meant more people to annoy Ronald Jr. For weeks, after losing the championship game, there was a "steady flow" of in-person house visits inquiring about his college-bound prospect. "This is my place of peace," Ronald Jr. would often recite when they came knocking.

The world seemed to be Eric's buffet for now. Remaining humble and reserved, he took the time to hear from all the college offers, who had one to give. Before he made his final decision, he made sure to discuss his final ruling with his parents. They were always there to help him; he just needed to ask. He loved having the option to go anywhere he wanted. And he loved seeing his hard work being noticed. He thought about this while he lay on the bed. And it led him to reminisce on the first recruiter he met. An individual that saw his talents for what they were, even on his worst game. It was Coach Derrick Clements that originally saw something in him. Good and bad, and still genuinely wanted Eric on his roster.

Shuffling through old papers on his nightstand. he then moved to his dresser, moving around schoolbooks that he's scheduled to return to before the school year ends. Trying to remember where he last placed that business card, Eric snaps his finger, recalling it was in his gym bag. Popping out his desk chair, he walked over to his bedroom closet, shuffling some more. After 30-seconds, he finally locates the card in the side compartment where he kept his spare ankle tape and weightlifting gloves. To Eric's surprise, the business card was still in pretty good condition, given how he threw his gym bag around aimlessly. As he started to fiddle the card between his fingers, he thought, "Why not?"

Eric picks up his cellphone to call head coach Derrick Clements. He wanted more information about the coach's "unofficial" offer. And the opportunity to play at Sojourner Truth University.

"... Good Afternoon, this is Derrick Clements."

"Hey. Coach? This is Eric Brewer. Not sure if you remember me."

Coach Clements, recognizing the voice, finally sat back in his chair. "I definitely do, Mr. Angry Man," he jokingly replied. He started to playback their first interaction in his head. "I'm glad to hear your voice Mr. Brewer- What's up?"

"Ugh, that was just that one time, sir," Eric said, giving his rebuttal. "Again, charge to my head, not my heart."

"Coach Clements' laughed, "I'm gonna have to steal that saying, and use that for when the men on my team get outa' line, thanks."

"No problem, free of charge," Eric replied.

As their cordial conversation grew, some of Eric's questions could be answered, and some couldn't be answered for legal reasons. Coach Clements' didn't want to get anyone jammed up, and Eric respected his honesty. He just wanted the answers to question's any kid in his position would sensibly ask. The energy between him and STU's head coach felt good, almost organic. He could sense that this coach wasn't going to bullshit with his future or his own, for that matter.

During their conversation, Eric discovered that this was Coach Clements' 2nd year as head coach for STU. He was on a mission, looking for weapons. So, when he got wind of Eric's skill set; seeing a few high school clips and got tickets to the hottest rivalry in Hollywood Heights. He had to check him out. Coach Clements was sold immediately, and that is what he told him over the phone. He just wanted to be sure Eric was willing to "commit" to this and prove to himself he could do it.

35 minutes later, as they were both getting off the phone. The last thing discussed by Coach Clements was a "personal task" he assigned Eric with. He wanted a typed, 400-word essay minimum on "Why STU would be a good fit for you?" Since this was just between them. He wanted it separate from Eric's college application. If he so chooses to apply to STU.

Eric Brewer's Response:

> *Most of us take things for granted in life. Instead of seizing the moment to better ourselves and our condition, we often succumb to the surroundings that keep us warm at night, no matter how good or bad it might be. In Hollywood Heights, Ohio- In my neighborhood- the Treetop district, there's a sign that reads, "Drug Free Zone," standing two blocks away from where I'm writing this letter. Yet, drug addicts continue to roam the streets at night, running rampant, even in broad daylight, or walking to school. You have people post up, some you have known, or seen your whole life. Some should be going to school with you. I've seen gunfights. Within an earshot- excuse the pun- as we walk to the corner store to grab a pop. Again, all of this, no more than a block from my house. People that live on my side of town are trapped. And I simply refuse to take this blessing for granted.*

When you approached me after the game, we had just lost to the Roosevelt Bears. I felt trapped in myself and defeated. And you saw me in a weak state of mind. Even though it's been months since we met. I sincerely apologize for my actions and rude commentary. I was in a battle with myself. Outside of the neighborhood life that I don't partake in, I care for my grandfather, who has looked out for me in more ways than one. At times, I feel it's my duty to tend to his needs. However, I feel at ease knowing my parents can step it up while I attend college.

That night you saw me, I wanted to perform well that rivalry night for my grandfather and fell short. A positive outlook in that- I guess- is that he doesn't remember a thing that night. To be blunt, he barely even knows me now; and I check on him daily. What I'm trying to get across is that for the last 3 years since I have known that he has Alzheimer and the older I get, it's not getting any better for him, or even my own mental compacity. Seeing him spiral downhill is getting harder to watch. My grandmother steps up amazingly for me and shows me what "love" is. They have been married for almost 50 years.

It is deeper than basketball for me. My family and friends are my support system. Without them, there wouldn't be an Eric Brewer that you see today. You don't know them. But Angelo, Jeremy, and Jacqueline are people I can depend on at a moment's notice. My friends are my family. My coaches, Walker and Lawry, who you saw chewing me out that game, has also been "blessings in disguise," as my mom would say. They always pushed me to be better and a leader on the team, even when I doubted myself.

It must be said- I'm more than an athlete. I'm an avid reader, and I love Marvel comics over DC. I also love shoes and rare coins. I'm honored by Sojourner Truth University's athletic scholarship offer. But I want to make sure I succeed in my schooling, as well as basketball. If not, my dad would kill me. My grandfather once told me, "If I get something in my brain, nobody can take it away from me"- I'm a firm believer in that statement, and I want to make him proud. Even though I'm 17, I want to leave a legacy one day. I have a future, and the sky is my starting point. And this scholarship will excel that path. As a student-athlete, I will not let STU, my family or my friends down. Especially my grandfather, Ronald Jervon Brewer, 2nd Battalion, 7th Cavalry.

In closing and transparency, I never heard of Sojourner Truth University or the person, but I'm glad I did my research. Sojourner's story is a remarkable one. Once a slave herself, she ran away only to come back stronger and as an abolitionist and a pioneer for women's rights. Forgive my ignorance, but they didn't teach us about her in high school. Only Harriet Tubman and Fredrick Douglas. So, if you could recommend some black history books to me, I would appreciate it.

Sincerely,

Eric Dwyane Brewer

Removing his fingers from the keyboard, he moved the mouse to click "Spell Check." Eric felt satisfied with what he wrote. But to make sure, he took to his parents to be proofread, again, as they sat over dinner. They approved. Eric still felt compelled to mention how his relationship with his shoes was tied to a deeper relationship with his grandfather, who always gifted them to him every birthday. However, once his parents saw he had exceeded the recommended 400 words. They thought it would be overkill. So, the letter was done.

-8 months later-

The sounds of squeaking basketball shoes sliding against the hardwood floor as players sprinted across the court. Stopping and touching the baseline, then sprinting back to the opposite side. Sweat drips off Eric's chin, hitting the floor each time his fingertips reach out to the navy-blue court baseline. His coach, making sure he saw each suicide, ran with execution and a purpose. "Make sure you touch that line, men!!" This is college.

"That's right, Brewer!" the coach screamed, "Hustle! Hustle! Finish it out!" Hands began to clap on the sidelines, mostly from the veteran players, mostly seniors. The good news is that most of his new teammates urged him to complete his suicide drill. But on the flipside, there were some mocking him as he ran. It was the "rookie treatment," that happens every year. And it was something he had to get familiar with, again. Head down, finishing out the run, Eric yelled as he ran through the line. Out of breath, he wiped his face with his grey t-shirt; written in gold cursive, with blue outlining were the words, "STU Trailblazers."

Coach Derrick Clements' continued to congratulate the team by bringing them in for a quick huddle before the end of practice. "Great stuff, men, everybody, especially the rookies… Seniors, clap it up for me."

As they clapped, they began to eye the "fresh meat" still getting acclimated to their new school.

"Study the playbook," Coach Clements continued, "And take care of those bodies; use ice if you need to. We got a long season ahead of us. Bring it in. Blazers on 3…"

As a freshman in a new school and a new state, Eric was still soaking in the environment, taking in the new gym, seeing the new sights. There was so much more to do here than Hollywood Heights, and he was thankful. STU smelled different from the Bucks' worn-down gym. The colors were different, more refined. The people and their accents were unique to the ear. One of his teammates, a local kid from Atlanta, checked to see if he wanted to join the other freshman for lunch. Eric said he would meet them there. But first, he wanted to shoot some free throws, his normal "cool down" after practice.

During this time, he would reminisce about his grandfather's lessons as a kid, the tough times, the good times, the tears, the smiles, and the love. Sinking his 3rd free throw in a row, he took a moment to pause. Eric then tucked the ball under his arm and ran over to the baseline, where he placed his gym bag. He reached inside, picked up his phone, and he quickly went to his "incoming call" log to find the number he wanted to dial. Pressing "send," he waited for a few seconds as it rang; and they picked up. "Hey, Grandma!! It's Eric!! How are you and grandpop!? I miss y'all already."

www.ingramcontent.com/pod-product-compliance
Lightning Source LLC
LaVergne TN
LVHW041626060526
838200LV00040B/1453